WHEN
SILENCE
SCREAMS

WHEN SILENCE SCREAMS

An Arthur Nakai Mystery

MARK EDWARD LANGLEY

Cover design by Z.K. Coffman
Author photo by Brittany Ghezzi

For my wife, Barbara—my toughest critic and best friend. And for Erica, Jerry, Makayla, and Molly Jaymes and Melanie Rae—beams of sunshine that never cease to amaze.

This book is also dedicated to the 5,712 missing and murdered indigenous women and girls of 2016, most of whose voices have yet to be heard.

Our women's and girl's voices have been silenced for too long. Our people walked this land long before anyone. Our history is written here. That is why their voices will once again be heard. That is why they will not be forgotten.

Unknown

ACKNOWLEDGMENTS

I wish to thank my agent, Richard Curtis, for his constant efforts and my editor, Eileen Chetti, for her words of wisdom and constant encouragement; Delane Atcitty, executive director of the Indian Nations Conservation Alliance, and Rochelle MacArthur for sharing their knowledge and understanding; Arnold Clifford for his constant words of wisdom concerning the Navajo people, their customs and their beautifully rich history; the New Mexico Department of Public Safety; Travis Tutt, one of the many fine Navajo jewelry artists and craftsmen in the Farmington, New Mexico, area; Shannon Lynn, pool player extraordinaire; and Vicki for sharing a part of her story with me.

AUTHOR'S NOTES

Although 98 percent of the locations in my novels actually exist, the other 2 percent have literally been conjured up by my imagination, and certain names have been changed due to creative license. I leave it up to you, the reader, to figure out which is which.

I would also like make it known that a portion of the sales from this novel will be donated to Missing and Murdered Indigenous Women USA. If you would like to learn more about this worthy foundation, please visit https://mmiwusa.org/.

CHAPTER ONE

April Manygoats' eyes flickered briefly, projecting snippets of images upon the canvas of her slowly awakening mind. As her consciousness sharpened, her eyes focused on the overwhelming darkness that surrounded her. The first sensation she became aware of was the icy chill of cold air that cloaked her naked body like a heavy blanket; the second was the rough and gritty surface of the wooden floor where she lay, which seemed to grip her adolescent shape like a thousand frozen fingers of the dead.

Through the foggy haze of her still emerging mind, she realized that her body was in a state of self-imposed weightlessness, a kind of transcendental void where all her senses could reset and begin to feel again. Her eyes fluttered once again as she became more aware of the damp, musty darkness that hung in the air like a cloying mist. Her first thought was to try to move, but the ropes that had been wrapped snugly around her arms kept them in place; she tried moving her legs, but once again the firm grasp of ropes kept them still. She could feel the bottoms of her feet resting flat against each other and the roughness of her heels as they shifted slightly.

As she lay there—her eyes staring into the shadow of captivity—her ears began to search for any suggestion of sound. Hearing nothing her cloudy mind could discern she felt her hear sink even lower as a feeling of hopelessness began to take hold. With all the will she could muster, she pushed that feeling down deep inside to a place where she would be able to deal with it later. She could only manage to move her heavy head slightly to th e left and right and backward. Forward wasn't a direction available to her because of something that had been woven into her long dark hair that kept her head from moving in that natural direction. Her mind thought back to when this was the norm for some of her clients—their sick, perverted game that made them feel like men. But this, she knew, was so very different. In her previous life, she had quickly graduated from back alleys to clubs and on to the luxury hotel rooms of Las Vegas, but this—this was terrifying.

She wondered if anyone was looking for her. She wondered if her parents had gone to the police after she had never returned to their spot under the covered sidewalk at the Palace of Governors in Santa Fe during the Indian Market. She took a deep breath and told her nineteen-year-old mind, *Of course they would be looking for you! Why wouldn't they? Even after all these months had passed.* The reality of it all, she conceded, was that there had probably been Amber Alerts and social media notifications and fliers posted everywhere her parents and friends could put them since the day she had disappeared. But had anyone actually paid attention to them? And, more important, had anyone who ever did even seen her?

As her senses tingled back to life one after another, she found the rough texture of the ropes that bit into her tender skin unrelenting. She tried to move again, but all that did was reinforce the fact that she had been hog-tied—as one of her gentlemen clients had once described it. With each jerk and twitch, she could feel the straitjacket of rope cutting deeper into the flesh of her shoulders and arms, tightening around her belly and thighs, strengthening its hold around her adolescent torso. She couldn't see them, but her breasts felt as though they had been compressed between several strands of rope and swollen to resemble something only Madonna could have dreamt about in her nightmares. Her nipples, protruding and tender, telegraphed swift shots of pain to the thalamus region of her brain each time they scraped the rasping surface of the wooden floor.

Her hands, which had been secured behind her back as part of this spiderweb of torture, were beginning to sting and tingle with numbness like the rest of her body. How long had she been like this? she wondered. Had it been hours or days? Days or weeks? As she began to move slowly, she could hear the ropes straining around her five-foot, two-inch, one-hundred-fifty-pound frame. Suddenly, she heard a recognizable sound from her past. It was the sound of the steel cable in the pulley that was attached to the winch that would lift her into the air so that whoever had done this to her could do whatever he wanted to with her.

She finally lay still in the darkness . . . realizing there was no escape.

Looking around was useless. She had no way of knowing where she was or the size of the room she lay in. She had no way of knowing what time it was or if it was even day or night. All she could do was begin the slow inventory of her body to see if any of her parts ached worse than normal. Aside from her legs, which were beginning to cramp in their immovable position, none of her points of entry seemed to feel any unrecognizable pain. She knew he had been inside her but had no way of knowing how many times.

Suddenly, a sense of her vulnerability began to set in again, a fact that the silicone ball gag filling her mouth brought into blinding clarity. As she lay flat on her stomach, all her numbing and tingling body could feel was the saltiness of her tears as they rolled down her face and trickled onto her lips and then crept into her mouth to place their salty kiss upon her tongue. And the only echoing sounds that pierced the darkness were those of her own breathing and periodic swallowing of the buildup of saliva being drained into her throat by the gag. The dank, thick, frigid air of her makeshift prison covered her trembling skin with goose bumps as she tried to stay in one place so that she could keep the wood warm beneath her.

She remembered her first time—how she had felt like a piece of meat hanging in a butcher shop freezer. She remembered how her client had used his cell phone to film every humiliating detail so he could relive it. And she remembered *him*. The tall, thick man with the clammy hands and breath that smelled like Italian dressing. Her eyes squeezed shut as she dragged her thoughts back into the harsh reality that this wasn't a hotel room, and she wasn't going to be paid, and she wasn't going to be allowed to walk out of here—wherever *here* was.

She struggled against her own mind to think back to the exact moment she had been stupid enough to let herself be manipulated by whoever it was that had done this to her. All she could remember was that she had finally gotten away from the sickening life she had been trapped into performing and had been trying to get back to her parents' home in Sheep Springs. She remembered hitchhiking with the trucker heading west out of Albuquerque and making it as far as Milan. The trucker had wanted a different type of payment for his trouble, but she had managed to turn his testicles into a pile of mashed grapes with a sharp thrust of her fist, giving her the opportunity to escape out of the passenger side of the semi as he writhed in pain.

He had parked the truck in the large lot north of the diesel pumps. She remembered running quickly from the lot, darting across some street, and moving past the people filling their cars with gas under the blue-and-white Chevron canopy of the Enchanted Mesa Travel Center. She recalled being eyed by everyone as she settled her stride to a fast walk toward the kachina-painted facade in her Coca-Cola T-shirt, jeans and sneakers, carrying her backpack with what little she had managed to quickly gather inside it.

The next thing that came to mind was the man she had noticed watching her as she walked through the doors of the travel center. She had learned how to be good at noticing men and separating the lookers from the buyers ever since she had been on the streets, where she had to learn fast. Except when she had been sold to the Cuban. He had always weeded out the wannabes before she had been borrowed for a few hours for a price. Money that she never saw. She thought back again to the guy standing by the glass cases displaying jewelry and pottery and other trinkets across from the short office chairs stationed by the bar-like craft table below the picture windows. The table was decorated with a row of magnifying-glass task lights at the ends of flexible arms, bent so onlooking tourists could watch the Native craftsman at work from the outside. The craft area had been separated from the glass cases by a short, spindled, urethane-coated log railing. She had noticed him eyeing her from across the store before turning and heading toward the Kachina Café. By the time she had reached the café's entrance, he had moved close enough to notice she looked distressed and asked her if something was wrong.

"No," she said politely. "I'm okay, just hungry."

"Traveling far?" he said.

"Heading home."

The man asking questions was dressed in a gray business suit and wore polished black shoes. His smile was placating. She gauged him to be in his mid- to late forties, another skill she had been forced to learn in the life she was desperately trying to escape. He was a little stocky, but not enough to make him unattractive in a fatherly sort of way. Maybe, she figured, she could end up with a good meal using the least amount of promising flirtation. Men were all stupid, she had come to realize, and could be swayed into doing anything given just the smallest whiff of it.

Suddenly, April's thoughts returned to a stark realization. A realization that felt like two big hands twisting her gut and wringing it out like a damp rag. He must have slipped something into her drink—probably Rohypnol or something like it, if she knew his kind. He had probably done it when she had gone to the bathroom. *That had to be it!* It was the only time she wasn't watching him. The suit must have slipped a roofie into her thirty-two-ounce cup, and then watched, satisfied, as she drank it all down. She scolded herself for being so stupid. The one time she had eased up on her lack of trust had brought her entire world crashing down into the dungeon of hell again. All she vaguely remembered after that was him walking her out of the building and herself getting more and more sleepy and disoriented and letting him put her into his car. After that—nothing.

She struggled pointlessly against the ropes again, fighting their constricting movement and feeling them bite further into her forgiving flesh. The tiny individual strands that made up the rope felt like miniature knife blades as she twisted and turned against their confinement. The more she fought, the more her bindings tightened; the more she thrashed, the more she felt the rope laced into her hair try to pull the follicles out of her scalp whenever she let her head move forward. She remembered being tied up in a similar way at the Cuban's as part of the harem of sex slaves that serviced his desires as well as those of his friends on special occasions. But she had been running away from all that, not looking to get thrown back into the ritualistic humiliation that always accompanied this kind of terror.

Suddenly, the rattle of chains and the unsnapping of a padlock drew her attention. From somewhere in the darkness, she heard the links of chain sliding through the rings of iron and saw the glistening snow on the ground highlighted by a pale sliver of moonlight that sliced into the room through the opening door. The cold outside air rushed in and rolled over her body like a sea wave as the moon's glow bathed her briefly in its milky-white illumination. The moonglow, however, was soon eclipsed by the dark figure of a man. He stepped in and, just as quickly, the moonlight vanished with the closing of the steel door, which resonated like the slamming of a prison cell. Soon rough hands were holding her face and reaching around to the back of her head. She felt his fingers work free the small buckle holding the ball gag in place. She felt the ball pop out of her mouth and a river of saliva run unashamedly down her chin and dribble onto the floor.

Moving her jaw quickly, in an effort to revive its full range of motion, she called out, "Who are you!"

No response.

"Why are you doing this to me!"

Again, no response. Suddenly, her ears picked up another recognizable sound. With the stroke of a match a small yellow flame seemed to float in the darkness above her. Her eyes followed it as it cast a dismal glow on a portion of the man's face as the tip of a cigarette blazed. All she could focus on were the two gray eyes staring back at her and an evil mouth that held the cigarette between lips that seemed to grin as if he were Satan himself. She heard the rush of his breath as he extinguished the flame.

"I'll do anything you want!" she pleaded. "You don't have to do this!"

The tip of the cigarette glowed again as he inhaled the toxins deep into his lungs. "Let you go?" his voice whispered softly. "Now, why would I do that? You and I are going to have such fun." He exhaled again, this time the acrid smoke clouding her face. "You do like to have fun? I do."

April Manygoats coughed against the smoke and didn't answer.

"I do so hope you enjoy having my kind of fun," the man continued. "The others did—or at least they did until I grew tired of them." She heard him inhale again, saw the tip of the cigarette glow, and heard him expel the smoke into the air. "But it doesn't really matter. I know that I'm going to be the one who will truly have all the fun. You will be what I want, when I want it, and for as long as I want it. Day or night. You are simply a pleasure toy for me. A submissive that will do anything to please her master. And no one will hear you scream, so you can scream all you want. In fact, I like it when the girls scream. It adds a whole new exciting dimension, don't you think? And no one will be here to save you, because your kind isn't worth saving. You have no name; you have no say. You have no history before me. All that you have ever been, all that you are now, and all that you will ever become is what I alone will create. Do you understand?"

"Yes," she whimpered through trembling lips, her breathing rushed. "But I just want it to be over. Why don't you just kill me and get it over with?"

"Because we have to play the game," he said, tilting his head slightly to one side. "This is all about the game. My game. And you are the one I have chosen to play it with."

CHAPTER TWO

The few inches of freshly fallen snow covering the metal roofs of the shed and barn of White Mesa Outfitters had Arthur slightly worried as he sat at his kitchen table with Billy Yazzie. Most winters when it snowed in the hi-lo country it always melted with the purifying rays and warming temperatures of the sun and lasted no longer than early afternoon. It was also the time of year when he and Sharon tried to take time for themselves. They would pick a day and load their horses into the Featherlite and head to Colorado. They loved riding in Echo Basin—the lushness of the forest, the sweet music of the creeks and the richness of the grassland sometimes did more for their souls than the high desert of White Mesa could, even though it was their home. Arthur remembered the early snows dragging down the Douglas fir branches and decorating the ponderosa pines, then hearing the melting droplets falling like a light rain to the ground beneath them in soft whispers. But this time it felt different. There was a wariness in his bones, accentuated by the recent string of cold mornings, that made him think it was going to be a very heavy winter this year. Winter coats were already covering the horses, and that told him that the plants and flowers would be flourishing the following spring; that the rivers and washes would flow strong with runoff from the mountains as the snowmelt once again transformed life for the Four Corners region of the San Juan Valley.

"I'll need you to check the hay in the barn," Arthur told Billy over his coffee. He was studying his latest literary acquisition after getting back to his roots as a bibliophile. His first edition of Ernest Hemingway's *To Have and Have Not* had arrived the day before, and all he could do was marvel at it. The book felt good in his hands. Unlike an electronic tablet, the weight and smell of its two hundred and sixty-two pages allowed you to literally cradle a piece of history in your hands. "If you see any mildew on it, throw it out," Arthur added, not looking at Billy. "I plan on going to NAPI today and picking up around ten more bales and enough four-way feed to get us through if we get what I think might be coming."

"Sure thing, boss," Billy said, pointing at the novel. "You get a new one?"

Arthur smiled. "Just another piece for my collection."

"Hemingway?" Billy queried. "He ever do any graphic novels?"

Arthur shot him a sideways glance. "No," he said flatly.

Billy had trimmed his mustache and let his dark hair grow longer over the summer to the point where it now hung midway down his shoulder blades. And the only weight he had put on seemed to be more muscle. "I love graphic novels," he said. "This dude really missed out."

"Hemingway didn't miss out on anything," Arthur corrected. "It would do you good to read some of his early works. Remember, the man who reads is an educated man."

Billy reached across the table.

"Not this one," Arthur said. "Get yourself a paperback. This is going on my shelf with the others."

Billy shook his head. "I don't get you, boss. Why pay good money for something that's just gonna sit around?"

Ak'is was curled up next to Arthur on the kitchen floor. Sometimes his breaths were so covertly measured it was difficult for Arthur to tell if his old friend was actually breathing. He would have to concentrate on the dog's abdomen until he saw it expand and contract. And the wolf dog's stomach was doing just that.

"It's called *collecting*," Arthur said. "A man should always have diversionary interests."

"I know how to please a woman," Billy said.

Arthur chuckled. "Really? Please pass on your infinite wisdom, oh great sage."

Billy crossed his arms, responded confidently, "You buy 'em whatever they want."

Arthur's chuckle transformed into an outright guffaw. "You're still wet behind the ears, Grasshopper."

Billy's expression was one of embarrassment coupled with a dash of vicenary confusion. "I'm almost thirty."

"I'll pass along to you the words my father passed along to me," Arthur said. "He said, 'Son, the way to really please a woman is to buy yourself a pack of gum. Pull out a couple of sticks and start chewing.'"

"Bullshit," Billy said, thinking Arthur was joking.

"That's what I said," Arthur agreed. "But then he explained, 'When you get the gum really pliable, use the tip of your tongue to roll it between the roof of your mouth and your tongue until you work it into a ball.' " Arthur waited. No question came. "Do that several times a day. That's how you'll please a woman.' "

"I don't get it," Billy said.

Arthur grinned. "You will … because no matter how skilled you think you are, you're not."

Billy drank a mouthful of coffee from his travel mug. "You want me to check the generator, too?"

"No," Arthur said, resting the book on the table. "I'll do that. I want you to make sure the tack is all good. I'll check the corral fence and gate, and then we'll both make sure the stalls are clean and ready."

Billy nodded.

The house was always quiet when Sharon was gone. Arthur didn't like that. It made him uneasy. Maybe it was because it reminded him of the last time she had been gone. He also wished they'd had a little more time this morning for pillow talk after their enthusiastic round of lovemaking. For the last few months, Arthur always felt like he was racing the clock. Ever since they had decided to try again, Sharon seemed to be concentrating more on her established timetable and the days of the month than on the passion that creates life. *Whoever thought lovemaking on a schedule was romantic?*

Unexpectedly, Ak'is' ears perked up and swiveled like military radar homing in on an unidentified object. As the big dog lifted his salt-and-pepper head off the floor, Arthur could almost see him triangulating the sound before he even stood and looked at Arthur in earnest. Both men recognized the slow roll of tires through crunching snow and went to the window over the sink. Arthur let his hand push aside the curtains enough to see the brown Monte Carlo come to rest at an angle by the side porch railing. The engine went quiet and the exhaust stopped smoking in the cold air. Through the lightly falling snow, Arthur could make out two people in the front seat talking before the driver's door swung open and a woman climbed out.

"Who's that?" Billy said.

"What makes you think I'd know?" Arthur answered. "I've never seen her before."

The woman looked to be in her late thirties, judging by what Arthur could barely see encircled by the furry hood of the black parka. She turned and gave an order to the other occupant and shut her door with a heavy thud. As she walked around to the front of the car, the passenger door opened and a boy got out. The kid looked young enough to be in his preteens and had to use both hands to push the heavy door of the old Chevy closed before walking to the front of the car to meet the woman, who Arthur deduced was his mother.

"Billy," Arthur instructed as the two visitors stepped onto the porch, rounded the corner of the house and went out of view. "I'll need you to put the horses in the corral. Let them stretch their legs a little today. Then make sure more ice hasn't formed in the water troughs we broke earlier."

Billy quickly drained the last of his coffee from his travel mug before replenishing it. "Sure thing, boss."

"And stop it with that 'boss' stuff."

Billy poured cream into his insulated travel mug and used a long teaspoon to stir it into a flawless shade of tan. "Would you rather I call you P.I. Nakai?"

"Hell no," Arthur said with a screwed-up face. "Stick with 'boss' until I can think of something better."

A knock rattled the kitchen door. Arthur crossed over in front of Billy to answer it, and the open door let in the afternoon cold. "*Yá'át'ééh*," he said. "Can I help you?"

Ak'is' nose went to work sniffing the chilly air for the scent of unexpected guests. When his golden eyes read them as nonthreatening, he turned away, walked back to his spot on the floor, and lay back down. Forming a loose crescent, he swung his back legs outward, rested his big head on his large front paws, and inhaled and exhaled contentedly.

The woman was Navajo, that was clear, but Arthur didn't recognize her as local. She looked as though she could have easily been crowned Miss Navajo twenty years earlier, and her eyes managed to capture the kitchen lighting in a way that made them gleam. The boy seemed shy and clung close to her right side as they stood on the porch.

"May we come in?" she asked. "We have driven all the way from Tó Hałtsooí to see you."

"Of course, where are my manners," Arthur said, waving a hand toward the kitchen table. "Sheep Springs is about a seventy-five-mile drive in good weather." He motioned toward Billy. "This is Billy Yazzie. He works with me."

The woman nodded, said, "*Yá'át'ééh*," and sat quietly with the boy.

Billy nodded and returned the greeting, feeling a bit awkward but curious too. Arthur closed the door. "Billy, why don't you make sure those things we talked about are done. I'll come out and help you when we're finished here."

Billy nodded, grabbed his wool-lined jacket and brown winter cowboy hat from their pegs by the door and left.

The young boy sat quietly and said nothing. He appeared to have no cell phone or electronic game that would have kept him occupied during the long drive, at least none that Arthur could see. He hadn't checked his pockets. For a kid today, he supposed, their trip must have been a boring one with nothing but the noise of a car radio. The woman pushed back her hood and placed her hands in her lap. "Thank you for seeing us," she said calmly. "I've heard about you and what you did for your wife and our people and told my husband you could help us."

"Can I take your coats?"

The woman shook her head politely.

"Would you like some coffee?" Arthur said. "I could make a fresh pot."

"That would be nice." The woman smiled. "The heater in the car isn't working very well—not at all, actually—so we could use something to warm us up. Do you have any hot chocolate? My son loves hot chocolate."

"I think I can find some," Arthur said. "My wife usually has a box around here somewhere."

The woman began. "I am Melanie Manygoats, and this is my son, Markham."

Markham whispered something in Navajo to his mother as Arthur got busy emptying the old grounds, filling the basket with a new filter and coffee and pouring in the water. Then he hit the button and was on the hunt for hot chocolate while the coffee percolated. It didn't take him long to locate it, put some water in a mug and place it in the microwave. He turned to face them as the cup spun slowly. "Are either of you hungry?"

The boy nodded.

"We don't wish to put you out, Mr. Nakai," Melanie Manygoats said.

Arthur smiled at the boy. "You're not putting anyone out. What's mine is yours. How's mutton stew sound? My wife made it yesterday, so it's had time to marry overnight."

The boy's face lit up and so did hers, though she tried to not make it seem so noticeable. "You are too kind."

"Not at all." Arthur pulled out the Tupperware container Sharon had placed in the refrigerator the night before, dumped its contents into a pot he found in a lower cabinet and turned on the stove. "How can I help you?"

The microwave beeped its piercing tone. Arthur removed the mug of hot water, tore open a pouch and emptied the chocolate mix into the mug, stirring with a spoon as he poured it, before placing it in front of the boy.

"Six months ago," Melanie said, "my daughter, April, disappeared in Santa Fe. We were selling our jewelry at the Palace of the Governors. My husband is a craftsman with silver and turquoise, and I do all the beadwork pieces." At a time when her face should have shown obvious pride, all that registered was helplessness. "My daughter went for some gelato and never came back." Tears welled up in her eyes and quickly spilled down her cheeks. She wiped them away swiftly as her son watched.

Arthur poured a cup of coffee for Melanie Manygoats. "Cream?"

"Yes. The police have been doing their best," Melanie continued, "or so they keep saying, but they still have nothing to tell us after all this time. They even asked us to give them DNA samples in case … to compare with any young girl that might need to be identified." She sighed. "Somehow I don't think finding a missing Indian girl is a priority to them."

"I'm sure the police aren't thinking that," Arthur said consolingly, pouring from a carton of half-and-half he had taken from the refrigerator. He sat it in front of her and went back to the stew.

"I'm not so sure," Melanie said. "When someone called the FBI in Gallup with a tip a few months back, they told her that she should call us, April's parents, and tell us. It was like they didn't even care."

Arthur pursed his lips as he stirred the simmering stew. "Was there anyone in Santa Fe she knew? A relative or an acquaintance?"

"No relatives. And I don't think she would know anyone there aside from the other artists and their children."

"Is it possible she may have run off with a boy?"

"Oh no," Melanie Manygoats said. "April would never do that."

"How sure are you?"

The girl's mother sat up straighter in her chair. "*Very* sure. Don't think that because she is young, she is stupid."

Arthur turned toward her while swirling the now bubbling stew. "I don't think that. Did you visit any of the hospitals, jails or morgues?"

Melanie Manygoats shivered. "My husband did. I couldn't bring myself to do that. He found nothing. Our girl was nowhere."

"Did you check homeless shelters?"

"Of course. Again nothing."

"I'm sure you've called her phone? Checked her social media?"

"Yes. Her phone used to go to voicemail; her social media accounts haven't been updated since she disappeared." Melanie sipped her coffee. "The police tried tracking her phone when we reported her missing, but there was no signal. The only reason I know she's alive is that she hasn't come to me in my dreams. That's what gives me hope. Because I know she hasn't walked on. If the time comes when I do see her, then I know she is gone forever."

Arthur paused stirring. "How has your husband been handling this?"

Melanie looked down at her coffee and followed her hands as she raised the mug to her lips. "He's changed." She sipped and set the mug down. "He's become very angry with the world. He wants to find whoever took our April and kill them."

Arthur turned slightly. "If my daughter were missing, so would I."

Melanie smiled softly. "At this point, he's begun drinking more than usual and seems to be looking for a fight with anyone who will give him one. No matter who it is."

"I understand," Arthur reassured her. "Could there have been any reason she would run away? Any history of any mental or physical abuse?"

"None at all." Her response was forthright. "She was … is a very happy girl."

Arthur continued to stir the stew. "Could she have been pregnant?"

"No!" Melanie Manygoats snapped. "How dare you!"

"I'm sorry I had to ask, but I'm sure the police have already asked you many of the same questions." Arthur finished stirring the mutton. "From what I can recall, Sheep Springs isn't a very large area on the rez."

Melanie Manygoats looked surprised. "You've been there?"

Arthur nodded. "My wife and I went to a flea market there one weekend."

Arthur took two bowls from an upper cabinet and filled them with stew, placed the hot bowls and spoons in front of his two guests. The boy was the first to fist a spoon and begin to eat; his mother followed.

"And aside from the visitors' center and the post office," she noted, "the only real business we have left is the gas station convenience store and the Church of Latter-day Saints."

"I remember stopping at that station," Arthur said. "The old white building with big blue lettering on it." He dumped some cream into his mug and poured himself another cup, letting the steaming coffee combine with the cream before sitting down at the table.

"That's right," she said, tasting the stew, her face pleased. "Your wife is a good cook. The squash is sliced thin, but not too thin, and the meat is very tender."

"I'll tell her you liked it." He sipped his coffee. "I know it sounds like I'm prying, but how profitable is the jewelry business?"

Melanie ate another spoonful before responding. "We've been doing it for about fifteen years and, like any business, our busiest time is tourist season. After all the traveling to shows and taking care of expenses, we still just make enough to get by."

Arthur nodded.

"My husband made April a silver necklace for her last birthday." Melanie smiled. "It was of a Native girl with a funny little grin. He said it reminded him of her when she was small and being mischievous. She had traditional hair and a little dress that had three small Arizona turquoise stones for a belt, and little moccasins."

Arthur said nothing, honestly not knowing what to say. Then: "What did the Santa Fe Police tell you?"

"They went through her phone records and interviewed anyone she texted or called in the weeks prior to her disappearance. None of them had anything useful to say." Suddenly, she stopped eating and looked across the table at Arthur. "It's not like April to just vanish. I mean, she's lost her phone before, but always used a friend's phone to call and tell me not to worry." She ate another spoonful, chewed the sautéed and boiled cubes of mutton and swallowed. "And she wasn't into drugs, either."

Arthur gave her credit for knowing where he was going with his questioning.

"The police asked us all sorts of questions six months ago and still they have nothing to tell us. We're tired of getting told there is nothing new. We've given every bit of information we have to the Santa Fe police, the tribal police, the BIA and the FBI, and still we have nothing to show for it."

Arthur sipped his coffee, swallowed.

Melanie Manygoats let her spoon rest in the steaming stew and looked across the table at him. "She's a good girl, Mr. Nakai. I never thought she would become one of the stolen and end up on a missing poster. I used to point them out whenever we saw them and warn her about the evil that lurks within this false world. But I never thought—" She collected herself quickly. "I sleep very little and think too much because I spend my nights crying. My husband spends each day brooding and being angry. Angry that someone had stolen his little girl from him and angry that he couldn't have stopped it from happening."

"I'm sure that's a heavy weight to carry for a father," Arthur said. "I'm sure he is doing his best."

Arthur had seen many posters of those missing as well. Each one stating height, weight, hair color, eye color and any other information that could help, but rarely ever did. Each flyer usually held a beautiful photograph of a smiling girl or woman taken at a happier place and time. If her worst fears were not to be realized, Arthur tabulated, the girl she would get back would not be the same girl she had lost. She would be a freighted, broken version of that girl … and hopefully not broken beyond repair.

Arthur said, "Did you bring a picture of April?"

Melanie pulled a photograph from her pocket, handed it to Arthur.

He stared at it for a good portion of a minute. She looked like her mother and had curled the ends of her dark hair into soft spirals that fell down off her shoulders in front of her. Her face was a beautiful adolescent palette of softly arching eyebrows that sat above sparkling brown eyes filled with promise and surrounded by natural lashes that had not yet been augmented beyond her years by Madison Avenue; the small set of pouting lips were shaded in a lip gloss Arthur had no way of identifying, and the choker that surrounded her neck sported a small black-and-white yin- yang symbol that rested against her contrasting skin.

"Lovely young lady," Arthur said. "May I keep this?"

Melanie Manygoats smiled. "Thank you. Of course, you can."

Arthur laid the photo on the kitchen table. "Was there anyone in Santa Fe she could have gotten to know online?"

Just then the boy leaned over and whispered again to his mother. Melanie looked at Arthur sheepishly and smiled. "He asked if he could use your bathroom."

Arthur grinned and took him upstairs to be out of earshot of his next question. Ak'is didn't move, just let his eyes follow them out of the room. The boy's mother took another spoonful of stew.

When Arthur returned to the kitchen, Melanie Manygoats said, "Mr. Nakai, I taught my daughter that women are sacred beings. That the Creator has selected us to become the gateway that connects the spiritual world with the physical world. That we are the only power on earth strong enough to navigate the unborn spirits into this realm." She paused, showing the resilience of a mother's love. "From what I have read and heard, I know that when you find her, she may not be the same girl that was taken from us. But she will still be our daughter. And she has a home ... and a family that loves her. Do you know the question those of us who have had daughters taken ask ourselves every day?"

Arthur shook his head slightly.

"We ask, how many more red dresses will have to hang in the wind before this terror will be over?"

The boy came downstairs, maneuvered through the living room, and stepped carefully over Ak'is' large, furry body as he returned to the table and continued eating. Arthur watched them both in brief silence, his mind running through all the stories Sharon had conveyed over the years concerning missing women and girls, and the horror stories involving some as young as eight. The thought of it sickened him. He considered Melanie Manygoats—and all the other distraught parents—and tried to put himself in their terrified shoes. He tried to understand all the things those parents had missed by having their children taken from them. How they had watched birthdays come and go in silence all while knowing nothing more than they did the year before; he thought of how there had been no high school graduations; no chance of walking their daughters down the aisle at their weddings; and no grandchildren to bounce on their knee. All those things would be gone forever if their child was never found—or if their worst fears were realized. Arthur shook the compounding thoughts from his mind.

"Who's the lead detective on your daughter's case?

Melanie Manygoats thought for a moment. "He is a man called Lance Gilberto. Do you know him?"

Arthur shook his head. "No. But I think I need to go to Santa Fe."

"You are going to help us?"

Arthur nodded. "I am."

"I don't know how we can pay you." Melanie's eyes dropped, then looked up pleadingly. "Even with the business, we don't have a lot of money."

"The way I see it," Arthur confided, "you can't put a dollar amount on your daughter's life."

"But we will certainly owe you something."

Arthur thought for a moment. "We could make a trade."

"A trade?"

"Yes. I will locate your daughter, and in return your husband can make me a silver bracelet."

"I don't understand," Melanie Manygoats said.

"Money comes and goes," Arthur explained. "There's nothing really permanent about it. It's transient. Your husband, on the other hand, is an artist. Whatever he creates will last forever."

CHAPTER THREE

"Did you ever have any contact with Detective Lance Gilberto of the Santa Fe PD?"

Arthur had already packed a bag, gathered up Ak'is and booked a room at the Anasazi Plaza in Santa Fe for a couple of nights, pool side, main floor. He had also placed his new Hemingway acquisition on the bookshelf with the rest of his dusty collection before calling Sharon at KZRV and leaving her a voicemail concerning what had transpired and where he was going. It was now after five p.m., and he was closing in on Bernalillo hoping to get Captain Jake Bilagody of the Navajo Nation Police Department, Shiprock District, to broker a meeting with the lead detective.

"He's with their Special Victims Unit, I think," Jake said. "Why do you ask?"

Arthur brought him up to speed on Melanie Manygoats and her daughter. He could hear the "I told you so" getting ready to sing over the 5G LTE.

"Aren't you glad I convinced you to get that P.I. license after that whole Patriot Security mess?"

And there it was.

"Thanks for helping out with the advisory board," Arthur acknowledged.

"Hey, your military and Homeland records did more for you than I ever could've. But having a friend on the board didn't hurt. At least you used the correct jurisprudence examination." Jake chuckled. "You'd be surprised at the wannabes who screw that up."

"That was the easy part," Arthur acknowledged, taking a moment to notice the hypnotic glow of the waning December day that surrounded him. "The hard part was finding a photo of me that looked virile enough for the license."

Jake's laugh roared over the digital airwaves. When it subsided, he said, "You want me to see if Gilberto has time to meet with you?"

"Give him my number and have him call me. I should be at the hotel around six thirty. I'm staying at the Anasazi Plaza."

"Sounds ritzy."

"Not as swanky as the Eldorado or the Hilton Plaza, but it's good all the same. It's where Sharon and I stay when we go away for a quick weekend."

Jake took a moment to remember those kinds of weekends. *But then again, that's always how love starts*, he recalled. Then, after the roller-coaster ride of years rolls by, it turns into weekends of not talking and being so frustrated with each other that infidelity begins to rear its ugly head and divorce seems to be the obvious next step. Jake took a breath. "I'll contact him as soon as I get a chance."

Arthur picked up on the sound of melancholy in his voice. "You okay?"

"I contacted a Realtor today. I'm gonna sell the house. Find something smaller."

"I'm sorry," Arthur said.

"Don't be," Jake reassured him. "There's just too many memories for me to keep it. I figured since she's moved on … it's time I should. I contacted a guy in Big Rock. Supposed to be good. Guess I'll see if he is."

"He can work in the Nation?"

"Yep. He handles about fifteen communities in and out of the Nation."

"Maybe it's for the best," Arthur said. "New place, new start. Time to get back in the game, find a good woman."

Jake snorted. "What woman would want me? I'm old, I'm overweight, and the only thing that gets stiff on me are my joints." He waited for Arthur to laugh. When he didn't, he added, "Besides, he's already got a few places for me to look at."

"That sounds promising."

Arthur could hear the shrug when Jake said, "Whatever. Right now, I've got a missing rez girl just east of Sanostee."

"Who?"

"Lucy Nez. Fifteen. Disappeared five days ago. She was riding her bike back home after hanging out at a friend's house."

"You've been looking for her for five days?"

"She wasn't reported missing until two days ago," Jake explained. "When she didn't come home, her family got some people together to help with a foot search, but they didn't turn up anything but her bicycle. Looks like whoever took her tried to hide the bike under a bridge over Sanostee Wash." Jake paused. "If it wasn't kinda funny, I wouldn't mention it, but Nathan Johnhat says it's probably skinwalkers. Can you believe that? Says one of 'em chased his son home one night about a month ago."

"People always fall back on the old legends when they can't explain the present day," Arthur said, remembering the first thing his grandfather had told him that truly scared him—that skinwalkers used something called corpse powder, a fine dust made from crushed human bones that would bring sickness and death to those who were poisoned by it. "But like all of us, I've grown up hearing those stories, so I wouldn't dismiss it."

"I'm not sure who took the girl," Jake said, "but I doubt I'll find her held captive by some witchy medicine man, no matter how terrifying the old stories are."

"Legends always have their basis in truth, Jake."

"I know, I know. Next thing you'll be telling me is the Hairy Man is out there stealing rez girls."

"Bigfoot wouldn't do that," Arthur replied.

"How do you know?"

"Rez girl attitude."

The roar of Jake's laughter filled his ear so loudly he had to pull the phone away from his head. When it subsided, he heard the police captain turn serious. "Trafficking is a big business, Arthur, and you don't need me to tell you that. Second only to drugs and guns. If it's not that, then we've got someone out there with other ideas. And every day one of our girls is missing is a day they're going through a kind of terror I don't want to even think about." Jake cleared his throat. "I'll have Gilberto contact you."

"Thanks." Arthur ended the call.

The area around Sanostee Wash, Arthur remembered, was just as barren and beautiful as most of the state. You could see around it for miles in any direction. And the only trees holding their ground were those that followed the snaking wash, sucking whatever water managed to flow through it at any given time of the year. *Focus on the highway, Nakai. Focus on how it meandered through the San Juan Valley, twisting and turning like a river of asphalt through the reservations on its way toward Bernalillo. Pay attention to the road.* The Anglo maps always showed Tamaya land as Santa Ana, but it would always be Tamaya.

Arthur reflected on how many times he had taken this route in the years he had lived here. Too many, probably. He liked staying in his own part of New Mexico, visiting friends and relatives on the rez and attending gatherings and the occasional ceremonies. But there was something about the comfortable familiarity of White Mesa that gave him solace. He even liked flying with Sharon—seeing the land as it rolled slowly beneath her Piper Saratoga. You couldn't get that perspective from the ground. In the air, you could understand the nuances, the subtle and dramatic changes of the land, the ancient depths of canyons that gave way to the even more remarkable heights of the mountains; from the elevations of jagged volcanic rock to the smooth layers of towering sandstone to the low mounds of delicately rounded basalt and ash and everything in between.

And then there was Santa Fe. Founded—or stolen, depending on which telling of history you agreed with—by Spanish soldiers and clergy who had pushed their way into Arizona and New Mexico after conquering Mexico in 1540. During that time, they had managed to seize more than one hundred pueblos and force whatever indigenous peoples they hadn't already slaughtered into a life of slavery, all while managing to excommunicate their gods in favor of pushing the one and only savior as they saw fit.

Arthur grinned happily as his new Bronco pumped the cabin full of warm, dry air. After discussing how much it would cost to repair his old beast, he had decided, with much sad reflection, to commit its soul to the junkyard. The very next day he hit the internet looking for a replacement. Ak'is now sat quietly in the passenger seat of the 1993 Bronco, staring out of the windshield, tongue dangling loosely and occasionally putting his face in front of the dash vent so he could taste and sniff the heated air spilling from it. Arthur continued grinning as his mind brought back the teachings of Mrs. Todacheene's class when she had explained that fateful August in 1680 when eight thousand Navajo warriors overwhelmed the Spanish settlements and unleashed their fury upon two hundred armed settlers, four hundred Spanish soldiers and twenty-one Franciscan friars. It proved to be a successful effort to reclaim their land from the colonists, forcing the remaining one thousand Spanish survivors to flee to the Governors Palace in Santa Fe. As the warriors laid siege, depriving the invaders of water for several days, the Spanish somehow succeeded in escaping to El Paso and saving themselves from further retribution. Arthur cocked his head in recognition of someone who had opened his adolescent eyes to the truth untold in *bilagáana* textbooks.

Arthur's thoughts were shattered as the factory ringtone blasted from his cell phone resting in the cup holder in the Bronco's center console. Ak'is moved his attention to it briefly before returning his grinning face to the dash vent. The profile picture of Sharon filling his screen made his heart skip and brought a knowing smile to his face. Now if he could just remind himself to change that annoying tone.

"Chaco Pizza!" Arthur said.

"Would you kindly explain to me again why you have taken the dog to Santa Fe and not me?" Sharon's tone carried with it more than a hint of humor.

Arthur elaborated more than he had on her voicemail at the station.

"I feel so sorry for her and her family," Sharon said. "Did you know there were one hundred and fifty-seven cases reported in the Southwest of missing girls and women this year? Most of them younger than eighteen. And that's only a portion of the five hundred and six lost to us in the US. If you listen to the media—of which sometimes I resent being a part—it seems like Native women and girls aren't considered justifiable victims. When some white girl goes missing from a golf course, it's plastered all over the TV.

When it's one of us, no one hears about it. I know that sounds harsh, but it's true."

Arthur said, "How do you know all this?"

"Perhaps it's because I'm an outstanding journalist who knows how to dig through a story and unearth the facts, or maybe it's because I don't just see the facts but the faces and the lives torn apart by this growing abhorrent reality." Sharon paused briefly. "Or maybe it's because I'm an indigenous woman first who wants to see all our sisters returned so that we can fight together and make sure that others will never suffer the same fate."

Arthur said, "I should listen to you more often."

"That's what I've been telling you since we met," Sharon said, her breathing slightly labored.

"Are you all right?"

"I'm fine," she said. "I'm just exhausted. When I get off the phone, I'm going to take a nice hot shower and wash the world off me, then I'm gonna eat the rest of the mutton from yesterday and sit by the fire and read for a while."

Arthur crossed the Rio Grande into Bernalillo. "Mutton?" he said.

"Yeah," Sharon said. "You know—that stuff you heated up today in the pot you didn't wash?"

"Oops."

"I'll give you *oops*," Sharon joked. "You know how I hate unwashed dishes in my sink."

"I love you."

"Nice try." Arthur could visualize the wry grin brightening her perfect face. "Are you going to make it back in time for our session with Dr. Petersen on Wednesday?"

Arthur winced. He had forgotten about that. They had been seeing her once a week for five months and making good progress—or so the shrink, as he called her, kept telling them. "It's too early to tell," he said. "Can you reschedule it so we both can go?"

Silence. Then: "I suppose I can. But I do think I should at least go. I'll just explain why you're not with me. Just promise you'll keep going."

"I promise, *she'at'ééd*."

"Don't sweetheart me, you—"

Arthur signaled and took the entrance to the fly bridge that curved onto I-25 and headed east toward Santa Fe as his wife's voice stopped abruptly. "What's wrong?"

"Was anyone in our bathroom today?"

"Melanie Manygoats' boy. Why?"

"It looks like he wrote a web address on our mirror with my lipstick," Sharon said. "Hold on."

Arthur could hear Sharon's fingers producing clicks with every keystroke she entered on her phone's screen. Then the muffled sound of people talking, followed by a millisecond pause, and then the deep moans and erotic screams of a couple in the middle of copulation.

"My God, Arthur," Sharon said, "you need to see this. I think it's the boy's sister."

"What?"

"What did you say her name was?"

"April."

"I'm going to send you this link," his wife said. "The girl in the video says her name is April."

CHAPTER FOUR

Arthur sat at the Ortiz bar in the Hilton Santa Fe Plaza Hotel on one of the red-leather-backed pub chairs, sipping a tall glass of Santa Fe Nut Brown and staring at the empty can next to the square white napkin on the bar. The can was of a bronzish color with a yellow Zia symbol emblazoned on it. His taste buds admitted that the nutty ale flavor was still there, but the more he stared at the can the more he realized how much he actually missed the feel and taste of the bottle. But he reluctantly conceded, one less carbon footprint the better—even though you could recycle a glass bottle as easily as an aluminum can. But as he was the only person in the bar, the whole consideration didn't seem to matter much anyway.

The bartender, a stocky Hispanic man named Blas—pronounced *Blaz*, as he had initially corrected Arthur—was wiping up the black marble bar with a white towel before getting back to his stack of room service bills piled up by the register. Arthur's observant mind noticed his dark blue long-sleeved shirt, black slacks and matching belt. He couldn't see his shoes but deduced they probably matched the gloss and color of the belt. Blas looked to be middle-aged, Arthur guessed, with a thick head of black hair that went well with the mustache that decorated his upper lip.

The University of New Mexico's basketball team had been running back and forth on the TV above the center of the bar for a while. They were putting their 5–7 season up against the 7–7 UNLV and, so far, had been holding their own. But, Arthur figured, there were still twenty more games left in the season, so he shouldn't worry just yet. Below the TV stood liquor bottles of assorted heights and diameters that were ready to fill the carefully stacked glasses on the flanking glass shelves. Ak'is was back at the room sleeping or sniffing or thinking whatever wolf dogs do when they were alone, while Arthur grabbed the red leather bar menu standing before him and began looking through it while awaiting the arrival of Detective Lance Gilberto.

"Would you like to order, sir?" Blas said.

"Just looking," Arthur said. "I'm waiting for someone. I'll take another beer, though."

"Yes, sir."

Arthur was enjoying the taste of his Nut Brown Ale when out of the corner of his eye he saw a thin, muscular middle-aged man come into view from the hallway that led into the restaurant/bar area from the lobby. Blas retrieved a new can from the fridge behind the bar and placed it in front of Arthur before going back to tallying his room service bills as the thin man turned and headed into the bar. His dark but slightly graying hair was raked backward over his head in a thick lion's mane, and if he was looking to be all about the Benicio del Toro brood, Arthur figured he had mastered that long ago. When he got closer, the man stuck his hand out in Arthur's direction. "Arthur Nakai?"

Arthur shook it. "Thank you for meeting me, Detective. Can I interest you in anything?"

"Corona," Gilberto replied.

Arthur motioned toward Blas and ordered. By the time Gilberto's leather jacket was off and draped over the chair next to him, his Corona was waiting in front of him on a white napkin square. Arthur couldn't help but notice the tactical holster Gilberto wore and the butt of the SIG Sauer sticking out of it, along with the two-clip magazine pouch that hung on his opposite hip; the matching handcuff pouch at the small of his back seemed at home, too.

"Captain Bilagody tells me you're here about the Manygoats girl." He took a swig of his beer and set it back down as he climbed into the pub chair.

Arthur sipped his Nut Brown, looked at Gilberto. "Her mother seems to think that when it comes to missing Indian girls, the police don't think it's a priority." Arthur studied Gilberto's expression. "By the way you said 'Manygoats girl,' I'm wondering if she was right."

Gilberto sipped his Corona again, grinned a little, then set the bottle back on the paper napkin. "I understand why she may feel that way, but I'm sure she doesn't realize what's involved and how many leads we're chasing on top of all the other cases we're handling."

Blas walked back up the bar to them. "Have you gentlemen decided on something to eat?"

"I'll have an order of those Award-Winning Meatballs in the Arrabiata Sauce," Arthur said, then looked at Gilberto.

"I'm easy," he said. "Make it two."

Blas smiled and left the two men to their conversation.

"As far as the Manygoats case, we still continue to get leads, but none of them pan out. This girl dropped outta sight like a witness in a Mafia trial." Gilberto took another mouthful of beer and swallowed, barely enjoying the coldness and none of the fruity-honey flavor. "It just seems like a case of the girl being a runaway, and the parents don't wanna believe it. I see it all the time."

Arthur's fingers spun his tall glass slowly. "And what leads you to that assumption?"

Gilberto shrugged. "Her home life, for one. The fact that they live below the poverty line, even with the jewelry business, means she probably wanted more out of life and she couldn't stomach living at home anymore." He drank another swig of beer, this time seeming to savor the flavor a little more. "If you ask me, I'm sure she found something— or someone—that she thinks could give her the land over the rainbow."

Arthur stared sideways, stopped spinning his glass. "So, you're just going to shove aside the option that she's become one of the stolen?" Arthur shook his head. "My wife was right."

"About what?" Gilberto said.

Arthur picked up his glass of Nut Brown, studied it briefly, drank a sip and swallowed. "That Native women aren't really looked at as justifiable victims."

"I didn't say that," Gilberto countered.

"Did you ever seen a rape tree, Detective?"

Gilberto looked at him. "No."

"I have. When I was in the Shadow Wolves. We caught up to some coyotes around two thirty in the morning. They had stopped under what seemed to be the only tree around for miles. It was a rendezvous point where they could pick up more supplies. The three coyotes had stripped this teenage girl and laid her out under the branches of the tree— branches that were already decorated with the underwear of previous females that had suffered the same fate. One was on top of her while the other two were keeping their weapons trained on the UDAs. They were going to take turns." Arthur drank a mouthful of beer, swallowed. "I've seen a lot of shit, Detective, but seeing that tree and what it represented was my tipping point." Arthur paused. "Do you understand how many families are still waiting for a phone call to let them know what is going on with their case? Some of them don't hear anything for months or years." Arthur exhaled. "It's hard to get closure when your child is simply gone. Not dead … just … gone."

Gilberto starred at his bottle of Corona. "Look, I'm not saying being taken isn't a possibility. But the girl didn't live a high-risk lifestyle. She wasn't into drugs or alcohol, but maybe had a self-esteem problem. Maybe she felt ignored or depressed? I don't know. I'm only guessing. And I don't think she hated her life enough to want to end it, so she just caught a bus and took off."

Blas arrived with two rectangular white plates of large meatballs drizzled artfully in a glistening red pasta sauce. He placed the plates in front of the two men and left as quietly as he had arrived.

"And when I spoke with her parents," Gilberto continued, "I didn't get the impression she was running from any type of domestic abuse." He picked up his fork and began to dissect his first meatball. "Of course, she could have been kidnapped, and we're not ruling trafficking out either. But the fact of the matter is, the girl's phone hasn't pinged anywhere in six months. You know kids today—they can't stay off the damn things. But this is like Hillary Clinton took a hammer to it."

Arthur remembered sitting on the corner couch in his hotel room while Ak'is studied the guests lounging poolside. He had played the video Sharon had sent him. He watched as much of it as he could stomach, pausing it in the opening sequence to compare the photo Melanie Manygoats had given him to the girl in the video. All that sadly did was confirm it was her. And she looked like she was either drunk or drugged and had no clue what was happening to her. But Arthur did––she was being broken in. And her younger brother had seen it. Arthur was willing to bet he had never shown it to his parents; it would destroy their memory of their sweet little girl. *Helluva thing for a kid to keep to himself*, he had thought. Arthur was also willing to bet he wasn't going to let Detective Lance Gilberto know the video even existed. Not yet anyway. Not until he had something more tangible.

Arthur cut a meatball in half and then half again, forked and ate it. "Is there anyone you can think of in Santa Fe who would know if she was being trafficked?"

Gilberto was still hewing on his first meatball. "Honestly," he mumbled, "we may see three or so cases a year of prostitution here." He swallowed and chased it with a mouthful of Corona. "In fact, the last sexual case we had was some jackoff propositioning a woman at a city bus stop." Gilberto snickered. "If there's trafficking, it's not on the radar. And I certainly haven't seen any suspected cases come across my desk." He patted his mouth with a white cloth napkin and tossed it back onto the bar. "That sort of crap happens in Albuquerque."

Arthur ate another piece of meatball. "What did you turn up there?"

Gilberto followed Arthur's lead and ate another bite. When the meatball wasn't obstructing his tongue, he said, "We work with APD pretty closely, but she's never shown up in their system and there's been no sightings of her anywhere. If someone's seen her, no one is talking. Either that or she's already been moved out of state. Which means she could be working every bus station, truck stop and pickle park between here and God knows where." He paused. "With your experience, you know the deal—after seventy-two hours there's a good chance she's already dead. And it's been six months."

Arthur emptied his pilsner glass by half deliberately and wiped his mouth with his cloth napkin. "What did local CCTV footage turn up? You did trace her steps?"

Gilberto nodded. "There's an EarthCam across the street from the park that faces the bandshell, but you can't see the Palace of the Governors because of the trees. And the store cameras we pulled footage from along the way to where her parents said she was going were spotty at best. None of them showed anything useful." He cut another meatball and ate the half, enjoying it before taking another mouthful of Corona. "I wish I could have saved you a trip. We could've done this over the phone, but then I wouldn't have had this delicious snack." Gilberto finished his meatballs and beer and pulled a business card from his shirt pocket. "If you come up with anything, I'd appreciate knowing about it."

Arthur took the card and placed it on the bar, gave Gilberto one of his cards. "As long as you do the same."

Gilberto inspected the card curiously. "Navajo P.I., huh? That's different."

Arthur smiled. "I'm not the first. And it makes everything legal."

Gilberto grinned and slid off the tall pub chair and into his jacket. He tucked the card into a jacket pocket, then held out his hand. Arthur took it. "Thanks for the meal, Mr. Nakai."

Arthur nodded briefly, finished his beer and waved for another as the detective disappeared back up the hallway. Arthur was using his fork to cut his final meatball in half when Blas pulled open another Nut Brown and leaned on the bar with his forearms.

"I didn't mean to overhear your conversation," he said, sliding the beer can toward Arthur, "but if you're looking for a runaway, I know who you should see."

Arthur's thoughts refocused instantly. "Who would that be?"

"Shirley Becenti," Blas said quietly, as if the empty bar itself could hear him. "She runs a women's shelter in Albuquerque. She's helped a lot of girls over the years." He took one of the small square paper napkins from a stack under the bar, clicked his pen, and scribbled an address on it and slid it to him. "See her. It would be a good place to start."

CHAPTER FIVE

Arthur Nakai pulled into the parking lot of the Arroyo del Alto Women's Shelter on Peterson Avenue in Albuquerque just as the double glass doors were being unlocked by a young woman with long blond hair that came to an end at her waist. It was 9:02 in the morning.

He had done an online search the night before and was thankful Blas had given him the address. Every listing that came up gave phone numbers but no addresses, maintaining protection for the women and children housed within them. The building itself was bland and nondescript. Almost four hours away from home, the morning temperature stood in the mid-forties, with an afternoon promise of fifty-one, and the weatherman's partly sunny was a gift he was happy to accept. The young woman's hair shimmered brightly against her black blouse in the morning sun and her black fitted skirt and matching cowboy boots made Arthur smile. Her glasses appeared to be narrow black rectangles, and the eyes that stared at him through the lenses, even at this distance, did so like she was sizing up an opposing enemy. There were no other cars in the lot.

The temperature reassured Arthur it would be okay to leave Ak'is in the truck—something he would never do during the blistering heat of the summer months. He cracked the windows a couple of inches behind the Ventvisors to give the wolf dog some new scents to ponder and got out. By the time he arrived at the unlocked glass doors, the blonde had already disappeared into the building. He tugged open one of the doors and stepped into an entryway that led to a set of doors to his right, this time steel and locked. From somewhere behind the opaque wired-glass window to his left, a young woman's voice spoke through an intercom: "May I help you?"

"I'm here to see Shirley Becenti," Arthur said as he gazed into the camera mounted in the left corner above the double steel doors. "Is she in?"

"Do you have an appointment?"

"I'm sorry, I don't, but I think she'll see me. Tell her it's about April Manygoats."

"One moment, please."

Arthur took turns staring at the floor, the ceiling and the walls while the blond woman behind the wired glass checked. He stared at the camera again in case Shirley Becenti wanted to see his face. Just then, the doors in front of him buzzed. He stepped forward and pushed them open. A different long-haired woman stood on the other side. Her skin was the color of a woman who was predominantly Native but had enough Caucasian blood to pass as white. Her eyebrows looked like they had thinned over the years and rested above dark eyes that seemed to see right through him as she sized him up. Her face had traveled the path of her life well, Arthur reasoned, even though he could see that her youth had long since faded with that passage of time. She wore a pink blouse under a black blazer with long black slacks that trailed down to matching mid-heeled shoes. The steel doors closed slowly behind him with that same mechanical hiss all hydraulic door closers have before the quiet latching of the mechanism.

Shirley Becenti smiled at him briefly, held out her hand. Arthur took it and felt her long, soft fingers wrap around his rough hand. "I hear you want to see me about April Manygoats?" She released his hand and clasped together her own in front of her. "How did you know she had been here?"

"I didn't. I was just putting it out there to see if I got a response. And I did."

"I see."

"Her parents hired me to locate her." He pulled a business card from the inside pocket of his lined denim jacket and handed it to her.

She smiled. "An indigenous private investigator. How unique. You see something new every day." She motioned across the empty anteroom with an open hand. "Have you had coffee yet?"

Arthur shook his head slightly. "Not enough."

Shirley Becenti grinned. "Follow me."

Arthur followed her across the gray anteroom, passing doors he presumed led further into the interior where the women and children were living safely, and one that obviously led to where the blonde with the boots had been sequestered behind the opaque glass. Once they were inside Shirley Becenti's office, she closed the door. She offered Arthur one of the padded armchairs that faced her desk, black metal with chrome legs. While her back was to him, he let his eyes roam over the wall to his right. It was plastered with fliers of missing Native girls and women. Arthur felt his jaw tighten at the sheer number of them, and the emotional reality of his task became much more of a weight on his shoulders. It had never really hit him until he saw the rows and rows of faces that made up the columns that were pinned to her office wall. Among them was a flyer of April Manygoats: *Age: 19, Hair: Brown, Eyes: Brown, Height 5'2", Weight: 150 pounds.* Last seen where and when and wearing what, followed by a phone number to call and a case number.

"Do you take cream, Mr. Nakai?"

"About an inch, please."

Shirley Becenti went about the task of creating a cup of coffee to Arthur's specs, then turned around to see him staring at the wall. "Are you wondering why those are up there?"

Arthur gave no answer. He knew she wasn't looking for one. He was getting good at knowing the right moment to speak when it came to women—even though it had taken years.

"That wall is filled with the alerts of our sisters that have gone missing just this year. Did you know that at least twenty-five percent are under eighteen? I had a woman in here last year that was brought into the sex trade at nineteen, and she was still doing it at forty-two." Shirley sighed. "The only time I take a flier down is when they're found safe … or otherwise. And I am constantly updating it." She exhaled heavily. "What really upsets me most is the fact that the media doesn't give a damn."

"That's because the media thrives on controversy," Arthur acknowledged. "They make it seem like one race is more worthy of coverage than another; like one color matters more than another or reaches more viewers or gets more clicks on a website. They don't understand that there's more than two colors in America."

"Exactly," she agreed. "But our people have always been subjected to that since the colonials invaded. To people like you and me, all of America is occupied Native land." Shirley Becenti half grinned. "People need to be reminded that the government didn't give us anything they didn't take away from us first." She absently stirred cream into his coffee with a spoon. "Any sugar?"

"No, thank you."

"I'm curious," she coaxed. "How do you think I can help you with April Manygoats?"

"I was hoping if you had any contact with her here at the shelter you would be able to give me some insight into her frame of mind, possibly tell me something that would help me find her."

Shirley Becenti turned and handed Arthur the hot mug, which featured the black-on-white designs reminiscent of ancient pueblo pottery, then poured one for herself. Black, no cream, one heaping spoon of sugar. She took her seat behind her desk, and, sipping her coffee carefully, she studied him over the mug's rim, then rocked back slowly in her chair so as not to spill any of its rich Colombian contents.

"She showed up here about two months ago," Shirley told him. "Just wandered in one day looking for help. She was in bad shape. Said she had been doped up with scopolamine among other things."

Arthur sipped his coffee, shifted his eyebrows upward, pleased at the perfect mixture of cream and caffeine. "Scopolamine?" he quizzed.

Shirley Becenti explained. "Scopolamine is a pollen. It's tasteless, colorless and odorless. I've heard the Colombians like to mix it in drinks or sprinkle it on food. Sometimes the bolder cartels simply blow it directly into your face." She sipped her coffee and went on. "It makes a person open to suggestion and extremely docile; submissive even. April guessed that's what was used on her the first time she was gang-raped. She said they kept her in that acquiescent state for weeks at a time. She said she just taught herself to simply float away and not feel anything while it happened." Shirley Becenti held her mug in her hands as if she were cradling an injured bird. "She was here a little over a month before she just walked out the door and never came back."

"Does that happen often?"

"No. But I'd be lying if I told you it never did." She took a mouthful of coffee and swallowed it. "The girls get scared, start thinking they have no place left in the real world, and go back to the only world they think they fit into … no matter how terrible it was. That's the one thing you have to learn in this job—you can't save them all, no matter how hard you try." Shirley sighed. "That's a hard realization to cope with sometimes."

Arthur drank some more coffee. "So, what made you want to open a shelter? I read your mission statement last night on the internet, but what was the catalyst?"

"You wanna know about me?" Becenti said. Her elbows balanced on the arms of her chair, her long fingers holding the mug in front of her. "Let's see, where do I begin?" She tilted her head back and rolled her eyes in thought. "How about when I was an unwanted child cramping my parents' style. How about when I was locked in a dog crate when I was small because I did something they didn't like. Let's add to that the thought that the Creator was punishing me for just being alive."

Arthur was holding his pottery mug with both hands now because the warmth emanating from the ceramic felt good. "The Creator was always with you," he said. "Taking care of you; protecting you."

"Protecting me?" Shirley Becenti's face was shaded with disbelief. "Where was the Creator when I was eight years old and taken from my mother and told that she wasn't my real mother and given to a woman I didn't even know? Where was the Creator when I was fourteen and my stepfather raped me over and over until I was seventeen, when he was killed by a drunk driver? Where was he when a man broke into my apartment when I was twenty-three and did the very same thing?" She gulped down the rest of her coffee and looked at Arthur—not for understanding or pity, but simply because she noticed the empathy registering in his eyes. "I figure the Creator was simply rolling the dice with me and kept coming up craps." She took a deep breath and let it out, clearing her lungs as well as her mind. "What I'm saying is that I can relate to the women and girls that come here for help. When I was a girl, I didn't have anyone I could talk to about it. Until my stepfather died, only he, my mother and myself knew what he had done."

Arthur said, "Why didn't she turn him in? Get you both away from him?"

"Because he was a verbally and physically abusive bastard. She was simply too afraid to rock the sinking boat." She paused. "When I opened this place ten years ago, I didn't want today's girls to have to go through all the shame and self-hate I had felt without anyone there to help." She huffed. "And all the well-meaning bleeding hearts in the world aren't going to be able to help these girls and women unless they've lived through it and can understand the kinds of terror they're running from."

"I didn't mean to pry," Arthur said contritely. "But don't you think all that happened in your life was meant to bring you to this point? Your past is everything that made you who you are today."

"Always the optimist, aren't you?" Her smile was one hard-earned. "In my late twenties through mid-thirties I did some pretty crazy shit and got into some pretty horrible relationships. I guess you could say I never knew how to pick a good man. They were all losers. I have two broken arms, a broken leg and a rod in my back to prove it."

Arthur watched her get up and pour herself another mug of coffee. She motioned to him. He declined.

"Let me tell you," she said, "after you've lived a hard life, your body doesn't hold up as well as you thought it would."

Arthur set his mug on the corner of her desk. "The young lady I saw unlocking the door, did she know April?"

"No," Shirley said. "That would be Liz Hanover."

"Is she here?"

"Not today. It's her day off."

Arthur nodded. "Can you give me her home address?"

Shirley thought for a moment. "We don't give out that type of information. I trust you can understand? But if you'd like to speak with her, you can find her at Bankshotz—with a z—around three o'clock today."

"Where's that?"

"It's a pool hall and bar off Central Avenue just south of the University of New Mexico. She practices there all the time before traveling to tournaments."

"She's a pool shark?"

Shirley grinned. "A very good one. Don't let her get you involved in a game; she'll take you for whatever you've got."

"How much contact did she have with April?"

Shirley thought for a moment. "I'm not sure, but Liz works with a lot of our younger girls in here, so I'm pretty sure she did. She's only twenty-three herself."

"Did she ever mention who took her from Santa Fe by name?"

Shirley Becenti sipped her coffee quietly. "Not to me. Just that she had met some asshole in some online chatroom."

"Through a gaming console?"

"No. Her family could never afford that. It was through one of those phone apps the kids all use. He did what they all do—started telling her nice things, pretended he was getting to know her so he could get her interested in him. They've got a name for that—the Loverboy Method."

"And young girls fall for that?"

"The younger the better," she said. "But all young girls are naïve. These parasites will work their deviate magic on girls as young as twelve. It's a long process, though. They may even be stringing along a handful of unsuspecting girls at the same time. They start by courting the victim, getting them to divulge information about themselves, their problems, their lives—all while never really telling them anything about themselves."

"And the girls don't think to question any of it?"

"You have to remember, Mr. Nakai, these are all very young and impressionable adolescents. To them it's just some guy taking an interest in them, someone that listens to their problems. A boy who builds this perfect world for them and tells them that they could be the center of it. And after a while of filling her head with bullshit, they'll move fast right when they know they have gained their trust and affection." She sipped her coffee again. "That's what happened to April. This guy lured her away from her parents, and she was never seen or heard from again. It's sad when you think about the possibility that everywhere you go in this state was the last place someone was ever seen." She shook her head slowly. "And the world just keeps on spinning."

Arthur had never thought of it that way, and it struck him to his core. It was safe to say he would never look at places in the same way again. "You said she just showed up here? Why didn't you contact the police or her parents?"

"I wanted to give her time to get clean before I subjected her to that," Shirley said. "In hindsight, I know I should have contacted the police, but I didn't know how they or her parents would react seeing her in the condition she was in. These people had stolen more than just her spirit. They had stolen everything from her."

"You said she never mentioned who she was sold to?"

She shook her head. "Mr. Nakai, the most useful side effect from scopolamine is a total loss of memory, so we never found out who had bought her. If she had any tattoos, she kept them hidden. But she always seemed afraid. And she just referred to the slug who sold her as her boyfriend." She shrugged slightly. "I guess she was still afraid of him, too. I get that."

Arthur pulled his cell phone from his inside jacket pocket. "I'd like you to look at something."

"Sure."

Arthur got up, walked around her desk, and positioned himself next to her. He could smell her perfume, a delicate sweet aroma that lingered in the air around her like a tantalizing aura. It was different from Sharon's, he quickly discerned, but it stirred his olfactory senses nonetheless. He focused as she leaned in to watch while the site loaded on the six-inch screen. The video began.

"My God," she said. "That's April."

"Who's the guy?" Arthur prompted.

After a while of watching the young Diné girl on the shabby mattress with the glazed look on her face going through the motions of passionless sex, they saw the man grab her legs and lay her on her side. It was only then, when he lay down behind her and resumed his rhythmic penetration, that he entered the frame enough to allow Shirley Becenti to see his face.

"I know that *zhinnie*," she scoffed. "His name is Jonzell Washington. Looks like he's graduated from hustling casinos for jailbait to shooting online porn."

Arthur stopped the video and turned the screen to black. "What?"

"This asshole used to hang around casinos and send in his minions to look for young girls and ask them if they wanted to make an easy fifteen hundred." Her face showed disgust. "I guess he found a safer way of doing that."

Arthur was still perched on the corner of the desk. He tucked his phone away into a jacket pocket.

Shirley looked up at him. "They would, of course, say 'yes.' The minion, usually a girl over eighteen, would take them up to a room in the casino hotel where he would be waiting to 'interview' them. If they seemed like the type to fall for his shit, he would tell them to get paid they needed to make a screen test."

"And that's how he got her to do this." It wasn't a question.

"I can't say for sure, but that's how he used to. Only when he's done, and they're putting on their clothes, the girls ask for the fifteen hundred. That's where he would tell him that this was just the audition, and he would have to pass around the tape to producers and try to get them interested."

Arthur said, "And they believe that?"

"Sometimes they're so desperate they'll believe anything." She raked her long fingers through her even longer black hair, shook her head to accentuate the length.

Even in her late-fifties, Arthur thought, *she is strikingly beautiful*. The ravages of bad men and a crazy life may have taken their toll on her body, but they hadn't damaged her looks.

Shirley continued, "Those that figure out he's fucked them, not only physically but figuratively, leave and never talk about it because they are too ashamed to tell anyone. But the ones who still think there's a possible contract with their name on it somewhere stick with him. Then, as you can see, he gets them hooked on something—heroin probably—and ends up supplying them for parties for a price."

"Heroin?" Arthur questioned.

"Everything old is new again," Shirley said. "Then, if they're good at fucking for the camera, he tricks them out for a while at a hundred bucks a pop. Even more for big doings like conventions and sporting events."

"A hundred bucks sounds cheap," Arthur said.

"When a girl can turn upwards of fifty tricks a day, a hundred bucks a john can turn into five grand a day. That works out to be around nine hundred grand a year if the girl makes it through half a year before dying of an overdose or committing suicide. Then multiply that by how many girls he's running and it's astronomical."

Arthur felt his jaw tighten again. His fist, too. He wanted to hit something. And hard. He despised men who used and abused women, but this was now taking him to a new level of anger.

"Where can I find him?" he said calmly.

"Last I heard he was using the Sonoran Motel off Sagebrush Trail here in Duke City."

"Albuquerque?"

"Yeah," she said. "Maybe he still does. It's been a while since I heard that. It's the kind of place where the rooms are cheap and the asshole manning the front desk doesn't care what's going on because he's being paid to keep his mouth shut and his eyes open."

Arthur smiled briefly. "You've been a great help."

Shirley touched Arthur's hand as he stood. "Whatever he tells you, keep in mind he's only the white spec on the top of a pile of chicken shit."

"Copy that."

Shirley Becenti walked him out of her office, back to the double metal doors. "I can tell when a man has seen a lot and done a lot more than he talks about." She paused when they arrived at the doors, turned to look at him. "When you find

April, make whoever has her pay for it because that would be true justice."

Arthur smiled cynically. "I think you're confusing vigilantism with justice."

Shirley Becenti's eyes sparkled in the fluorescent lighting. "The Cherokee have a story that tells of the battle that rages inside us all. Inside each of us there are two wolves. One wolf is filled with anger and jealousy, greed and resentment, lies and ego. It embodies everything evil."

"And the other?"

"The other embodies all that is good. It is filled with joy and peace, love and hope, humanity and kindness, empathy and truth."

"What determines which wolf will win?" Arthur asked, remembering full well the answer to a similar story, told to him by his grandfather when he was young.

Shirley Becenti cocked her head to one side and replied, "The one you feed, of course."

CHAPTER SIX

It was 9:56 in the morning when Arthur Nakai pulled his Bronco into a slot across the street from the Sonoran Motel in Albuquerque, New Mexico. The spot set him up at a twenty-five-degree angle to the motel and ensured him a clear view of the arched entrance and a good portion of the parking lot. Arthur wondered if whoever had hung the lackluster Christmas decorations in the windows actually thought they added joy to the thirty-year-old dive or fleabag or whatever places like this were called in today's PC world. Ak'is had stationed himself in the passenger seat, ears at attention, and followed everything that moved with his golden eyes like a cheetah tracking prey on the Serengeti.

The color scheme of the two-story U-shaped motel was a mixture of fading paint and old concrete that had once displayed a horizontal bright red stripe on the original white paint running close to the edge of its flat roof. The establishment's sign advertised weekly rates, and according to Arthur's cell phone research, conducted as he sat there bored to death listening to his copilot pant, it was located in one of Albuquerque's worst crime zones. In fact, Duke City's finest had received so many 911 calls concerning prostitution, drug dealing and violence that Arthur wasn't looking for it to get any five-star ratings anytime this century.

Arthur and Ak'is had been gnawing on a bag of beef sticks he had picked up when he stopped for gas on his way to his stakeout. Arthur had washed them down with a bottle of ice tea taken from a small cooler on the front seat floorboard while making sure his partner had been drinking from the expandable urethane cup he had bought for this little demonstration of unmatched perseverance. As the hours slowly ticked by, the pair would take a bite of beef stick, followed by a swig of their respective drinks, and simply stare at the entrance. Arthur wondered if Sam Spade or Boston's own Spenser had ever gotten used to this part of their chosen profession. At least Spenser had Hawk. And Hawk could actually speak.

The office of the motel had five tall, shaded windows—all street side—with an office door that faced the arched entrance. Arthur had already read all the restaurant and business signs in the area more times than he cared to remember and was now looking for the street signs to grow his vocabulary. *Ah, boredom. Stakeouts aren't as glamourous as Hollywood makes them out to be.*

Arthur opened the center console and pulled out his first-edition copy of Tony Hillerman's debut novel, *The Blessing Way*. He swore he had heard it taunting him from inside its hiding place. If he opened it up and got involved in the story, he might miss seeing Jonzell Washington and never get a chance to confront him about April Manygoats. On the other hand, if he did open it, and gave glancing looks at the entrance every other paragraph, there was a good chance he would catch the spider bringing the unsuspecting victim back to his web. Arthur pursed his lips and weighed the possibilities of executive decision-making. Better leave it be, he decided, and returned the book to its hiding place inside the darkness of the console and closed the lid. He ruffled the fur on Ak'is' head and returned his gaze to the motel entrance.

With the windows of the truck rolled up, and the lined denim jacket keeping his Glock 19C warm and snug in its shoulder holster under his left arm, he was glad the temperature hovered in the mid-fifties. If this had been June, July or August he'd be sweltering inside an oven. And he had learned long ago not to keep a vehicle running in really cold weather because the wafting exhaust fumes would give you away to anyone looking for a reason to spot you, but it was still too warm for that to be bothersome. And then there were bathroom breaks. Arthur had trained his bladder well in service to his country, but as he had gotten older, curtailing its functions seemed to be a difficult task sometimes.

Suddenly, his hand pulled his keys from the truck's ignition and stuffed them into his jacket pocket. The spider had arrived. He recognized him from the video, but not the young girl he had on his arm. Jonzell Washington walked toward the entrance of the motel as Arthur climbed out of the truck and shut the door, not paying any attention to the comforting hollow sound it made as it slammed home.

"Guard the truck," he told Ak'is through the slightly opened window, "and try to keep your nose off the glass. That's just nasty."

Arthur Nakai quickly checked both ways for traffic, then trotted across the three eastbound lanes, pausing only briefly in the gravel median before continuing across the three westbound lanes unimpeded. Reaching the opposite sidewalk, he quickly moved through the motel's entrance. Jonzell Washington and his young protégée were angling across the interior parking lot. Arthur walked slowly past the motel's office and moved to his left toward the lower rooms of the two-story motor inn. He skirted an older Ford sedan and positioned himself out of view beneath the walkway above him. From his vantage point, he could see

Washington lead his latest star up the stairs at the end of the building. Arthur moved quickly, running beneath the upper walkway until he heard the wannabe porn director attempt a joke and the girl feign the kind of uneasy laughter you hear nervous teenagers make when they are unsure how to react.

This wasn't the kind of place that would have card keys. Arthur recognized the sound of an actual key being inserted into a doorknob and the door being opened. He jogged to his right in time to see the door close on room 206. After looking around the motel's interior to make sure no one had seen a strange Indian sneaking around the parking lot, he took the stairs in twos. His heart picked up its pace as the adrenaline raced through his veins, his lungs hardly laboring in his chest as he leaned a warm ear to the cold steel door of room 206.

Should he knock on the door pretending to be management or maintenance and hope that Washington opened it? Or should he try to kick it in like he used to do during door-to-doors in Kabul? He could hear nothing inside the room, but he recognized the bright light that suddenly backlit the vinyl curtains. Now all that remained, he quickly thought, would be Washington saying *camera* and *action!* Arthur briefly rethought his kicking-in-the-door option, but this wasn't Afghanistan; this was Albuquerque and this door was made of insulated steel, not desert-baked wood.

Arthur took a deep breath, pulled the Glock from its sling, and wrapped the knuckles of his free hand against the cold steel. "Maintenance!" he said loudly.

Nothing.

"Maintenance!" he said once again, wrapping his knuckles harder this time.

"Whatchoo want?" Jonzell Washington yelled from inside.

"I'm checking the heat in all the rooms, sir," Arthur lied. "We've had some complaints, so all the rooms have to be checked."

"It's workin' fine," Jonzell argued forcefully. "Don't need yo ass to look at nothin'!"

Crap. Arthur had to think fast. "I understand, sir, but my boss won't. It really won't take long to check, and I'll be outta your hair."

Arthur heard Jonzell bark an expletive before the deadbolt clanked loudly as the tumblers rolled the bolt back from the doorjamb. Arthur then heard the chain that wouldn't stop anyone determined to get inside move from its slot on the other side and tap the inside of the steel doorjamb as it dangled in place. Arthur took a breath, felt his fingers instinctively flex and reset themselves around the grip of the Glock, which he now held at his belly—the gun he was sure was out of view of the peephole Jonzell Washington had surely used to base his decision on. Arthur readied his left shoulder for the inevitable thrust against the door that he hoped would rock Jonzell Washington back into the room and stagger him off-balance enough so that he could rush him.

Arthur counted in his head as he watched the doorknob turn; then, just as the door cleared the jamb, he rushed in. Jonzell Washington rocked backward from the unexpected force and collided with the camera tripod first, followed by the lighting stand, both of which toppled over along with him. The bulb inside the silver aluminum cone popped as it hit the thin pile carpeting and went dark. The girl screamed. Arthur's eyes shifted momentarily to her before refocusing on Jonzell. Washington hurled a litany of obscenities as he untangled himself from the camera and lighting. Slamming shut the door behind him, Arthur locked it as he held the

Glock squarely on the low-life wannabe smut peddler, as Shirley Becenti had called him.

Arthur looked again at the girl on the bed. Her coat and clothes were off; the only thing saving her innocence was a black eyelash-lace bralette and matching panties. She was a frightened young Latina whose brown eyes still shined like those of a girl who hadn't been compromised, used and thrown away. Her dark hair fell straight over her thin shoulders and flat against the cinnamon skin of her adolescent body; the small mole that dotted the left side of her upper lip seemed to add to her adorability even as she cried uncontrollably.

"Who da fuck are you, muthafucka?" Washington exclaimed angrily.

"Me?" Arthur said. "I'm the guy you're going to help find a girl." Arthur looked at the frightened teenager on the bed. "Get dressed and get out of here."

The girl didn't move, just sat there shaking and continuing to cry.

When Washington moved to get up, Arthur moved closer. "Stay down until I tell you to get up!" He turned again to the girl, softened his words. "What's your name?"

"Alyssa," she said, embarrassed.

"Alyssa? Why don't you get dressed and leave this place and never come back? You don't need him. You're special. You're priceless."

"I'm nothing," Alyssa said.

"You're worth more than you know," Arthur reassured her. "Do you have any family? Someone you can call? I'm sure someone is worried sick about you."

She wiped the mascara-blackened tears from her eyes and reached out for a purple blouse that rested on the pile of her ensemble at the edge of the bed. "No one is worried about me," she said. "No one misses me."

Arthur stared at Jonzell as the girl reluctantly slid off the bed and got dressed. He could see the porn director's anger building while he felt his own rage growing in his body. By the look of Washington, this punk hadn't been where Arthur had been and done what Arthur had done. He was a poser, a player, and he was the one who was worth nothing. The asshole no one would miss.

"Whatever future this man claimed to be able to give you is a lie. Whatever love he told you he would lavish upon you is a lie." Arthur moved his index finger through the trigger guard. Jonzell bristled but stayed on the floor. Alyssa got into her coat, slung her purse over her shoulder and started to walk past Arthur. "Grab that pen on the table by the window," Arthur instructed.

The girl walked over and picked up the pen that lay next to the thin motel pad resting on a round table flanked by two chairs.

Arthur said, "I'm gonna give you an address, and I want you to go there." He glanced toward Jonzell. "Stick your fingers in your ears!"

"Are you fo' real?" Washington said.

"Be like Nike and just do it!" Jonzell did as he was told. Alyssa jotted down the information as Arthur rattled it off. "Do you have any money?"

The girl shook her head. "Well, a little."

Reaching into his front pants pocket, Arthur pulled out a handful of crumpled bills the gas station clerk had given him as change for his snacks and gave them to her. "That should be enough for cab fare. Be sure you go straight there and don't look back. She'll help you."

Alyssa looked at him. "Why are you doing this?"

Arthur smiled sympathetically. "Because you're worth it."

Alyssa smiled back, unlocked the door and left. Arthur locked the bolt behind her and slid the chain, then waved his gun in a way that told Jonzell he could take his fingers out of his ears.

"Man, you fuckin' crazy!" Washington barked. "You come all bustin' up in here and fuck up my shit!"

"Get up!" Arthur's tone was flat, hard.

Washington got to his feet and stood close enough that the muzzle of Arthur's Glock pressed against his belly. "I ain't 'fraida no fuckin' half-a-gas-can. You wanna go, muthafucka, le's go."

Arthur's left fist clinched and swung too quickly for Washington to react. The punch landed hard against the right side of Washington's head and sent him sprawling onto the bed. Arthur followed him and had the Glock's muzzle pressed into the flesh on Washington's forehead when he tried to sit up in a failed effort to fight back.

"That's Athabaskan, asshole, and this is how this is gonna go. You're going to tell me what happened to April Manygoats. And you're going to tell me where I can find her."

"Many what?"

"Manygoats," Arthur repeated. "The nineteen-year-old you stole from Santa Fe? Ring any bells?"

"I don't know shit about no Navajo bitch!"

"Who said anything about her being Navajo?" Arthur pulled his cell phone from his jacket pocket. "You know what the trouble is with society these days, Jonzell? You can find anything on the web because everyone has a cell phone." Arthur held up his phone with one hand and tapped the video Sharon had sent him with his thumb. "This jog your memory?"

Arthur let Jonzell's eyes study the screen up until the point where he appeared lying behind her, then clicked it off and shoved the phone back into his jacket. "How 'bout now? Anything? Because that was you, right?" Arthur pushed the semiautomatic's muzzle harder into Washington's forehead and asked again. "Right?"

"She came back here a few months ago." Jonzell was sweating now. And his eyes were wide enough for Arthur to see every frightened blood-filled vein. "She needed a fix and a place to stay. I gave her some candy and let her crash."

"Good. Now we're getting somewhere. She still around?"

Washington gulped down a hard swallow and shot a sideways look to the door.

"Don't look over there!" Arthur ordered. "You look straight at me!"

"She was hurtin' bad, know what I'm sayin'? I hooked her up with some Mexican brown so she could get back in the game, know what I'm sayin'?"

"Heroin?" Arthur cringed. "You shot her up?"

"Fuck yeah, man. Like I said, she was hurtin'." He swallowed hard and licked his dry lips. "Yo, look, I don't need no beat-up pussy around here, know what I'm sayin'? I got that bitch fixed up and back to her owner."

Arthur pushed the muzzle of the Glock harder, forcing Jonzell's head to rock backward, the cords in his neck muscles straining to keep his head vertical. He didn't think the lowlife's eyes could get any wider, until he said, "You ever see a man with a headshot? A nine-millimeter hole goes in—baseball-sized hole comes out. What's his name?"

"Fuck you, man! I ain't gonna tell you shit! He'll kill me!"

Arthur kept the muzzle of the Glock firmly against Washington's forehead while he reached inside his denim jacket.

"Whatchoo you doing?"

"You ever heard a nine-millimeter round fired in a closed room?" Arthur said, his fingers screwing the suppressor on the end of the pistol. "It's really loud. And your ears ring. And then there's the smell." Arthur's hand cranked the suppressor onto the threaded barrel of the gun. "This kinda puts a damper on that. Especially when you're using hundred-and-forty-seven-grain rounds like I do. Don't want to give your neighbors cause for alarm."

Jonzell Washington sat up straight on the bed; the vision of fear mapping his face was priceless. "I told you, man, he's gonna fuckin' kill me if I tell you!"

"I think whoever *he* is, is the least of your worries at this point in your life," Arthur said, immediately placing the tip of the suppressor over Jonzell's heart as he filled his free hand with the porn director's scrotum and squeezed. "I'm going to ask you again … who is he?"

"Fuck you, muthafucka!"

Arthur's hand tightened like a vise around walnuts.

"FUCK! I'M GONNA KILL YOU!"

Without hesitation, Arthur cocked his arm back and drove it home, slamming the side of the pistol against Washington's head like a boxer landing a roundhouse punch. Arthur's grip on the wannabe porn director's balls kept him upright as blood began to flow from the long gash that now decorated the left side of his face.

"FUCK!" Jonzell yelled against the pain.

As Jonzell's mouth gaped, Arthur quickly shoved the suppressor into it and watched as the blood ran from the gash in his jaw and ended up decorating his bare chest. Jonzell's mouth closed around the cigar-sized suppressor.

Arthur said coldly, "I'm done playing with you. Tell me what I want to know or you can say good night."

Washington tried to speak, but only garbled sounds managed to come from his swollen mouth.

Arthur removed the suppressor.

"Chino Ignacio Garcia!" Washington blurted. "I sold her to Chino Garcia!"

"Where can I find him?" Arthur's hand continued to squeeze Jonzell's testicles to the point where he could almost imagine the pain himself.

"FUCK!" Washington screamed. "He's gotta place on the northwest side!" Tears welled up in the porn director's eyes and ran down his sweating cheeks. "He moves drugs, sells guns and runs girls."

Arthur enunciated each word succinctly. "Tell. Me. Where. I. Can. Find. Him."

"He runs his shit outta some fancy-assed Cuban restaurant, Casa Caliente. Offices are upstairs. The building is bigger than it looks. He has private rooms in a building next door that used to be an old hotel back in the day. That's where the girls are."

Arthur lessened his compression of Jonzell's now swollen family jewels. "What's Garcia look like?"

"Like a fuckin' Cuban, man! Wears his hair slicked back, little fuckin' mustache, and he's got a tattoo across his chest."

"What's it of?"

Arthur released the pressure on Jonzell's balls and stood beside the bed now, flexing his left hand while keeping the Glock trained on Washington's chest. "I asked you what's that tattoo of? I didn't get an answer. I don't like it when I don't get answers."

Washington looked at Arthur, his hands gently cupping his throbbing testicles, and then at the end of the suppressor. "It ain't *of* nothing! It says *mano del diablo*. Hand of the devil."

Arthur waited a moment, letting Jonzell's fear build a little more. "How do I get in?"

"Why should I tell you, man?"

"Because I'll kill your worthless ass if you don't."

"Shiiit! You haveta go up to the bitch at the podium when you walk in and tell her you're looking for a dance partner. If you bluff your way past her, you'll be taken over to a pair of big-ass doors. There's usually a giant motherfucker there makin' sure no one gets through who ain't s'posed to. He takes his cue from the bitch up front. He'll take you through to where you'll meet the woman they call the Den Mother. She a tough ol' bitch. If you convince her, she'll bring out the ho parade. Then you take your pick and get to it."

Arthur unscrewed the suppressor, slid it back inside his jacket, then holstered his Glock and turned toward the door.

"I see you again, I'm gonna kill you, motherfucker!" Jonzell warned. "I promise you."

Arthur paused at the door, turned the deadbolt, and looked back at Jonzell sitting naked on the bed holding his balls. "Yeah," he said. "You keep thinkin' that."

CHAPTER SEVEN

"You think it's Lucy Nez?" Officer Brandon Descheene said, his right hand rubbing the spot on his chest where his medicine pouch hung under his shirt. The leather bag carried sacred herbs and an arrowhead talisman blessed by a *hataałii*—a medicine man. When you're out here, Descheene always believed, you can never tell how the afterlife will affect you. To the colonists, their ways were considered superstitions and myths, but to the Native peoples, they were—and had always been—truths that were to be respected.

Jake Bilagody watched the prevailing winds that traveled east from the Rock with Wings, otherwise known as Shiprock, across the dry and rugged landscape of the Navajo Nation. It rolled freely over the Hogback, as the Navajo once had, and rippled across the warm waters of Morgan Lake. He lowered his eyes to study the clear blue seventy-five-degree water gently lapping at the cold flesh of the dead girl's lower legs, which lay on the silt edges of the shore.

The girl's lifeless body was lying prone at the water's edge. She was clothed in red sweatpants and a matching hoodie with the words *Rez Power* emblazoned on the back in scripted white letters. The hood had managed to drape itself over her right shoulder and the right side of her face, which lay in the sand. Her long dark hair was matted to the back of her head, even though the back of her head had been caved in by something as yet unknown. The proverbial blunt object, Jake told himself. And there were no shoes on her feet.

"Does she look like she's fifteen?" Bilagody said. "This girl is in her early twenties, I'd say." Jake studied her features more closely. "And she looks more Mexican than Navajo."

Descheene nodded. "Definitely not a suicide."

"Ya think?" Jake responded. "Don't know too many people that drown themselves in a lake after hitting themselves in the back of the head with something. Over the last twenty-five years I've seen people weigh themselves down with cinder blocks, buckets filled with concrete ... even saw a guy use a bowling ball once."

"A bowling ball?"

"Yep. Took a heavy ball, put it in his bag, chained it to his feet. Then jumped off the end of a dock. Left a note in his car parked nearby telling whoever found it where to look."

Descheene said, "Daaaamn."

Jake added, "Whoever brought her here took her out into the lake and tossed her in the water. Wonder what made them think she wouldn't float? Normally the lungs fill with water and the body sinks. Then the body bloats with gases and rises to the top. She didn't."

Officer Descheene shook his head. "Boat launch is over there. They would have backed up and put the trailer in the water with her body already in it."

Jakes eyebrows raised. "Who says they trailered a boat? Coulda had a canoe or something strapped to the top of the vehicle. Wouldn't take much to pull it down, get the body out of the vehicle, put it in the canoe and paddle her out there."

"Would have taken at least two people," Descheene said.

Jake shook his head. "Not necessarily. Some canoes weigh as little as thirty or so pounds. One guy could handle it."

The young cop had lost most of the weight he had been

carrying over the last five years. Jake Bilagody attributed that to the strict workout regimen and diet he had been sticking to for the past year and a half. Even his posture seemed more erect and his uniform looked more fitted because of his stronger physique. Those were the days, Jake remembered. To be light on your feet and tight with muscle everywhere. He inhaled deeply at his remembrance as he let his jaw continue to feverishly work on the two pieces of grape chewing gum that his tongue had been rolling around since he had climbed out of his Suburban.

Jake looked at Hector Tom. "Let's go over it all again, Hector."

"I was just fishing, you know?" Hector said.

"You usually drive an hour to fish?"

"I live west of Beclabito. You show me a lake around there, and I'll fish it."

Jake grinned. "Go on."

"Caught me a handful of juvie bass about eight inches long." Hector held out his hands to emphasize the size. "I toss 'em back, you know? Just catch and release. I've got my permit. You wanna see it?"

Jake declined. "Tell me again how you found the body."

To the layman, Hector Tom simply looked like a ragged old man with flat, unwashed silver hair who always wore dirty and tattered clothes because he spent most of his time trudging around studying the geological timescale of the Navajo Nation. He had tried to educate Jake once, but lost him quickly trying to explain surficial deposits. Hector also spoke Navajo most of the time and English when he deemed it necessary. This time, standing over something as horrible as this, Hector had deemed English necessary.

"I hooked her," he said, hanging his head respectfully. "Hooked her clothes, I mean. I removed the hook when I got her to shore. Didn't think it was right leaving it there, you know? I had to show respect." Hector glanced back at the body, pale and discolored with a bluish-purple tint. "Never caught anything that felt that heavy before, so I was curious to see what I'd latched onto." He rubbed the side of an index finger against his chin. "Never thought it would be something like this."

Jake studied his elder. Hector was around seventy now, yet still reminded him of the disarming and beguiling Lieutenant Columbo. Jake had concluded thirty years ago that his appearance was one of intentional misdirection after learning Hector Tom was considered by many to be the foremost historian and geologist of the Four Corners region and had lectured at several of the western universities. Jake knew the aging eyes that peered at him from behind Hector's round, wire-rimmed glasses had a challenging and precise mind working behind them.

"Yeah," Jake agreed. "You don't eat anything you catch outta here, do you?"

Hector shook his head. "I don't trust the water enough to eat anything I catch. I just catch and release, like I said. This lake is used for cooling the APS plant, you know?"

The Arizona Public Service Company Four Corners Generating Station had gone online in 1963 and was one of the largest coal-fired generating stations in the United States. It provided power to some three hundred thousand households in four states. Jake recalled reading in the *Navajo Times* about seven or eight years ago when they were closing three of the coal-burning units built in the early 1960s, while keeping two of the other units built in 1969 and '70 active.

Jake nodded. "Didn't Navajo Fish and Wildlife do something out here?"

Hector said, "Dumped a bunch of donated Christmas trees under the water as habitat for the fish—otherwise all there was out here was that spiny naiad grass in the shallows."

Jake nodded and grunted, flexed his fingers against the march of old age stiffening his joints.

"You know what's good for arthritis?" Hector said. "Turmeric. Works for me, anyway."

Jake nodded. "Been using a cream. Maybe I'll try that, too."

Hector Tom nodded, then looked around nervously, as if he were fearful of any *chindi* that might be hovering around the girl's body. "You need me anymore, Captain? I don't like hanging around the dead. The older I get, the more I feel uneasy around them. I'm going home and burn some cedar and charcoal. I don't want the contract the ghost sickness, you know?"

Jake huffed and looked at Hector from under his furrowed brow. "I'll smoke myself later. I don't have the luxury of being distracted by the old ways on duty. You have to take those thoughts off when you put on the badge."

Hector Tom nodded. "I understand. Still, it must be lonely, my friend, not knowing which world you must walk in. One day you will have to make that choice. And I hope you choose wisely."

Jake stared at the old man briefly. Hector had just turned eighteen when he was plucked up and shipped off to Vietnam in 1968. He had survived in the jungles and on the rivers and found himself on the rooftop during the fall of Saigon seven years later. Jake had heard the stories. Mainly from the old man himself. Hector had seen his share of death in war, but this young girl had shaken him.

"Officer Descheene has your statement," Jake said. "We know how to get hold of you, so you can go."

Hector threw his hand up, said, *"Hágoónee',"* which meant "goodbye" in Navajo. "I need to get back. My grandson is watching the flock today. Several of us graze in the Carrizo Range during the summer in the clearings and lost some sheep up there a few months back. Now my sister lost a few of her goats last week in the pens by her own home."

"Mountain lion?" Jake ventured.

"Most likely. Came down from the mountains. The tracks we saw up there last summer matched the ones we saw in her corral. Same cut on one of the paws. Her goats had their throats all ripped out. Blood was everywhere. One lamb even got carted off. She lost eight altogether before she ran it off with her rifle." With that, Hector simply stopped talking and headed for his beat-up copper-colored F-150 with the blue doors and faded bed cap.

Jake Bilagody and Officer Descheene watched as the old man climbed into the cab.

"You think he'll ever get a grille and bumper for that?" Descheene said. "Looks like two headlights hanging on a radiator."

"It works, doesn't it?" Jake laughed as he watched Hector drive out of sight.

Hector's old truck was soon replaced by the bouncing light-colored truck of Field Deputy Medical Investigator Delores Mendoza. Her SUV came to a stop a short distance away from them, just off the edge of the graded road in the open area by the concrete boat ramp at the water's edge. The crime scene was a little over a doglegged half mile south of Indian Service Route 36, on the north side of the man-made twelve-hundred-acre cooling lake.

The dust churned up by the SUV's tires had been kept to a minimum since the hard-packed ground had been hardened even more by the onslaught of the recent cold snap. A photographer that had arrived just after Jake and Descheene had chosen to remain warming himself in his foreign hatchback until he was called upon. When Jake gave him the nod, he got out of his heated car and began walking toward them. Jake instructed him to start taking pictures of the crime scene while Descheene scanned the ground for anything that could be considered a clue. The balding man in the baggy jeans and dark North Face jacket went to work snapping photos. Jake stood with one hand on the butt of his Glock 22, the other resting on his dual magazine pouch loaded with two clips of stacked .40-caliber rounds as FDMI Mendoza sauntered up. She was carrying her usual bag of tricks and set it down on the ground next to the body as she squatted down to get a closer look after acknowledging them both.

She said, "You think this could be your missing girl?" as she opened her case and began tugging on a pair of blue latex gloves.

"I don't think so," Jake said. "She looks older than fifteen."

"Have any of your people touched her? Moved her in any way?"

"None," Jake assured her. "Old Hector Tom literally fished her out of the water, pulled her to shore, then called us. All he did was remove his fishing hook from her because he didn't think it was right to leave it."

Delores Mendoza's blond hair shone brightly in the chilly late morning sun. Jake watched as fine, single strands of it were picked up by a short burst of wind and fanned out like shimmering tendrils of spun gold.

Delores Mendoza brushed away some of the woman's wet hair. "Looks like someone bludgeoned her with something very heavy. Notice the deep indentation in the back of the skull." She studied the woman's body from head to toe. "The fact that your fisherman pulled her up in this condition means she's probably only been in the water a short time. Less than five days, I'm guessing. Decomposition in water like this is slowed because of the water temperature and freshwater fish don't do the kind of damage saltwater fish do." She looked up at Jake.

"Hector hooked her near the top of the water; don't bodies sink?"

"Bodies tend to sink to the bottom as soon as the lungs fill up with water," Mendoza said. "Full livor mortis discoloration like hers takes place between eight and twelve hours after death. Then rigor sets in and finally algor mortis—the time when the body meets the temperature that surrounds it. This girl looks like she tried to keep herself somewhat fit but has some noticeable cellulite. And there's no sign that something weighed her down, even though the hoodie would be heavy wet, so she could have been floating a few feet from the surface where he was able to hook her. She may have been tangled in the trees they dumped in for the fish."

"How do you know about those?" Jake was flexing his aching fingers again.

Delores Mendoza grinned. "I've been known to enjoy a few Four Corners BassMasters events held here over the years." She noticed his hands. "My mother has arthritis, too. You know what's great for that?"

Jake said, "Turmeric?"

"No, tart cherry," Mendoza declared. "My mother swears by it."

"Is that a fact?"

"Oh yeah." Mendoza pushed up the sleeves of the dead girl's hoodie. "Look at the bruises on her forearms. It looks like someone held her by the wrists, too. See the bruising here? They appear to be defensive marks. She was a fighter." Mendoza checked the tops of the woman's hands. "She's lost a nail—possibly during the struggle. One of those long stick-on jobs is missing from her right index finger. See how the actual nail's been exposed?"

"Looks like one hell of a struggle," Jake said as he made a mental note of the woman's nails. He had seen that kind before. His wife—ex-wife—had worn them a few times. Each finger had been decorated for Christmas, and judging by what he saw, the missing nail most likely had a snowman painted on it.

Delores Mendoza wedged both of her gloved hands under the girl's left hip and torso, leveraged her weight and slowly rolled the body over onto its back. Immediately, Officer Brandon Descheene felt his gut wrench, desperately trying to hold down his Blake's Lotaburger with green chile and cheese, seasoned fries and strawberry shake. Turning abruptly, he staggered away, barely making it five feet before his efforts failed him. The photographer turned away briefly to compose himself, then returned to his job of cataloging death.

Jake stared down at the mutilated body, grinding his chewing gum hard enough to make his jaw hurt. Descheene pulled a bandanna from his back pocket, wiped his mouth and struggled to remain standing as he made sure he kept his attention away from the body on the shore.

Delores Mendoza had already rocked back on her haunches and swallowed hard, put the back of a blue-gloved hand against her mouth while her wide eyes became instantly fixated on the battered face that had been dragged through the silt and sand when Hector Tom had reeled her in. The forehead, nose and jaw had been crushed with a vengeance she could only describe as evil. And—like the two officers of the Navajo Nation Department of Public Safety—she was struggling to keep herself composed enough to continue working.

"This was definitely done by someone in a heated rage," Mendoza said as she leaned forward slowly to examine the crude incision that ran like a jagged smile from hip to hip on the young woman's abdomen. Carefully pulling back the serrated flap of skin with the tentative fingers of a gloved hand, she muttered, "No wonder she fought."

Jake looked on, his jaw now agitatedly working the lump of flavorless gum while his courage continued to examine his own intestinal fortitude at the sight his eyes told him he would never forget.

Mendoza swallowed hard again, looked up at the large Navajo cop. "She was pregnant. They probably thought she was dead when they started cutting. My guess is she may have woken up, and the killer panicked and ... did this before removing the baby."

CHAPTER EIGHT

April Manygoats dealt with the throbbing pain of unremembered physical abuse that coursed unforgivingly through every fiber of her nineteen-year-old body. Each nerve pulsated painfully between her legs and anal entry and seemed to struggle with the distant, smoky haze that kept her brain from elusive consciousness. She tried, somewhat unsuccessfully, to control the movement of her arms and legs, letting her mind seek out each pain in an unproductive effort to overcome it. At least she could open her eyes and breathe—although her breathing seemed shaky and sporadic and appeared to only echo inside her chamber of horrors.

The thick leather collar surrounding her neck had been fastened loose enough to allow her to swallow and have a limited amount of movement, yet remained tight enough to amplify that what was happening to her was real and not simply some kind of imagined, terrifying nightmare. The leather straps that bound her wrists had been fixed snugly by chains to the bottom of two poles where she sat and gave her only a limited range of movement. When she shifted, even slightly, she could hear the jingling of the chains that ran from her neck collar to the tops of the four metal poles as they sang the tune of her captivity.

Her hands slowly traced the four chrome chains that led from the collar to the four steel poles at the corners of her fur-padded, open-air cell like individual suspension bridges attached to her soul. The cell resembled a table turned upside down, the legs affixed with eyelets so that each secured the ends of the chains that had become her shackled world. Looking down at her thighs and feet, she recognized the tracks where the ropes had been tied around her ankles and had held her suspended as he had spun her slowly around, admiring her body, allowing his fingertips to caress the suppleness of her skin and gently knead her tender muscles and breasts with his cold, rough fingers before making her relive the memories of her past that she had tried so hard to forget.

The chains felt cold to her touch, singing their tune of imprisonment while she tugged uselessly at them in an effort to free herself. *How could I have been so fucking stupid?* she thought. She again felt the residual pain of rough sex that throbbed deeply inside her pelvis and backside. The same kind of undeniable pain of forced and frequent entry she had often endured under the care of the Cuban. The kind of pain she had been introduced to during a life that fell somewhere between childhood and this moment. The only difference in being part of the Cuban's world was that she knew what was going to happen and why. Like all the girls under the Cuban's thumb, she had her regulars, but this was different. This was like she was inhabiting someone else's body. Or maybe, she thought, she had done what she told many of the other girls to do—to simply drift away to a place where nothing would hurt . . . until you woke up and the pain trembled through your bruised and sore body.

The glare of the single bare bulb stabbed her eyes and sliced sharply into her brain. She squinted against the harsh light as the chains continued to signal their presence. Hopeless, she began to sob. She could feel her tears dripping onto her breasts, running down the canyon between them, and racing across the length of her quivering belly, where they stopped and began to dry.

Maybe this is the way my life is supposed to end, she pondered as she wandered the darkened halls of her broken mind. It felt like she had but one path to follow, and no matter how hard she struggled to escape that path, it always had a way of finding her and keeping her imprisoned within its narrow confines. She continued to sob with the reality of the indiscriminate hand of fate that had somehow taken control of her life since the day she vanished. Her body had been used by so many different men so many different ways since she had last seen her parents in Santa Fe that she could barely remember any one of them except for the first one, who gave her the promise of love, only to lie, and who succeeded in sending her down this unwanted and inescapable path. The second, the Cuban, had succeeded in taking away what was left of her soul and dignity by training her and then passing her around like a party favor every night.

Those were the ones who had come and gone under the Cuban's watchful eye. Every man paid up front to do whatever their fantasies dictated. Every man, large or small, thin or fat, old or young, all had a hand in destroying her life and abusing her body. And none of them had even cared. To them she was nothing more than a commodity to be bought and paid for so they could be given the chance to feel like real men. Wearily she shook her head. What her mother had always told her, numerous times a month, had been true—boys and men only want one thing. And they will say anything or do anything or pay whatever the going price is to get it.

April sniffled and leaned forward to wipe away more of her escaping tears. At nineteen, her body felt like what she imagined fifty or sixty must feel like. *So much for being sacred.*

Tenderly, she tested the skin of her face with her fingertips. From her dampened eyes she watched her dirty fingers shake as they moved closer to the area of her cheek below her right eye. She felt the oil and dirt and mascara that had by now sealed her pores and the swollen patch of flesh below her eye where he must have hit her, though she couldn't remember why or when. But she did remember her *training*, as the Cuban had called it. She remembered his men starving her for days, only to *teach* her the art of oral pleasure. In the beginning, they wanted to make sure she could supply their clientele with what they had come to expect. At first, she would be beaten in an effort that was designed to break her will; then she was put through days of humiliation and degradation until she was too weak to struggle.

Her mind suddenly filled with their constant threats of murdering her family if she didn't do exactly as they said. Then they would drag her out of her cramped cage and sit her on her knees in front of a man standing naked in a room. They would position her in front of him and drizzle something sweet on his stiffness. She remembered her stomach twisting and groaning with the pain of hunger. And all it would take to get her to feed was the belt slamming across her back. She remembered how the trainer would shout commands while the standing man took her head in his rough hands and forced her to swallow his shaft time and time again. She remembered the sweet and sticky taste of honey mixed with the aftertaste of semen and vomit until she had learned to take it all freely.

What she had endured during her servitude wasn't the worst of it. The girls were always kept apart and working, but on those rare occasions when they were together, she learned of an even deeper cruelty—the disease, the torture, the pregnancies and the resulting abortions and forced miscarriages so the girls could keep working and earning. She tilted her head back and sighed as more tears escaped her eyes and raced down her face. She remembered hearing stories of the girls who had been forced to lie on their stomachs while someone jumped on their backs to ensure that they lost the unwanted child, which would have slowed the commerce of business and decreased profitability.

For the smaller kids, the five- to twelve-year-olds, the torture would be even more unspeakable. Their bodies weren't designed by the Creator to be abused in such incredibly cruel ways. They would have to be loosened up for the deviates that preferred that type of prepubescent pleasure. They would have to be taught not to gag, as she had been, and have unimaginable things pushed inside them to open them up. And most of the men that craved that kind of pleasure were never gentle. They were all rough, angry men who always preferred their girls scared so they could feel the rush from their loins as it fed the evil in their souls. The monsters her mother had warned her about actually did exist. For every desire there was a service, she had been told. And they were merely the product that provided that service. And there were always other girls out there to take their place.

Suddenly, her resolve steeled and her mind began working on a way to get out of this repulsive prison. Obviously, someone had tried before by the look of the desperate claw marks on the wooden floor in front of her. Turning her head, she noticed the same markings on the wall behind her, frantically created by other terrified girls finding themselves trapped in this insane nightmare.

Had they been successful? Probably not. But how was she to know?

As her eyes scanned the elongated, narrow room, she fixated on the pulley where she had been hooked up, raised off the floor to just the right height, and made to suffer whatever sexual pleasures her captor's sick mind needed to experience. In front of her and to the left was a bench where he had done God knows what to whoever had been here before her. It was a safe bet that she and the ones before her had not been the only ones who had been forced to play his game. On the wall above the table hung the tools of his perverted nature. She had seen most of them before, even used some of them on paying customers who had a pain level they wanted to reach to heighten their erotic sensations. And some of the very same had been used on her while under the care of the Cuban. All except for the machete. The blade looked to be eighteen inches long and honed to a sharpness that could easily slice through flesh, while the serrated top edge did more than hint that it could saw its way through the thickest of bone. *Was that how he got rid of his girls?* she wondered. *Is that how he is going to get rid of me?*

What scared her more now than her memories was what she could see decorating the wall to the left of the table—a collection of saws, pliers, and tools that would have seemed more at home on farms and ranches or in backyard sheds than here. And there was something against the ceiling, something she couldn't quite make out. She cleared her eyes and strained to pick out the image of something large and round hanging in the darkness in the corner of the room. Her body shivered as her hands tried desperately to reach the buckle on the neck collar but startled her when they stopped just inches away from it. He had planned her captivity well, she considered. Probably because he had managed to become so well skilled over what could have been years or even decades of doing this. No matter what happened, she knew she had to free herself and get out. This wasn't a movie. There wasn't going to be any action star or comic book hero showing up to save her. Freedom was going to rely on her alone. And she had to start right now figuring out how that was going to happen.

CHAPTER NINE

The delivery entrance to Casa Caliente was an old converted two-story firehouse on the northwest side of Duke City. The rest of the block was taken up by what Arthur could only envision as a Cuban villa, the building Jonzell had mentioned that had been attached to the firehouse when the club was built. The black-and-gold main entrance was sprinkled with a terra-cotta and cream-colored motif, and the words *Casa Caliente* in gold script loomed large above the vertical black panel doors.

A bell tower rose above the second-floor wall of windows of the Cuban villa, where Arthur assumed the Cuban would sit and control his empire. As Arthur drove slowly by, he scoped out the large double red doors beyond the long glass wall of the front of the club—an area probably off-limits to most of the staff—which stood to the left of the club where Jonzell had mentioned the girls could be found and which led to the Cuban's pleasure palace. They were the palace gates, where any prospective client, or even a seasoned one, would receive the nod that would allow them entrance to the interior of the villa, where a wide variety of female delights of all ages awaited their most inner desires. Arthur Nakai parked his Bronco across the street and studied the entrances he could see as well as all the windows and the gated front garden area, which resembled a Mediterranean tropical paradise.

During this time of day, Arthur understood, the place would be vacant and dead. But when the cool afternoon of a bright December day gave way to the colder temperatures and the nighttime crowd, the place, he was sure, would come alive in a flurry of lights, music and flowing booze. Arthur checked his cell phone, clicked on a local business's unguarded guest internet connection and did a quick search that told him the club's opening time was four p.m. daily. Placing his phone in the console's cup holder, he turned the ignition and drove the Bronco around the club to check out any way in besides the front and delivery doors. Ak'is panted against the passenger window, fogging it up and leaving the occasional nose print; all the while his tongue continued to dangle happily.

As Arthur drove the truck down the alley and around the block, he toyed with the idea of calling Detective Lance Gilberto. But this wasn't his jurisdiction, and he really didn't want him involved until he knew more. His plan was to get inside the club, somehow make his way past the gorilla that guarded the large double red doors and gain entrance into the inner sanctum. And for that, he would have to formulate a believable cover—one that would be easy to assume and even easier to play out.

Since Arthur had a discernable amount of time on his hands, he decided the hour-long drive back to Santa Fe would give him a chance to quietly think about how he was going to accomplish edging his way into the Cuban's alternative world.

* * *

The usual bustle of the historic Santa Fe Plaza was missing, the crowd sparse since it wasn't tourist season, but the plaza still managed to thrive in spite of the cooler weather.

Arthur had parked in the Anasazi Plaza's private lot and, after leaving Ak'is alone in the room with the TV on for company, he made his way to the lobby. His overwhelming need for a bison burger had him heading out of the double Spanish doors of the hotel, passing a handful of late vacationers relaxing in the large patio furniture under the broad portico. He angled across the lot to the stairs that descended to a small stone courtyard by a statue of a friar releasing a dove and wended his way briskly down West Water Street toward the Del Charro Saloon.

Standing at the corner of Don Gaspar and West Alameda after his five-minute walk, Arthur entered the front door of the bar. He was greeted straightaway by a tattooed young woman wearing a pair of tight jeans, some form of dark running shoes he couldn't figure out, and a black T-shirt sporting the restaurant's logo. She flashed a lovely smile and had long ponytail that bounced when she walked like another part of her did. She led him over to a small table by a window that overlooked West Alameda.

"My name's Adriana. I'll be your server. What can I get you to drink, hon?" Her eyes were a deep brown and flashed with the vitality of unbridled youth.

"Did you ever add Santa Fe Nut Brown?" Arthur said.

"Sorry, sweetie, no. Just the Pale Ale."

Arthur shook his head. "That's fine."

Adriana nodded smartly, said, "You got it, honey," and rattled off the day's specials.

Arthur declined.

"Do you know what you want or do you need a minute?"

Her bubbly attitude and dangerous curves made Arthur smile. And since he and Sharon always made a point of eating here, he didn't need to see the menu. "I'll have the Cowboy Bison Burger with a side of chips."

Adriana wrote down nothing. She appeared to keep it all in her head, small order that it was. The consummate waitress. Arthur also figured that the usage of *hon, honey* and *sweetie* had often led to good tips from businessmen and unmarried vacationers and possibly even some married ones.

"I'll be right back with your Pale, honey." She gave a wink, turned and swayed her way over to the red-and-black leather chairs that stood guard in front of the polished bar.

Arthur's table was near the crackling fireplace, next to a tall, multipaned window. He passed his eyes over the wood paneling on the walls, the wooden beams in the ceiling, the dark brick walls and the even darker plank floors. He glanced at the traffic passing outside on West Alameda Avenue and studied the few locals and tourists making their way to wherever it was they were going. He listened imperceptibly to the bar patrons talk of things only they could understand before Adriana returned and placed the green bottle on a napkin in front of him.

Arthur smiled again. This was getting to be a habit. Maybe Adriana was having her desired effect on him. Perhaps her siren song had captivated his libido enough to empty his wallet. He cleared his head and studied the bar. Every bar, he thought, always had a glass jar of some kind for businessmen to toss their calling cards into and win something. He hoped that Del Charro was no different.

It didn't take him long to spot the fishbowl. It sat on the right side of the bar and would be on his way to the restrooms. All he had to do was head to the john, dip his hand in as he passed by—making sure no one had seen his sleight of hand—and go through them in the bathroom. It wouldn't take much to pull it off. Just luck and a distracted bartender.

Adriana returned with his bison burger and chips, set them on the polished black table and asked if he needed anything else. He said he didn't, and she went away.

As Arthur chewed his way through the bourbon-glazed onions and bison meat, he kept an eye on the bar patrons. He took note of who the bartender seemed to be keeping happy as they watched the large flat panel that floated above the bar. The bartender, an athletic-looking young man with muscles that gave shape to his black T-shirt and styled dark hair, was currently keeping himself occupied with a group of middle-aged women who spent their time reciting stories of bad marriages and faded loves that had been lost to the ages of time. Only one spoke of love and passion and sexual encounters in a shower while eyeing the muscled mixologist with a cougar's stare. That seemed to make the others drink even more.

Arthur washed down his burger with the Pale Ale in the time it took to binge-watch three episodes of his favorite half-hour comedy. Adriana had appeared four times in that stretch and went away disappointed that he was going to order no more green bottles to increase the restaurant's bar receipts.

With his burger finished, Arthur got up and made his way toward the restrooms. He quickly dipped his left hand into the fishbowl as he passed and stuffed the cards into his jacket pocket. Once in the men's room, he locked the door and pulled out the cards and began to thumb through them. The chiropractor was out. So was the dentist and the guy who owned a car wash in Gallup. But the firearms sales representative from Phoenix was right up his alley. He pocketed that one and palmed the rest before leaving the bathroom.

The bartender was now involved in a close conversation with the cougar, so Arthur dumped the remaining cards back into the bowl and returned to his table to finish his drink. He had only taken two swigs of his half-empty bottle before Adriana reappeared asking if he had room for dessert. He told her no and asked for the check, feeling sorry he had disappointed her again since she had worked so hard fondling his male ego.

When she left the check, he studied it, then tossed down a ten-dollar tip, thinking that her siren song had probably worked after all.

CHAPTER TEN

Arthur went back to his hotel room and changed into a leather jacket that would fit the standards of a firearms salesman out for a casual night on the town. He hated putting a leash on Ak'is, but city and hotel regulations being what they were, he reluctantly conceded. The pair left their room, navigated the parking lot and crossed West Alameda by the First National Bank of Santa Fe.

As the pair crossed at the light, Arthur pondered his next move. Shirley Becenti had mentioned Liz Hanover and that she probably knew more about April Manygoats than Shirley did. He glanced at his watch. Twelve twenty p.m. Less than three hours until Liz was supposed to be at the pool hall practicing her craft, and plenty of time to snag Sharon a gift at one of the shops around the plaza.

Walking his large furry friend through West De Vargas Park, Arthur studied a few skateboarders in hoodies riding the concrete waves of the board park while Ak'is went about his business. And, given the looks he was receiving, he figured he'd better follow city rules and use one of the bags supplied at the closest bag station to leave the park as he had found it.

* * *

Bankshotz stood in the middle of the block and looked like your typical college bar. It had been placed strategically near the UNM campus, and Arthur was fairly sure that the hardworking students who attended the University of New Mexico had always found time to set aside their vigorous quest for the brass ring to enjoy its flavor and sports bar ambiance. Arthur parked the Bronco on the street, cracked the windows again for Ak'is, and went inside.

As in most places like this, a long wooden bar was stationed to Arthur's right, with rows of bottles and glasses standing like regimented soldiers on a parade ground beneath three large flat-screens playing whatever golf tournament was taking place, an NBA game that already had a lopsided score, and the Chicago Bears, who seemed to be surviving another battle in Green Bay, leading at the half by a field goal.

Arthur looked past the tables that filled the area between the bar and the booths against the wall to his left and spotted a group of six people drinking and shooting pool on the green tables in the back. The bartender looked at him. He looked at the bartender and walked over.

"What can I get you?" the bartender said.

Arthur looked at the young man with the Justin Bieber haircut and tattooed forearms. "I'm looking for Liz Hanover. Is she here?"

Haircut swabbed the bar with a wet rag. "Who wants to know?"

Arthur rolled his eyes. "Someone who is looking for Liz Hanover."

Haircut stopped swabbing, looked at the people shooting pool. "See the tall chick with the long black hair? That's her."

Arthur smiled. "Thanks. I'll take a Nut Brown."

Haircut pulled a bronze can from an iced cooler under the bar, popped the top, and sat it on a napkin in front of him. Arthur paid and walked toward the pool tables, beer in hand.

Liz Hanover stood all of six feet, three inches tall in the red high heels she wore as she balanced herself artfully over the green wool and lined up her corner-pocket shot. With the crack of the balls, Arthur watched the green-striped 14 ball bank off the opposing bumper, split two solid balls, and sink itself in the corner pocket to her left. Her small crowd cheered as she stood and chalked up her cue for the next shot.

Arthur said, "Liz Hanover?"

She looked at him. "I don't know you. I don't talk to men I don't know."

Arthur sipped his medium-bodied English ale, then produced a card and handed it to her. "That's a good philosophy."

She stopped chalking, took his card and looked at it. "Private dick, huh?" She grinned. "Or maybe just a dick?"

"Where'd you get that from, some old seventies movie? Shirley Becenti told me where to find you."

Liz Hanover handed him back the card. "Now, why would she do that?"

Arthur told her to keep it, then sipped his beer as he watched her slip it into the front pocket of her tight jeans. "Because I'm looking for April Manygoats," he said. "She thought you might be able to shed more light on why she disappeared from your facility."

Liz Hanover flicked her head in a Cher-like way and let her hair waft like a horse's tail. In the harsh lighting of the elongated Corona pool-table light, her eyes flashed and her fingernails glinted a vibrant red, with the third fingernail of each hand sporting snowflakes for winter. Hanover looked at her friends and laid her cue across the table. "Take ten, guys," she said, then looked at Arthur. "Buy me a drink?"

Arthur nodded. "Of course."

Liz Hanover smiled and waved him to a pub table surrounded by four tall chairs, then motioned to Haircut. He nodded. Liz grabbed a towel from a chair and cleaned off the chalky residue from her hands. After they sat, her drink arrived—a red margarita rimmed with salt and a slice of lime straddling the lip of a glass bowl that floated atop a green cactus stem. Liz Hanover took a sip, licked her ruby lips and set the glass down.

"If Shirley told you where to find me, she must have trusted you. What do you want to know about April?"

Arthur took another sip of his Nut Brown, felt it tantalize his pallet. "Did April say anything to make you think she was unhappy at the shelter?"

Liz sat back in her chair. "Not at all. I thought she was coming along well, but I guess you never know. Maybe her cravings for a fix were too strong. She was in pretty rough shape when she showed up."

Arthur nodded slowly. "She disappeared from Santa Fe six months ago. Did she ever tell you anything about her life after that?"

Liz crossed her legs. Arthur noticed the red high heel of temptation dangling sexily from one foot. "She told me about the first guy but never mentioned him by name. And when it came to whoever controlled her the last time, she clammed up completely."

"She was afraid?" Arthur said.

"I'm sure of it. She wouldn't tell me a thing. But I did notice her coming out of the shower one day and saw the crown tattoo on the front of her left shoulder." Liz let the fingers of her right hand rub a spot just below her left collarbone. "And she had a scar on the back of her neck."

Arthur sat back in his chair. "Was there anything else besides the crown?"

Liz thought for a second. "There were initials under it. *CIG* in script, I think."

Chino Ignacio Garcia flashed in Arthur's mind. "You said she also had a scar?"

"Yeah. I guess whoever owned her microchipped her." She paused to shake her head. "Owned," she repeated sadly. "It's common practice among traffickers so they can keep track of their stock at all times."

"Stock?" Arthur quizzed.

"To a trafficker, they are no different than cattle," Liz explained.

Arthur took a deep breath, let it out. "Did one of the other girls at the shelter help her get it out?"

Liz shook her head, cringed a little saying it. "She dug it out with her fingernails in a gas station bathroom after she escaped and flushed it down the john. She said if they were hunting her, she wasn't going to make it easy."

"Did she ever mention by name anyone she got close to where she had worked last?" Arthur said.

Liz Hanover sipped her drink, rolled her brown eyes in thought. "It was around two in the morning once, and we were talking over sandwiches and some Cokes. She mentioned a girl named Nikki."

Arthur was finding it difficult to sexily dangle one of his Justins from his foot, so he gave up. "Go on."

Hanover's left hand twisted the margarita glass slowly by the bowl. "She said Nikki was thirteen and had already been there three years. She was the only girl she had a chance to get close to. And that wasn't very often. They liked to keep the girls working, not talking."

"How did she describe her?"

Again, the roll of the eyes. "Nice-looking Asian girl with brown eyes and long black, maybe brown hair. Like that chic in *Crazy Rich Asians*." She studied Arthur's face and chuckled. "You have no idea what I mean, do you?"

"Not a clue."

"It's a movie."

Arthur's eyebrows rose. "Oh." He drank some more Nut Brown. "Did she ever mention Casa Caliente?"

Liz was raising her margarita to her lips when she stopped abruptly. "No. But any girl under that roof never leaves." She sipped her drink nervously, then sat it back down. "Holy shit. Is that who you think she got away from? The fucking Cuban?"

"You've heard of him?"

"Everybody's heard of him," Liz exclaimed. "Holy shit! Am I fucking stupid? The initials I saw tattooed on her stood for Chino Ignacio Garcia."

Arthur let that revelation sink in for her. Then, "What did you mean by 'they never leave'?"

"Guess I should've said they never leave alive. They just tend to disappear." Liz glanced back at her friends at the bar watching the TVs, then turned back to Arthur. "I've only heard stories, mind you, but I've heard they work the girls hard every night, never giving them any time to rest between customers. They're doing anywhere from forty to fifty johns—excuse me, clients—from the time they open at four p.m. till the time they close at four a.m." She shook her head, disgusted. "And when the girls become damaged, they just vanish one day and no one knows where."

"What do you mean 'damaged'?"

"Okay, look, you can sell a pound of drugs or an assault rifle only once, but you can sell flesh until the product becomes too damaged for your regular clients to want. Then the girls simply move down the food chain to the type of men that are allowed to do anything they want to them. That's where the sex is always painful, and it's continually violent."

Arthur drank another sip of his Nut Brown but found it hard to swallow. "Did April mention anything else?"

Liz took a big drink of margarita and licked the salt from her lips. "Just that she'd seen a lot of crazy, disgusting shit go on." She shook her head in disbelief and whispered, "Caliente." Then she added, "I've heard he runs that place like a real fucking bastard, and he never gets his hands dirty when it comes to discipline. He has 'trainers' for that."

"Trainers?"

"Yeah. The guys in charge of making sure the girls can do their jobs. Especially the young ones. What I've been told happens to them makes me sick."

Arthur remembered some of the stories he'd heard bouncing around the green zone in Afghanistan about the girls outside the wall and could imagine what the Cuban did was no different. "Are these 'trainers' in the building all the time?"

"Somewhere, I guess. I've never been there, thank God. It's just talk on the street."

Arthur figured there would be plenty of security, and not just for the club. His first feat would be to get past the podium at the club, then the mountain guarding the big doors, the same ones he'd seen through the windows earlier during his light recon of the premises.

Arthur changed the subject. "Are you good enough at pool to win tournaments?"

"Why? You wanna play?" Liz continued to dangle her shoe, her toes rocking it playfully.

Arthur shook his head. "I haven't played in years."

Liz Hanover smiled. "Playing pool is about finesse. Much like sex. It's not how you handle the balls, but how you hold the stick."

Although it was hard for someone indigenous, Arthur could swear he felt himself blush. He said, "Why the high heels?"

"It gives me an advantage." She grinned slyly. "Most guys are dumb. Not only do these heels give me a good view of the table; they also keep the boys off-balance by focusing their attention on my assets and not my game."

"I see," Arthur said.

Liz shrugged. "A girl's gotta pull out all the tricks to get the advantage these days." She turned and motioned for her friends to come back and resume their game, slid off the pub chair and downed the last of her margarita. "Mr. Nakai?"

Arthur stood. "Yes."

"There's something I need to tell you about April. It's the reason she ran away from there."

Arthur waited.

"She's pregnant."

"What?" Arthur's look of shock was unbridled. "Did Shirley know?"

"No. It just came up when we were talking that night." Liz wet her index finger and ran it around the rim of her glass, collecting the remaining salt, then put her finger in her mouth and sucked on it. "She didn't want them to do to her what she had seen them do to the other girls in that situation, so she worked on a plan to escape."

"How far along is she?"

"At that time, about four weeks. She's been gone from the shelter more than three weeks, so she won't start to show for another five. But she may have morning sickness by now—unless she's one of the lucky broads that don't get it."

"So, whoever has her now might not know she's pregnant?"

"Maybe not," Liz said. "But, in her case, she'd be better off losing it."

Arthur looked at her, confused. "Why would you say that?"

Liz shrugged. "Who'd want it?"

CHAPTER ELEVEN

The late afternoon sun had already transformed into twilight when Arthur arrived at Casa Caliente. He parked on the street and walked to the big black doors he had seen during his drive-by and went inside.

He had spent the last hour and a half thinking about April and her baby while going over his story. Maybe Liz Hanover had been right, he pondered. Why she would want to keep a child conceived in violence and degradation was beyond his thinking. Nothing good could ever come from it. Just then he heard Sharon's voice counseling him in his mind—the child was simply an innocent life that had no say in the matter of how it came to be. And now its heart was beating inside her, and April could probably feel it; and in that way had its own grip on her soul. Arthur exhaled to clear his mind and refocused. He was a firearms sales rep from Phoenix with a penchant for young Asian girls. He could make the name on the business card work because he spoke fluent Spanish as a result of his work on the Arizona border with the Shadow Wolves. All he had to do was be believable enough to get himself in and find Nikki and hope she could tell him something useful.

The smartly dressed woman at the podium smiled as he walked up. She was an exotic representation of how Havana must have looked before Castro, when the hotels gleamed and the booze and money from the American tourists flowed freely like the waters over Niagara Falls. Her hair was twisted into long strands of curls that reminded him of how Gloria Estefan looked when he was growing up.

"Good evening," she said over the loud Latin music blasting from every speaker and reverberating off every patron. "What is your pleasure tonight?"

"I'm not sure," Arthur said. "The club looks tempting, but that's not the kind of dancing I'm looking for." He smiled and handed her his firearms card. "I'm looking for more of a private lesson."

The woman's eyes flashed when she glanced at the card. "I see. This way, sir."

She led him through the dancing and drinking crowd toward the tall red double doors and the monster who looked like Manny Pacquiao, except he looked five sizes bigger. She spoke to him in Spanish. The monster looked at Arthur indignantly.

"Manolo will take you the rest of the way." She gave Arthur back the card. "Enjoy your lesson."

Arthur turned to watch her leave. When he turned back, Manolo wore no expression. The big man turned and made the door handle disappear with the palm of his huge hand before opening the door and waiving Arthur through. He walked past him into an empty waiting room with walls covered with tapestries of Caribbean colors, three matching elegant sofas and another door opposite the one they had walked through. The crystal chandelier floating from the ceiling was an attempt at an elegant touch. Arthur heard the door close behind him. He turned. Manolo was still there. Still saying nothing. Manolo moved past Arthur and pulled on a long piece of cloth with a gold tassel at the end of it. A few moments later, the other door opened and a middle-aged Latina in a long elegant dress walked in and smiled with her hand out.

"I am Madam Sofia. How do you do, Mr. …?"

Arthur told the Den Mother—as Jonzell had called her—the name on the business card, then handed it to her.

"Gonzalez," she repeated, giving the card only a cursory look. "It's awfully nice to have you here with us this evening. I trust you can tell me the type of dancing instructor you're looking for, so I can properly assist you with your choice."

"I'm looking for an Asian instructor," Arthur said. "Preferably very youthful, if you know what I mean. Do you have anyone like that?"

The woman smiled. "I believe we will have quite the array for you to choose from. Let me have them come in, so you can make your choice."

Arthur nodded. "That would be nice."

Madam Sofia disappeared for a few minutes and returned with five girls, all preteen and early teen. Arthur looked back at Manolo. Still no reaction. The words *muscle-bound eunuch* came to mind. Arthur turned his attention back to Madam Sofia.

"Is there anyone you like?" she said.

Arthur studied the girls. They all wore silk robes tied at the waist and no shoes. They stood still. Too still. It was a scared type of still that filled the small room with an anxiety Arthur didn't like feeling. "May I know their names?" he asked.

"Girls," Madam Sofia said. "Tell the gentleman your names."

The first three looked at him and said their names, or whatever names they had been given to make them more appealing to the clientele. Number four said her name was Nikki, and that got Arthur's attention.

"Her," he said. "I believe I would like to choose her."

Madam Sofia smiled and clapped her hands twice quickly. "Excellent choice," she said as the other girls filed out the door they had entered through. Nikki smiled a little-girl smile and walked up to him, took him by the hand.

"Do you have a credit card we can bill, Mr. Gonzalez?" Madam Sofia said, noticing his wedding ring. "I assure you it won't show up on your statement as anything but a restaurant bill for your expense report."

"I don't trust credit cards," Arthur said. "Will cash be acceptable?"

"Of course. In that case, the price for a one-hour lesson is five hundred."

Arthur let go of the girl's small hand long enough to pull his wallet from his hip pocket. He fingered out five one-hundred-dollar bills and handed them to her. She took them and folded them into a pocket of her dress as he returned his wallet to its home.

Madam Sofia said, "Nikki will take you to a private studio for your lesson."

The girl opened the door and led him into a hallway that could have been in an ornate hotel. They passed several doors bearing scripted gold numerals before Nikki pushed the elevator button at the end of the hallway and waited for the doors to open. When they did, she waved for him to enter first and then followed. Arthur watched her press the button for the third floor. The doors closed. He glanced around the elevator searching for an ideal spot for a hidden camera. One that allowed the clientele to be watched and recorded in case someone got rough with the girls prematurely. Blackmail never went out of style. When the elevator stopped, the doors opened, and they stepped out onto a third floor that looked like the first floor. Nikki led him to a door halfway down the hall marked 321. She opened it with a card key and ushered him in.

The room was decorated with high-end colors, furniture and accessories and a had full wet bar off to the left.

"Would you like a drink first?" Nikki asked softly, using all the seductive prowess of a thirteen-year-old professional.

"No, thank you."

Nikki's eyes searched his own as her small hands released her sash, letting the silk robe fall to the floor. Her body was slim and pale. It was the body of a girl lost in a world of despicable people who had taken control of her young life at an even younger age and made her do despicable things that most people couldn't imagine could happen to a girl her age. Arthur's eyes noticed the crown tattoo with the scripted *CIG* initials below it that Liz Hanover had spoken about. In Arthur's mind, Nikki should have been following some annoying teen popstar or aggravating her parents on a daily basis; instead, she was trapped here in this hellish world of depravity.

Arthur averted his eyes. "Put your robe back on," he said.

"What's the matter?" Nikki pouted. "Don't you like me? I like you. I love you."

"Just put your robe back on and let's talk for a while," Arthur gently suggested, his eyes still staring at the minibar. "Can we do that?"

Squatting down slowly, Nikki picked up her robe off the floor and shrugged into it, then tied it and stepped over to the bed and sat down. She patted the sheets with a delicate hand. Arthur walked over and sat next to her.

Nikki said, "What do you want to talk about? How hot I can make you?"

Arthur said, "April Manygoats."

The girl's eyes remained indifferent. "I don't know her."

"She knows you," Arthur said. "And I'm looking for her. Her mother asked me to find her."

Nikki looked around the room nervously. It was a foregone conclusion that here, too, were cameras that had been strategically placed to focus on the bed from different angles, the shower and wherever any of the girls and women could please a paying customer.

"I'm not paid to talk," Nikki said flatly. "I'm paid to fuck. If you want to know anything about her, you've come to the wrong place."

"Turn your head," Arthur said.

Nikki did.

Arthur said, "Are all the girls microchipped?"

Reflexively her fingers reached up and touched the small scar at the base of her slender neck. "Yes. I feel like a fucking delivery van. They know where we are all the time."

"What if I try to get you out?" Arthur offered. "I'm sure your parents have not given up looking for you."

Nikki scoffed. "They probably don't even give a shit. I left after my father raped me while my mother was at the store." Tears formed in her young dark brown eyes, which had become devoid of life. She wiped them quickly. "I'm sure he's moved on to my little sister by now. My mother never woke up from her dreamworld to even notice."

Arthur felt a churning in his gut that ground away at his soul. "How long have you been gone?"

"Three years, I think. I caught a bus from Phoenix and got as far as here. I was heading for Dallas and just hanging out in the station waiting for another bus when this guy came up to me. He talked a lot of shit that I fell for. Next thing I know, I'm here doing this."

After three years of hell, Arthur thought, this girl's view of the world she lived in was as cold and forged as a steel beam. "When was the last time you saw April?"

"She left here, maybe two months ago."

"Did she say where she might be going?"

"Back to her parents, I think. Some dinky Indian town I never heard of."

"How did she escape?"

"She got close to a boy in the kitchen, and one day she was just gone. And so was he. I didn't know if she made it out or was sold to someone else or was killed. We all figured the boy from the kitchen was killed for helping her."

"Did you know April was pregnant?"

Her little eyes widened. "God no!"

Just then the door to the room opened, and Manolo thundered his way in. Nikki instinctively stood as the big man moved across the room at an astonishing pace and let a big hand smack the side of her head, sending her flying to the carpeted floor. Arthur jumped to his feet and instantly felt a powerful backhand that crashed into his jaw and sent him sprawling onto the bed and bouncing to the floor. Manolo shouted something in Spanish and another man grabbed Nikki and pulled her kicking and screaming out of the room.

Manolo's large hands filled with Arthur's shirt and jerked him to his feet before tossing him toward the door. Arthur stumbled but regained his footing just as Manolo's hand punched flat into the back of his right shoulder and made him lunge toward the open door. Arthur managed to make it out of the room before Manolo slammed him into the opposite wall of the hallway and closed the door to room 321. Their next stop was obviously the Cuban.

CHAPTER TWELVE

"The victim's name is Angelina Martinez," Delores Mendoza said over the phone.

"Are you sure?" Jake said. He was sitting at his desk in his office flexing his fingers and rubbing arthritis cream all over them to numb the pain.

"The killer pretty much made a dental record search impossible, and a photo ID was worthless, but she still had fingerprints."

"*Still* had them?"

"Normally in water the skin starts to get a bit loose after a week, but she was about three days short of that, so I was still able to pull them. I found nothing under her nails, so there's no DNA of the killer, which leads me to think she may have known her attacker. The birthmark on her right hip also matched the description in her juvie file."

"Was she married?"

"No. But she had a boyfriend who could be the baby daddy."

"What's his name? Jake asked.

"Emmanuel Ruiz," Mendoza said, then gave Jake the last known address of Angelina Martinez.

"And you're sure about the baby?"

The sight of Angelina's body remained fresh in Jake's mind, and he felt it would be for quite a long time. After almost thirty years in law enforcement, nothing really surprised him anymore concerning what one human being could do to another. But this … this had really disgusted him.

"I'm sure," Delores confirmed sadly. "All the signs are there. Toxicology found prenatal over-the-counter supplements in her system, and depending how far along she was—I'm guessing almost full term—the child could still be alive."

"Could?"

"The average gestation period is forty weeks, so my guess is she was just about to give birth. Our killer performed a crude attempt at a C-section using some sort of small knife—possibly a thumb knife or paring knife with a three-inch blade. Without any medical care, Angelina was just left to bleed out." Mendoza stopped to swallow. Jake heard it through the phone line. He swallowed, too. "Makes me sick to my stomach that someone could do that."

"I gave up trying to figure out society a long time ago," Jake said. "Was there any evidence on her body that could tell us anything?"

"Nothing," Mendoza said. "If she had any carpet fibers or anything else that would shed some light, they were most likely washed away by the water of the lake."

"How good are the child's chances?"

"Pretty good if there were no immediate problems with the birth, but the child really should have been taken to a hospital right away to be checked out."

Jake said, "But wouldn't they be able to tell if whoever brought the baby in had given birth to it?"

"Of course," Mendoza said, "if they let them examine them. Which is why they probably didn't go to a hospital. It's more likely they are taking care of the infant themselves and keeping a low profile until they can show the baby off as their own." She paused. "She was a pregnant mother fighting for not only her life, but the life of her child … and she fought like hell."

"I'll have my officers hit the local clinics and hospitals just in case," Jake said.

The phone line went quiet for a few moments. Then Mendoza said, "You know, I became a medical examiner to give people a voice."

"How so?"

"Back home in Chicago when I was small, I saw kids in my neighborhood—hell, on my own block even—get shot down in the streets or end up flame broiled in a burning car or tossed out like trash in an alley dumpster. Ever since I came out here, seeing these girls go missing almost daily really bothers me—as a woman of color, I mean, because they hardly ever show up again. And when they do, like our Angelina here, they've died in some truly horrific fashion." Mendoza exhaled. "They couldn't speak for themselves when they were alive because no one ever listened to them before they were taken; but when I have a chance to listen to the story they tell me, that's when their silence screams volumes. And I listen very carefully … because I'm the last person that will ever hear them."

Jake took a breath. "I'll have someone visit the boyfriend or whatever tonight. See how he reacts."

"You think he's involved?"

Jake said, "My experience tells me it's always the first place to start."

CHAPTER THIRTEEN

April Manygoats startled when she heard the chain on the door rattle as it had done when he had brought her food. If you could really call it that. Smoked sausage, mac and cheese and water were filling but held little nutritional value on their own. But it was a way to stay alive, and she felt lucky he even gave her that.

He had always made sure there were no utensils she could fight back with, so she was forced to eat from the plate with her fingers. The plate, of course, came from one of those cheap bundles of paper plates, so she couldn't smash it and use the shards as a weapon. She was watching the door as it opened and saw him step in. He said nothing as he walked over to her, picked up the paper plate and plastic cup and took them over to the workbench, then went back outside without saying a word. When he came back with another girl, April's eyes widened and her stomach tightened.

She looked young—younger than April was—but not by much, and was bound behind her back at the wrists. The girl's eyes were just as wide and staring back at her, the fear in them measurable. The ball gag strapped to her head and filling her mouth had ensured she wasn't able to scream. And the fact that this new girl was already naked, April was sure, had heightened their captor's anticipation about whatever "playtime" he had imagined in his demented mind.

His large hands had a firm hold of her upper arms as he guided her in, her dirty feet shuffling grudgingly across the wooden floor, her legs buckling every other step, her body trembling as much from the cold as from the terror. April understood it all.

April watched as he led the girl over to the far wall, unlocked her handcuffs and used them to shackle her to an iron ring bolted to the wall. After he closed the metal door, he turned on the light. The childlike whimpering of the girl seemed to echo in the confines of their dungeon and fill him with a type of evil contentment.

"It's all right," April said, trying unsuccessfully to comfort the terrified girl. "You'll be okay."

The big man glared at her sitting on her furry nest. His other plaything. Now he had them both in one place and could double his fun anytime he wished. The grin that spread his thick lips matched the wicked twinkle in his eyes. He walked over and leaned down slowly, placing his mouth close to April's ear, and whispered, "Now you can watch me with her."

He stood as April's eyes teared and followed him as he walked over to the young girl cuffed to the wall. She watched him grab her jaw with a rough hand and whisper something to her. Then, as her whimpers changed to sobs, she watched him bring over a roughly made padded bench and slide it between the girl and the wall, forcing her arms to stretch and bending her body at a strained ninety-degree angle. He strapped her ankles to the base of the bench, which spread her young legs wide and taut. She watched him jerk the bench toward him, forcing her into a tightly bent position that offered her to him unwillingly and completely.

Once again April said, "It's all right. Don't think about it. Put yourself in a faraway place."

In three quick steps, the big man was hovering above April. She watched his hand swing back before feeling the swift and powerful force of it against her face. The strength of it spun her head violently to the right so that her neck popped from the blow.

"That's enough!" he growled. "You're spoiling my fun. Say another word, and I'll throw you into the pit. We'll see if that shuts you up."

April turned her head, the left side of her face now stained with the reddish handprint of her captor, and watched him drop his pants. He reached out a hand and grabbed a handful of the girl's long black hair as he positioned himself behind her haunches. He toyed with her virginity with his swollen head as he pulled her hair backward roughly, then proceeded to begin the process. April simply closed her eyes and turned her head. But she couldn't close her ears—they heard every cry, every muffled scream and every hard thrust that filled the ten minutes of torture the girl suffered at the hands of this foul creature. When he finished, he pulled up his pants and buckled his belt with a satisfied deep breath. After removing the ball gag, he tossed it onto the workbench and left. April heard him chain the double doors. The single bulb still glowed.

The girl was crying, gasping for every gulp of humiliated air she could find.

"You're okay," April said. "You survived. That's all we can do until we figure a way out of here."

The girl, still bent and strapped over the bench, strained to look back at her. "We're never getting out of here."

April could see the pleading in her eyes, the utter destruction of any free will that she had realized back in the other world, which now seemed only imaginary. The tears that streaked her young face April understood too. They were the tears she had cried after Jonzell had sold her to the Cuban. Now that she had someone to talk with, to plan with, they could conjure up a strategy that could free them. But how long that would take she had no way of knowing. He would have to make a serious mistake for them to take advantage of. Or they would have to plot using the tools that surrounded them if they managed to free themselves. Either way, it was going to take more than luck. It was going to take a strong will to survive and quiet determination. And time. She mustn't forget about time. It was the one thing they both had, but they had no way of knowing how much of it he would give them.

April studied the girl as she sobbed. Her body shook as her mind unleashed her fear and let it consume her thoughts. Her dark hair had fallen over her right shoulder, so April could see her face. The drooling from the gag had dappled the floor in a glistening pool below her, and the glaring light of the single bulb that hung from the ceiling helped her to notice the rivulets of blood that now trailed down the inside of the girls trembling legs. April squeezed her eyes shut, realizing this monster had robbed her of her purity, her very spirit.

"What's your name?" she said. "My name is April. April Manygoats."

"Lucy," the girl muttered, trying unsuccessfully to control her sobbing. "Lucy Nez."

"Lucy, we have to work together if we are going to get out of here. We have to combine our efforts in order to get him to make a mistake."

"We're never getting out of here … alive."

"Yes, we are!" April encouraged her. "This is not where I am supposed to die, and I know it's not where you will. The only way we can get out of this is to work together. Even if it means giving him what he wants."

"I can't do that," Lucy sobbed.

"He's going to take it from you anyway," April said. "I've known his kind before. He's going to use us until he's tired of us. I don't think we want to know about what happens after that."

"I just wanna die," Lucy cried. "I. Just. Wanna. Die."

"Lucy!" April pleaded. "Lucy! Don't you think your parents are worried sick about their little girl? I know they are. I know mine are. We owe it to them to fight back and get the fuck out of here!"

Lucy responded with, "Look at me. Look at you. You think we're honestly going anywhere?"

"Yes!" April said. "I do! We're getting out of here and going home."

"He told me he'd kill my family if I tried to escape."

"Does he even know where they live? Does he know anything about them? Where your father works or your mother? Does he know anything about your family?"

Lucy Nez's sobbing shortened, then stopped. She turned her head to look at April. "No. He knows nothing about them."

"That's what they all say when you figure out what's happening after you've been taken. They prey on us and instill fear in our heads because we're young and they think we're stupid."

Lucy tried pulling herself up, but the bench kept her bent over. She could feel the pain that throbbed between her young thighs and strained her lower back and neck; the weakness of her arms and the straps snugly wrapped around her ankles.

April said, "How did he take you?"

"I was riding my bike. On my way home from a friend's house. When I got to the small bridge over the wash I couldn't pass because there was a car coming across."

April had heard the stories circulating the rez about white vans, typically unmarked, traveling the graded roads day and night in search of prey. But the fact that this guy had used a car was odd. Maybe, she reasoned, it was because he knew the rez was always on the lookout for the unmarked vans. That or he was simply arrogant.

"I was waiting as he drove over the bridge, and then he stopped near me. He said he thought he was lost and would I mind helping him get back to the highway."

"And you did," April said.

Lucy Nez hung her head. "Yes. I was so stupid."

"How old are you?"

"Fifteen."

"You're not stupid. You just don't know anything about the real world. The real world sucks. And people like him prey on people like us. I was just like you. I didn't know anything either. The internet is full of these fuckers. Most girls think everyone on social media is who their profile says they are. That was my first mistake. Yours was just being naïve."

Lucy's legs tensed and relaxed as she struggled to maintain blood flow and ease the tingling sensation of neuropathy. She tried arching her back as much as she could to relieve some of the strain and stiffness resulting from hanging by her tired arms. April could tell she was confused enough not to realize she was bleeding from her *ajóózh*—the Navajo term seemed a gentler way of referring to the girl's vagina.

Lucy said, "Did he pick you up, too?"

"Yes," April said, "but not like you. My story is too long to tell now. I just let my guard down when I shouldn't have."

"I'm cold," Lucy said. "And I hurt inside."

"I know, *she'at'ééd*, but the pain will go away. You have to be strong, and the cold will pass once your body becomes acclimated to it. Let the anger inside you warm you."

"Are you sure about the pain?" Lucy said. "I've never felt it before."

"The pain is natural, even though the way it happened wasn't."

Lucy sniffled and coughed. "I've never made love before."

April's eyes flashed. "What he did to you wasn't love. What he did to you was disgusting and humiliating. That's not what love is. He's a sadist."

"What's that?"

"Someone who gets pleasure from giving pain to someone else, making them suffer. Humiliating them."

"Have you known real love?"

April hung her head mournfully. "No, but I've been with plenty of men, and none of them my choice." She looked at Lucy. "I gave up on love a long time ago. No man in his right mind would want what's left of me."

Lucy's eyes shifted away from April. She shivered. "Aren't you cold?"

"I don't notice it anymore."

"How long have you been here?"

"What was the day you were taken?"

Lucy Nez thought back and told her.

"I've been here for three weeks, then." She looked at Lucy, then stared at the doors. "He thinks he broke me. But that's what I let him believe. I was broken a long time ago."

Suddenly the chain rattled off the double metal doors, and they groaned open. He stepped in carrying another furry pen replete with chrome chains of its own for his new plaything. After closing the door, he walked over and placed the pen on the floor next to April and glared at her knowingly. After releasing Lucy Nez from her bondage, he led her over and forced her down on her knees onto the fur. She looked up at him, her face glistening from spent tears and saliva that had spilled over her chin. He said nothing as he buckled the leather collar with the chains linked to it around her neck. After releasing her from her handcuffs, he locked them into the leather straps attached to the remaining chains of her pen, then stood for a moment towering over his two young captives. He noted different things lurking behind their eyes, saw different thoughts working through their adolescent brains. He smiled demonically. As long as he had them, he was going to enjoy them. And they were going to enjoy each other, if that was what pleased him.

Goose bumps had already formed on Lucy Nez's skin. From the cold, he was sure, but mostly from the fear he had instilled in her before making her walk the fifty yards naked from the house to the container in the chill desert night. He also noticed the rivulets of blood that decorated the insides of her thighs, now dried, but still managing to glisten in the light given off by the bare light bulb that dangled above. His chest swelled with maniacal pride knowing he had been the first to break her seal. He hadn't had that privilege with the other girl, the girl from the truck stop, and only a few of the ones that had come before her. That was always a rare pleasure. They had all been simply a mixture of young girls that tantalized and middle-aged women lonely and searching for excitement. But this—this was different. This always added a feeling of newfound exhilaration to his games.

But the other girl, he considered, hadn't seemed to mind it as much as the others. She had somehow already become used to his type of gratification. He could feel it every time he had been inside her that she had grown used to it long before he had slipped that drug into her drink and helped her to his car. But she was ceasing to excite him, just like the others had. It only stopped being fun when their minds became so fragmented they gave up fighting. When that time came, and it always did, he would do with these two as he had done with the rest. He would return them to the earth, where they would never be found.

April Manygoats watched him standing there, her gaze never leaving his empty, dark eyes. What terrified her was that she saw the frightening thoughts working behind those empty eyes. She could see he was already thinking of the time when he grew tired of her. The fact that he had brought this new child was proof of that. But if they were going to get out of this alive, she would have to give him the kind of sick pleasure he desired in the way he expected it. She would have to scream even though there was no fear in her heart; she would have to register the pain though she no longer felt it; she would have to make him work for the release he craved. And she had become good at that—knowing what men like him wanted. And knowing how to give it to them without scarring her soul even more than it already was.

"You two get a good night's sleep, now," he said, reaching out his big hands and brushing their hair softly. "Tomorrow is going to be a very busy day." April watched him reach into his pocket and pull out a cell phone. He held it up, making sure the shot focused properly before tapping his thumb on the red dot. The flash filled the container with every shot. Through flickering eyelids, April watched him take a photo of Lucy Nez and one of her, then another of them both. "A very busy day, indeed."

CHAPTER FOURTEEN

The oversized hands of the giant Pacquiao guided Arthur through the double doors of the glass-walled office he had seen at the top of the tower during his recon. They forcefully shoved him into a contemporary chair of white leather and chrome design and kept him there momentarily, then lifted their hydraulic pressure so his shoulders could regain their feeling.

Arthur looked around. Manolo stood blocking the double doors like he was guarding a stack of gold bars at the national repository. The office was filled with more contemporary furniture made of white leather and chrome that complemented the glass walls and the night lights, including a spray of Christmas lights that glowed beyond them. Scattered on the bookcases, furniture and desk were several small items that Arthur could only assume made Chino Ignacio Garcia think of his island home. The Native pottery and statues that decorated the office Arthur could relate to, but only as far as their indigenous similarity, while the paintings that decorated the two solid walls seemed to be more a mixture of Afro-Cuban and what were called naïve styles.

Suddenly, the big man moved away from the doors and opened them. Chino Ignacio Garcia walked in with two other men in suits following him like obedient puppies. Garcia looked to be in his mid-thirties, with striking Cuban features, and seemed impeccably dressed in his tailored dark suit. His puppies probably carried nine-millimeter semiautomatics under their suit jackets, Arthur figured, as he sat there watching them flank him. Garcia took up his position in the high-backed white leather throne behind the contemporary desk.

Garcia smiled but said nothing as he opened a wooden humidor on his desk, pulled out a cigar and snipped off the end. He lit it with a gold lighter he took from his suit jacket pocket. "Would you like one, Mr. Nakai?"

Arthur declined. "What are you going to do with me?"

Garcia pulled in a deep drag off his cigar and blew the smoke into the air away from him. "Do?" he said. "What makes you think I'm going to do anything with you?" His accent was a mixture of Cuban and American.

"Oh, I don't know," Arthur replied. "Just a feeling I get when I don't like the odds."

Garcia smiled, then reached over and pressed a button on his desk. Moments later, the double doors opened again and Jonzell Washington walked in, took up a position on Garcia's right.

Jonzell grinned like an idiot. "Told you I was gonna kill you, motherfucker."

Garcia made the tip of his cigar glow again and blew the smoke toward Washington.

Jonzell coughed and waved his hands. "Whatda fuck! C'mon, man!"

"Mr. Washington," Garcia said confidently, "when you have a man of Mr. Nakai's talents you don't kill him—at least not until you determine if he can be useful. Besides, every man has a price. We just have to find out his."

Arthur said flatly. "And what do you want?"

"I want the girl, of course."

"What girl?"

"Please don't disappoint me," Garcia said. "The one you were asking little Nikki about." He tapped a fat ash into a large glass ashtray. "You see, not only can I see into every room; I can hear as well. In my business, you can never know when such information may become useful as a way to obtain a desired response from certain individuals at a later date."

Arthur paused as if he were thinking. "What do you want me to do?"

"You can find her and bring her back to me. Where she belongs."

"You gonna let this motherfucker live?" Jonzell snapped. "Man, that's bullshit! You're even lucky I was here tonight and saw this asshole walk in. Without me, that little bitch would have told him everything."

Garcia gave the Jonzell the fisheye, telegraphing his displeasure at the interruption. "Sometimes, Mr. Washington, it is in one's own best interest to form unlikely alliances to achieve one's goal. This is simply a negotiation." Garcia returned his attention to Arthur. "But, as Mr. Washington so crudely points out, I can't have my girls thinking they can leave whenever they desire without consequences." He paused. "What do you say? Can you find her?"

"Why do you want her back?" Arthur said. "I know it isn't because you have a shortage of young girls. You lose one, you can simply replace her with another one Jonzell lures from a bus station or finds sleeping on a sidewalk."

Anger flooded Garcia's face, followed by a heavy-handed fist brought down hard onto his desktop. "Because she is mine! Bought and paid for! I own her!"

Arthur remained still, just like he had numerous times in the red zone while in-country. He knew he was nowhere near out of this yet. It still had a chance to go south, and he was going to ante up to make sure it went the other way. Adrenaline now flowed through his veins like lava coursing through an underground tube, but Arthur managed somehow to keep his expression bland, like a card player holding a winning hand. He only hoped his bluff didn't turn out to be aces and eights.

"I apologize for my outburst, Mr. Nakai," Garcia said graciously. "My hot Cuban blood, eh?" He tapped another fat ash from the end of his cigar into the large crystal ashtray. "We are both self-made men. Did you know that my father came to this country during the Balsero Crisis in the nineties? Your news called it the Cuban Raft Crisis. If it had not been for him risking his life on a piece-of-shit raft, I wouldn't have achieved the American dream and become the man I am today."

Arthur said, "I live by the teachings of my people. I am proud of who I am. Can you say the same?"

Garcia took a long, slow drag on his cigar that matched the look he gave. Arthur could see his calculating mind working somewhere behind the callous brown eyes. He began thinking maybe he had overplayed his hand.

"The girl is simply my property," Garcia said coldly. "I want her back. You will get her back for me. In fact, she was one of my best girls. A real professional."

"I doubt that," Arthur said. "She's a kid."

Garcia grinned devilishly, pointed his cigar at Arthur. "She was a professional. Her clients loved her." His eyes roamed the office in thought. "Let me put it to you this way—would you pay for a girl that would gag on a straw or one that could swallow a radiator hose?"

Arthur didn't answer.

"I believe you will find her for me," Garcia said. "You know why? Because you've got skills and very big balls.

But I warn you, don't fuck with me or you'll lose more than those big balls."

"Her parents hired me to bring her home. I can't not do that."

Garcia rolled his tongue between his teeth and lower lip. "My friend, I'm not giving you any choice in the matter. You have a wife, I understand. And a business. It would be a shame for something to happen to both of them."

This was no place for heroics, Arthur reasoned. The stakes had just been raised and it wasn't looking like he had anything close to a winning hand. Arthur said, "Can't your people find her?"

Garcia waived his cigar absently. "They rely too much on technology. If the little blip doesn't appear on the screen, they don't know what to fucking do." Garcia crossed his legs, rocked back in his high-backed white leather nest. "You, on the other hand, rely on other ways—ancient ways—of locating someone. That is what I need. Someone who can show me results."

Arthur studied Jonzell briefly. He was fidgeting too much. Maybe it was a nervous tic or maybe the recent memory of having his family jewels crushed and a semiautomatic shoved into his mouth was making him anxious.

"What do you say?" Garcia queried. "And I expect only one answer, so make sure it is the correct one."

Arthur nodded reluctantly. "I'll find her for you. But it goes against everything I believe in. And if I'm going to trample over my morals, you're going to have to compensate me very well for doing so."

The smile on Garcia's face was a broad one. "You see, Mr. Washington, every man has a price. You just have to negotiate it. How does five thousand dollars a day sound, Mr. Nakai? She is costing me more than that in revenue each day. I'll give you fifteen upfront before you leave here. That gives you three days."

"Sounds good to me," Arthur said. The two puppies flanking him smiled smugly and nodded, never losing their enforcing poses. If what Arthur was thinking of doing actually worked out, he would make sure the money was put to good use. Now, he wondered, would John Sykes be able to help him when the time came?

Garcia laughed and leaned forward slowly. "Like I said, don't fuck me over … or you or your wife will die. I do not care which."

Arthur nodded. "Understood."

"Good." Garcia grinned, taking another drag off his cigar. "We understand each other, then." Garcia opened a desk drawer, lifted out three stacks of banded bills and placed them on his desktop, then closed the drawer and rocked back in his white leather chair again. "Take it."

Arthur did.

Garcia swiveled his chair, admiring the shimmering lights of Duke City, which mingled sparsely with the abstract blotches of Christmas lights twinkling beyond his window walls.

"Now, get the fuck out of here."

CHAPTER FIFTEEN

Arthur sat for five minutes in the Bronco letting his muscles relax and his pulse return to normal, reflecting on just how close he had come to fulfilling Jonzell Washington's fantasy. He had no reason to disbelieve Garcia—that an operation of that size had hidden cameras in every room watching every sordid transaction that took place, catching anyone in the middle of fulfilling their deepest, unbridled desires. *Who knows what secrets hide in the dark places of someone's mind?* Arthur turned the ignition and pulled the shifter into gear, thinking it was a good thing Chino Ignacio Garcia saw him as an asset instead of a liability.

Arthur drove away from Casa Caliente west on Sagebrush Trail, turned south on University Boulevard and easily piloted the three blocks that moved him onto Lead Avenue. He was heading west when his phone vibrated inside his leather jacket. He cranked the wheel of the Bronco with one hand while fishing it out with the other and tapped the screen with his thumb.

"What are you up to, sexy?" he said.

"I'm up to my neck in relaxing suds while a glass of red wine balances precariously on the edge of the tub in a bathroom that smells wonderfully of lavender candles," Sharon replied. "How about you?"

"I think I'm realizing what I'm missing."

"Suffer, baby."

Arthur heard Sharon chuckle.

"How did today go? Uncover anything useful?"

Arthur grinned. "I tracked down the last place April worked and spoke with a young woman at a shelter where she stayed briefly."

"Sounds like progress."

"Somewhat," Arthur confided, holding back the revelation of April's pregnancy and the threat to their lives. "I still don't know where she went or if anyone came into contact with her after she left Albuquerque. The only thing I know is she was heading back home."

"Well, if she couldn't afford to use a ride service or fly, she probably hitchhiked. It's still dangerous as hell, but kids do it anyway. Especially desperate ones."

Arthur let his mind work through that suggestion. "She'd need to find someone traveling long-distance to grab a ride with to have any chance of getting far enough away from here quickly. No local would want to make that kind of trip."

Sharon sipped some wine, savoring its rich currant and plum flavor. "My bet would be a truck stop. There has to be one off I-25 or I-40 somewhere."

"I'll check into that tomorrow," Arthur said. "Right now, I've got a couple of calls to make. Listen, I'm going to have Billy stay with you until I get back."

"What? Why?" Sharon said. "What the hell's going on?"

"This isn't just about a runaway," Arthur told her. "This is about April being stolen and sold to the highest bidder."

"What?" Arthur heard the bathwater splash.

"The video you sent me was just the beginning," Arthur explained. "The guy in that filth turned her into a junkie, used her for a while, then sold her into prostitution." Arthur could hear Sharon gasp. Telling her that she herself might be in danger wasn't an option. "I'd just feel better knowing he was there instead of you being alone."

Arthur heard her pause to drink some wine. "I know where your guns are," she said. "And I know how to use them. You taught me. I can take care of myself."

Arthur paused at the stoplight on Oak Street by the Presbyterian Hospital complex, saw no opposing traffic, turned right and headed up the long ramp that shot him onto I-25 North.

"I know you can take care of yourself. Just humor me, all right?" Arthur eyed his side mirror and merged into the middle lane beneath the digital message board and the interstate sign indicating the exit for Dr. Martin Luther King Jr. Avenue. "Grab my Colt .380, if you want to, but Billy is coming over."

"Too small," Sharon remarked. "I like the SIG P365 better. It's got a ten-round mag, and I can have one in the pipe. If I can't take someone down with less than eleven shots—"

Arthur smiled and interrupted. "I love it when you talk firepower."

"I'm not going to be a victim again," Sharon said. "Dr. Peterson may be helping me work through my past, but you are the one who is showing me my future." Sharon paused, waiting to see if her husband had a reply. When none came, she continued. "Speaking of our future—when you get back here, we're going to get back on our schedule."

Arthur shook his head, thinking it was a good thing she couldn't see him doing it. Being on a schedule had taken most of the fun out of their lovemaking. There used to be times when the anticipation was thundering through his body like a summer storm, wild and uninhibited. But now it often became just an act shared by the two of them and not the meaningful, passionate exchange it was meant to be. Could his attitude be the reason she hadn't conceived? he wondered. If it changed, would then the result not change? He couldn't remember how many pregnancy tests she'd already gone through, none of them showing the desired response.

"Are you sure planning this like we're doing is such a good idea?" he said. "It may just happen on its own."

There was quiet. Arthur didn't like when there was quiet. It usually meant the calm before the monsoon. "You want to give up?"

"I'm not saying that. I'm saying it will probably happen the one time we're not trying so hard. Remember in the beginning? All it would take was for you to brush against me or me to brush against you? It wasn't regimented; it wasn't tied to a clock."

"Things were different then," Sharon said. "Things were new, and we thought we had the world figured out." She paused. "Then everything changed."

"I know," Arthur said. "What I'm saying is let's just not focus so much on the clock and let our emotions drive everything. We want our child conceived according to love, not according to Timex. Can we do that?"

Arthur heard the quiet again. Or was it more of a deafening silence this time? Then: "Maybe you're right," Sharon conceded. "Like those times you used walk up behind me and softly kiss my neck. I'd feel your hands circling my waist and pulling me against you. I miss those times."

"So do I," Arthur reassured her. "And I want them again. If I were there right now, I'd be seeing if there was enough room under those bubbles for me."

"Pity you aren't here to find out."

He exhaled. "I'm going to call Billy and send him over to stay with you, so you might want to put some clothes on."

Sharon said, "Why?"

"Because I don't want him to see you naked."

"That's not what I meant."

Arthur grinned. "Because I'm not taking any chances. The people involved in April's disappearance aren't good people."

"You think I'm in danger?"

Arthur pursed his lips in an effort to moderate the truth. "Not really, but I'm not taking anything for granted. Just go along with me."

Sharon sighed. "After I finish my wine, then."

"Good."

"If you were here, you could dry me off. And maybe that would lead to something intriguing."

Suddenly, the thunder of a medical helicopter's blades roared overhead. Arthur watched the chopper spin effortlessly in the dense December air and complete its inbound dust-off on the pad at Heart Hospital. He caught himself smiling.

"I wouldn't want to dry you off," he said. "Your skin tastes better wet."

"Mmm," Sharon moaned. "You really know how to tease a girl."

Arthur moved through the spaghetti bowl where I-25 and I-40 came together like capillaries between arteries and veins. "I know how to do more than that," he teased further.

"You'd better pay attention to the road, and I had better get out of this cozy tub. I'll feed Billy when he gets here."

"Ayóó'ániinísh'ní," Arthur said tenderly.

"I love you, too," Sharon said softly. "Stay safe."

"Always," Arthur said before ending the call. He quickly located and dialed Billy Yazzie's number. "I need you to go to my house and hang out with Sharon for a while."

"What's up, boss?"

Arthur gave him a heads-up.

"Not a problem," Billy said. "I'll head over after we've dropped off the last of the firewood to some elders. Don't worry, boss."

Arthur grinned. "You're the one who should be worrying. She'll be packing the SIG Sauer."

Billy laughed and hung up.

Arthur's stomach churned, and he recognized the coinciding growl. An interstate food sign announced four upcoming restaurants, and that didn't help matters either. He still had less than an hour's drive ahead of him before he reached the hotel, so he decided to take the Montgomery Boulevard exit, cross back under the interstate bridge deck, and turn into the IHOP parking lot. More than anything, he felt like breakfast.

Arthur paused before getting out to make another call. He located the number quickly and tapped the call button. John Sykes answered in three rings.

"What's up, LT? I've been wanting to call you."

"I'm working on something," Arthur said. "I may need your help."

Without hesitation, Sykes answered, "What's the mission?"

Arthur went through the story up to a point. "You in, brother?"

"You even have to ask?"

Arthur smiled. "This thing is stringing out in different directions, so I'll call you when I need you. Be ready."

"Copy that." Sykes took a heavy pause. "Like I said, I've been meaning to call you."

"What about?"

"I've been having some really fucked-up dreams, LT. It's like every time I fall asleep, I feel like I'm hunting ghosts. You know?"

"I know," Arthur said somberly.

Sykes huffed. "You ever see the faces of the men we served with in your dreams? I mean the ones that bought it right there in front of you?" There was another pause. A longer one. "Because lately I can't stop seeing them."

Arthur inhaled and let it out, remembering. It didn't take much for him to remember those days. Almost anything could do that. No matter how much harmony he had found. "I know they're hard—the memories. Because with every man that died, a part of you died with them. Whether you liked them or not, they were our brothers; a part of our team. They depended on us as much as we depended on them. I used to have nightmares a long time ago, too," he said. "Back when a bottle of whiskey kept them away for a while. Don't have them as much anymore."

"Yeah," Sykes lamented, "the whiskey just clouds them over until next time. Trouble is, the next time keeps coming faster and faster. Someday I think it'll be all I dream about. And when that day comes, I'll have to decide whether it's better to be part of the world that makes me remember … or a part of the other world that doesn't."

"When we joined up, they shaved our heads and took away our names so they could destroy who we were, so they could create who we would become. We need to get together when this is over," Arthur said. "Bring things out of the shadows where they can be dealt with. Maybe get the other guys, too?"

"All, sir?"

"You think I was kidding about the support group?"

"It would be good to be able to talk about it," Sykes said. "Rosheen's a good listener, but she hasn't a clue. Most of the time, I think I just scare the hell out of her. But it's not like talking with somebody who's been there." There was a moment of silence. "She's my angel, LT. I know what I tell her worries her. I can see it in her face."

"We all need to have someone who understands us," Arthur confided. "Even if they don't understand what made us. Keep it together, bro. I'll call you when I need you."

"Roger that."

Arthur ended the call and walked across the parking lot to the restaurant, where the host escorted him to a table and went away before a young lady arrived.

Jeanie looked to be in her mid-twenties, smiling face, youthful skin, with dark hair pulled back into a ponytail. Arthur noted her red shirt, black pants and matching sneakers along with a small black apron. He smiled and gave her his order and she left; then he pulled out his phone and scrolled through his contacts. He tapped Detective Lance Gilberto's number and waited. Jeanie reappeared with a pot of coffee, a mug, and apron full of creamers that she dumped into the empty little white bowl. Gilberto answered as she began to pour his coffee.

"Who can you contact in the Albuquerque PD?"

Jeanie looked at him oddly, finished pouring.

"Why?" Gilberto said. "What did you come up with?"

Arthur waited for Jeanie to go away. When she did, he continued. "What do you know about Chino Ignacio Garcia?"

Gilberto's tone changed. "I know he has all the appeal of a urinal cake."

Arthur told him the story, and the angle he wanted to work that had been swirling around inside his head. "I need someone here in Duke City to be in the loop to pull this off."

"If you pull it off, you mean," Gilberto said.

Arthur said, "O ye of little faith."

"I have as much faith as the next guy. I go to church and everything. But I'm also a realist. What you're talking about is taking this man down, and that isn't gonna be easy. But I do know a guy in the Child Exploitation Detail of their Juvenile Crimes Section that could help you. Eduardo Espinosa. He's a good man. You can trust him. I'll text you his number and then give him a call, bring him up to speed."

Arthur poured some creamer into his coffee and stirred.

Gilberto added, "Did Garcia give you any money?"

"Not yet, but I'm supposed to get five grand what I turn her over to him," Arthur lied. "He did let me leave with my life, though."

Arthur Nakai had plans for the fifteen grand up-front money, and he was going to make sure it did some good, not just collect dust in an Albuquerque evidence lockup waiting for Garcia to go to trial. And he wasn't about to see it get lost in the system, never to be seen again or know that nothing good had come from it. Even if Garcia told them he had paid him, he was going to make sure that cash was never found. After all, it would be Garcia's word against his.

Arthur paused, looked around the restaurant for any unwanted ears. Seeing none, he explained further, "I'm going to let him think I'm working this the way he wants. Except when I find April, I'm going to make sure she gets back to her parents. Then I'll call him and tell him I'm bringing her to him. That's where your cop friend Espinosa comes in."

"Okay. But you can't meet with Garcia alone because he sure as hell won't show up alone. You'll need backup. Espinosa can provide that."

"As long as Espinosa has no problem with me, I'll have no problem with him."

"Absolutely." Gilberto sneezed.

"Catching a cold?"

"What do you think?" Arthur heard him sniffling. "Over-the-counter shit doesn't work worth a damn. Hold on …"

Arthur heard the receiver get set down on a hard surface—probably the cop's desk—and Gilberto blowing his nose. When he picked the phone back up, he said, "Any leads on the girl so far?"

Arthur explained how she escaped from the Cuban and removed the tracking chip. He added the story of little Nikki. There was no telling what the Cuban's trainers had done to her after she had been taken away. Arthur said, "The girls I saw there looked to be all underage. How come this asshole is still in business?"

"Somebody's in his hip pocket would be my guess," Gilberto speculated. "Politicians, cops, someone with power enough to make it happen. He's either greasing a palm or he's got something on someone he can use as leverage. Maybe a kinky sex tape of someone powerful, like that asshole in New York that ended up dead in his cell." Gilberto scoffed. "Like hell that was a suicide."

Jeanie returned with Arthur's stack of pancakes and green chile omelet, sat them in front of him. She smiled and asked if he needed anything, then went away when he told her he did not.

Gilberto said, "Where are you heading now?"

"Back to the hotel. My dog's been there by himself, and I don't want to have to pay for steam cleaning the carpet." Arthur snorted a laugh as he poured maple syrup onto his buttermilk pancakes. "Knowing him, he's probably found a spot to sit and watch the pool. I'll take him with me tomorrow when I check out the truck stops, see if anyone remembers seeing April."

"Good luck." Gilberto sneezed again.

"Good luck with that."

"This place is like an incubation chamber for every virus known to mankind."

Arthur cut and forked some of his green chile omelet. "Call your guy. Have him call me in the morning before I hit the truck stops."

"I sure hope you know what you're doing," Gilberto said, sniffling.

"Yeah," Arthur replied. "So do I."

CHAPTER SIXTEEN

Officer Brandon Descheene's headlights picked their way through the night as they guided him up Highway 491, just north of Shiprock District headquarters. He slowed, crossed over the southbound lanes, and gunned his white Tahoe onto Bluff Road before the semi bearing down on him got too close.

Bluff Road itself was a mixture of degrading asphalt, loose gravel and semi-packed dirt that followed the San Juan River as it rolled lazily and wound its way into the open desert. When the orange sign rolled past the glow of Descheene's headlights, he could feel the town's namesake—the rock with wings, or Tsé Bit'a'í in Navajo—standing like an ancient guardian somewhere off to his left and slightly ahead of him, shrouded now by the cloak of darkness. The scientific explanation was that it was the remnants of a throat from an ancient volcano, one of many on the Colorado Plateau, that had formed almost thirty million years ago. But to his people, the Diné, it was the sacred swan that carried his ancestors on its back safely away from their enemies.

He passed more orange street signs and his dread grew as he thought of how Emmanuel Ruiz was going to take the news that the mother of his unborn child had been found murdered brutally and his child had been stolen. The big question circulating in Descheene's mind was why Ruiz hadn't immediately reported her missing instead of waiting the four or five days. Did they have an argument that resulted in her storming out? Had she gone to visit a relative? Did she maybe get pissed off and leave him before the baby was born? Or had he killed her and hidden the child somewhere? Descheene had been in similar situations before, but they had not had the tragedy this one seemed to encompass.

After he turned onto Seventh Lane, his mind racing, the small stones his tires threw into the fender wells made the only sound he heard, along with the occasional dispatch from his police radio. After half a mile, the headlights of Unit 18 washed over the open white tubular gate where Descheene turned; he drove up the gradual incline, parked his unit by a pair of rusted horse trailers and sat, observing the layout.

There were two other houses on the property. The one to his left was an octagon shape—meant to resemble a hogan—with tan outer slat walls and a brown shingled roof with a stovepipe sticking out of the center of a smaller raised roof. Directly in front of him sat a cream-colored trailer with a large, makeshift corrugated overhang with no vehicle beneath it nor any lights on inside it. To his right was the small house of Emmanuel Ruiz and Angelina Martinez. It was yellowish in color with a basketball hoop standing tall off to the right next to a large tank of some kind he thought belonged buried under a gas station holding fuel. Two glowing lights hanging from two tall wooden poles would give off enough light for Descheene to make his way on foot to the yellow house. There were no lights on in the octagon, but he could see a light in the yellow house of Emmanuel Ruiz.

He radioed in his location and said that he would be out of the vehicle, then got out and stepped up to the front door. He knocked and took three steps back.

No answer.

He knocked again and took three steps back.

"Who is it?" a voice said.

"Officer Descheene, Navajo Police," Brandon replied. "I'd like to talk with you for a minute."

Descheene heard shuffling around inside the house before the door opened. He was greeted by a young man in his mid-twenties with a beer in one hand and a cigarette in the other.

"Is it about my Angelina?" the man said, his Mexican accent coming through his English. "Is she all right?"

Descheene said, "Are you Emmanuel Ruiz?"

The man nodded.

"May I come inside?"

Ruiz nodded again, stepped back inside the house. Descheene followed and closed the door behind them. Ruiz stood in the front room, took a drink of his beer and a drag from his cigarette.

"It's about my Angelina, isn't it?" Ruiz said again.

Descheene said, "Did you report her missing?"

Ruiz looked around the room. "No."

"Why not?"

"I said some stupid shit the last time we talked on the phone," he revealed, ashamed. "I just thought she got pissed and laid low with one of her friends." Ruiz took another swig of beer. "Did she come to you? Did she send you here?"

Descheene pursed his lips and took a breath. "Mr. Ruiz, I'm very sorry to have to tell you that Angelina's body was discovered yesterday morning in Morgan Lake."

His eyes went wide. "She's dead?"

"I'm sorry."

Ruiz's face screwed up. "What da fuck you talkin' about?"

"I was hoping you could tell me what she might have been doing out there."

"She didn't have no reason to be out there," Ruiz said. "That's bullshit!"

"What was she doing the last time you spoke with her?"

Emmanuel Ruiz fell back on the blanket-covered couch, the stunned look on his face telegraphing his worst fear setting in. He rubbed the beer can over his forehead as if his brain were heating up and it could somehow cool it down.

"Did she drown? Because she could swim. You can't drown if you can swim, right?" Suddenly, his eyes stared in a frightened gaze. "What about the baby? She was pregnant with our daughter. Is the baby okay?"

Descheene sat himself down on the edge of a coffee table in front of the couch, pursed his lips and swallowed. "We haven't located the baby yet."

"What da fuck does that mean? She was carrying her. She had a week to go!"

Descheene couldn't tear his eyes away from Ruiz's. "She'd been in the lake for a few days. There was no baby."

Ruiz winced. "You mean someone took her? Someone killed Angelina, and then took our daughter?"

Descheene looked down at the sweat forming on his palms and wiped them on his uniform pants. "We've got officers hitting the hospitals now to see if anyone has come in with a newborn in the last week. We'll hit the clinics and doctors' offices in the morning. Was there anyone who'd want to hurt her? Old boyfriends or anyone she may have had contact with that may have threatened her?"

Descheene watched the emotions welling up in Ruiz to the point where they broke him down. He began shaking and crying because his whole world had been destroyed. The hand holding the beer suddenly heaved it forcefully across the room in anger, slamming it into the wall behind

Descheene's left shoulder and sending its contents spewing streams of white foam.

"There ain't nobody that would hurt Angelina," he argued. "She never had trouble with anyone."

"I'm sorry to have to ask these questions right now," Descheene proceeded, "but I need to know what she was doing the last day you spoke with her."

Ruiz wiped his eyes and sat up straighter, took a couple of deep breaths. "She made breakfast before I went to work."

Descheene pulled a small notepad and pen from his uniform pocket, flipped open the pad and began writing. "Where do you work?"

"Mesa Verde Mining. I used to work for Black Mesa, but they closed and we moved here."

"But Mesa Verde's in Colorado," Descheene said.

"The name refers to the Mesa Verde formation of the San Juan Basin field.

Dez nodded. "When did you leave for work the last morning you saw her?"

Ruiz thought briefly. "Around six a.m. Because the baby was close to coming, they put me on day shifts for the last few weeks so I could be home at night with Angelina."

Descheene continued to scribble. "Go on."

"She said she was going to Diné Laundry and wash clothes before heading across the street to City Market for some groceries."

"Did you talk to her later that day?'

"I called her around two in the afternoon. I always called her on my break to see how she was feeling."

Descheene smiled. "What kind of car was she driving? Make, model, license number, if you have it."

Ruiz took a second. "Nineteen ninety-eight Explorer. White. It's got rust around the fenders and used to have sidebars, but they rusted off." Ruiz leaned to his left and pulled his wallet from his hip pocket, retrieved his insurance card. He handed it to Descheene, who took it and copied down the VIN. "Her belly was the size of a watermelon, you know? She couldn't hardly sleep at night with all the hip and back pain. Her legs and feet and hands all swelled up something awful."

Descheene handed him back the insurance card. "Was she going anywhere after the grocery store?"

Ruiz returned the card to his wallet and slid the wallet back into his hip pocket. "She said she was going to see some woman about baby clothes they were selling online. She was always trying to save money."

Descheene said, "Do you know who or where this woman was?"

"I know she was in Waterflow somewhere. I don't think she ever mentioned her by name. She was just happy to get baby clothes cheap."

"Do you remember her telling you an address?"

Ruiz shook his head. "No." Then he added despondently, "I should've paid more attention to her. I should have listened to her when she told me stuff. And I shouldn't have let her go alone. It's all my fault."

Descheene asked Ruiz for Angelina's phone number and received it. If his questions weren't bringing out any useful information, perhaps he could have the phone tracked. "Is this when you two had the argument? When you called her?"

Ruiz nodded, took another drag off his cigarette. "Yeah. I was an idiot. Now I'll always remember the last time I talked to her I was angry." He looked at his hands and wrung them out in his lap, then began to break down into tears. "I never told her I loved her."

Descheene felt uncomfortable. He never got used to giving people this type of news. Learning how to handle suspects at the academy in Chinle was one thing, but all of the training that made up the twenty-six weeks never really taught you how to handle this situation. Only experience could do that. And sometimes not even then.

"I'm sure she knew," Descheene told him. "And I'm sorry, I have to ask you if you can account for your whereabouts for the last five days."

Ruiz bristled visibly. "You think I had something to do with this?"

"I want to find Angelina's killer," Descheene sidestepped, "and get your child back safely."

Ruiz repositioned himself on the blanketed couch. "Like I said, I've been working. The rest of the time, I've been sitting here waiting for her to come home." He looked around, lost in the fact that she would never bring her light to their home again. "It's really quiet here without her."

"Has anyone seen you here?" Descheene said. "Have you talked with any of your neighbors?"

"The dude in the trailer, and the couple in that hogan." Ruiz rubbed his face and ran his hands over his head and down the back of his neck. "I've been pulling long hours underground, man. All I've been doing is come home and sitting around waiting for a phone call or for her to walk through that door. And every night when she didn't, I went to bed and got up the next morning and did it all over again." He paused to look at the Navajo officer. "Now you're telling me she's never going to come back. I have no girl, and I have no daughter."

Descheene decided he wasn't going to push any further. He had enough information for now. It would be easy to corroborate his work schedule with the mine and the conversations with his neighbors. "What do you do at the mine?"

"I work on the long wall with a couple other guys."

"What's the long wall?"

"It's where a long wall of coal is ground away by a shearer—like a giant drill bit. Chunks of coal fall onto a conveyer and it get taken it away. As the shearer moves down the wall, a hydraulic roof support moves up to stop the roof from caving in."

Descheene said, "Sounds dangerous."

"The shearer can grind up to thirty feet of coal from the wall in a minute. I wouldn't wanna be chewed up by it. But the pay is good," Ruiz said.

Descheene scribbled his name and number on a blank page in his notebook and tore it out before folding up the notebook and putting it away in his shirt pocket along with his pen. "I know it doesn't mean much coming from me, but I'm sorry for your loss." He handed Ruiz the small piece of paper. "If you think of anything else, please call me anytime. That's my cell number. If we get any more information, we'll be in touch with you."

Ruiz looked up blankly, then nodded absently. He had already slipped away and fallen deeper into his own dark abyss. Descheene showed himself out.

In the front seat of his patrol unit, Brandon Descheene keyed the mic and contacted dispatch. "Navajo Eighteen."

"Eighteen," Alicia Tom responded.

"I've got a twenty-eight."

"Go with twenty-eight."

Descheene read off the VIN number he had jotted down and asked her to run the license plate.

"Navajo Eighteen, VIN comes back to a 1998 Ford Explorer, white in color with gold trim." She rattled off the plate number. "No violations."

Descheene relayed the dead woman's cell phone number. "Have someone contact the cell phone provider for dispatchable locations for the last five days regarding that number."

"We'll need to get a warrant because there's no imminent threat to the life of the victim," Alicia Tom informed him.

"Tell them there's an imminent threat to the life of the child," Descheene urged. "Tell them the killer has her baby."

"Ten-four, Eighteen," Alicia Tom responded.

"Eighteen, clear."

Descheene fired up his unit, circled around the trailer with the corrugated awning, and headed back down the gradual slope toward the tubular gate. As he drove south on Seventh Lane, he put himself in Emmanuel Ruiz's shoes. How could he not? Even though he had been taught to keep an objective distance, this, to him, was different. A girl like Angelina was old enough to be his sister, Tiana. And that reality hit too close to home for him. He had witnessed in person the ghastly way Angelina had been found. The image of her crushed face and crudely cut abdomen would stay with him forever. He turned left onto Bluff Road and was back on 491 heading into Shiprock when his radio crackled.

"Navajo Eighteen," Alicia Tom's voice said. "Come in, Eighteen. Dez, you out there?"

Descheene fisted his microphone. "Eighteen."

"Be advised we've been notified by San Juan County of a burned-out vehicle west of the Jewett Valley power station on Indian Route 38 close to the Hogback. One of the power station's workers was checking power lines on the way to the substation and found it. Engine 4 is on the scene."

He caught the light and turned east on Highway 64 and was passing Shiprock Fleet Management on his way to Waterflow to try to get ahead of the game in case the phone company could give them a last known location of Angelina Martinez. "Any word on the tracking yet?"

"Lieutenant Begay is working on the warrant."

"We don't have time for that!" Descheene insisted, the frustration clear in his voice.

"We can only go as fast as things can happen, Dez," Alicia Tom replied, then paused. "I told county you'd meet them on scene."

"Why?" Descheene said. "You're not making any sense."

"Because it's your victim's Ford Explorer that got torched."

CHAPTER SEVENTEEN

"We have to work together," April Manygoats told Lucy Nez, "if we're going to get out of here alive."

"How?" Lucy whimpered. "How can we do that? We're always chained up."

"He's a sick fuck. He likes us hard, dirty and submissive. I think he took you because he thinks I'm too old and too used to his kind of fucked-up sex."

Lucy turned her tired head and looked drearily at April. "Are you?"

"Am I what?"

"Too used to it?"

Every time Lucy or April moved, their chains reminded them of their imprisonment. April gazed back at Lucy, hung her head a little. "Yes. I'm used to it. But you don't have to be. We need to stop this asshole and get the fuck out of here."

Lucy wiped her runny nose, pulled her legs up to cover her naked torso, and wrapped her arms around them to hold them close for warmth. "We're never getting out of here. He's going to kill us."

"Not if we play his game. We're going to have to be smarter."

"What do you mean?"

"We're going to have to work together."

"I don't get it," Lucy said.

"Look, he's been fucking me for three weeks and using me like one of those lifelike dolls jerkoffs buy because they can't get a real woman. If I can get him to free me, even for just a minute, that might give me time to grab one of his own tools and beat the shit out of him with it. Then I can free you, and we can get the hell out of here."

Lucy shook her head. "No! That'll just make him madder. If you fail, he'll kill you and then you'll leave me here alone with him."

"Look," April reassured her, "what choice do we have—to sit here and be abused whenever he likes? I don't know about you, but I'd rather die out of these chains fighting for my life. All you have to do is distract him when he unlocks them."

Lucy shook her head fervently. "I can't."

"You have to," April argued. "If we don't at least try, then he is going to kill me anyway and use you like he did me until he gets tired of you and kidnaps another girl. Maybe younger than you."

Lucy stared at April, her eyes wet and scared.

April said, "If he keeps you chained up here for two or three years, destroying you every day, you'll never survive it. We need to stop this now."

Lucy began to cry. April's arms couldn't reach out to comfort her. She needed to make her see the only way to survive together was to work together.

"Do you want him doing this to you every day?" April probed further. "Do you want his big, ugly hands all over you going places and doing things no one has ever done to you? Do you want him to break you down so much that you will never be you again?" April looked at the wall by the workbench and pointed with her chin. "Do you want him to use any of those tools on you and make you beg him for death?"

Lucy's eyes raised to the collection of instruments she knew nothing about but was terrified of. "No," she whispered. "I don't want any of that."

"Then the next time he comes in, I'll keep him away from you by telling him what I want him to do to me. That should make him release me, and if you distract him, maybe I can grab something and try to knock him out or kill him. Then I'll unchain you, and we can walk out that door. We'll lock that fucker inside here."

Lucy whimpered, "I don't know."

"Listen!" April barked. "If we can get out that door, I'm sure he has a car out there. That means we can get the fuck out of here and go to the police."

"I don't know if I can."

"You have to," April stressed. "Look, guys like him are fucked in the head, you know? Their brain is wired like a bowl of worms." April took a breath. "You follow my lead if I get him to go along with it. It might be our only chance to get out of this hell alive."

Lucy's tears slowed, and her demeanor turned to apprehensive resolve. "I guess I'll try."

April's eyes flashed. "Do more than try. Like I said, if I can get to those tools, I'll bash his head in!"

Lucy felt her stomach feeding on whatever small amount of fat her body contained, her system searching for sustenance anywhere. "What if it doesn't work?" she asked.

April looked at her flatly. "Then I'm dead. Or we're both dead. Either way, we have no future if we don't try."

CHAPTER EIGHTEEN

The Ford Explorer was toast. There was no body inside the burned carcass that Descheene could see as it sat beneath the bright glow of four pole lights that had been erected at the imagined corners of the crime scene. Eighty thousand lumens of pure white sunshine illuminating the burned-out skeleton exposed the fact that everything that could burn did burn. Whatever could melt had melted. Descheene noticed the rear hatch of the SUV was blown out and twisted by the force of the gas tank explosion, yet still somehow managed to hang on precariously. He also noticed the sparkling glass shards that had once been the truck's windows scattered on the ground. The tires were blown from the heat, and the acrid smell of rubber and melted plastic still hung in the air, attacking his nostrils. As far as the San Juan County deputy sheriff could tell him, it had all the earmarks of an arson job, especially since it could be involved in his murder case.

"Looks like someone tried to get rid of incriminating evidence," the middle-aged deputy told him. "We'll have it towed back on a flatbed where the arson squad and forensics can go over it." They both looked at the blackened hulk sitting before them. "I'll get you a report tomorrow sometime."

Descheene nodded as his cell phone rang in his pants pocket. He didn't recognize the number but answered it anyway. It was Emmanuel Ruiz. Descheene wasn't going to mention the scene unfolding before him.

"I found the address and phone number of the woman Angelina was going to buy the baby clothes from," he said. "She must have written it down so she could put it in her phone and then thew it away."

"Hold on," Descheene said, hurrying over to his unit. He laid the phone on the hood, pulled out his notebook, and tapped the speaker prompt. "Go ahead."

Ruiz read off the information as he scribbled. "Thank you for the information," Descheene said.

Ruiz said nothing; the call simply ended.

* * *

Officer Brandon Descheene pulled up in front of the rundown trailer off Route 6899 around nine thirty p.m. During the summer, he could imagine the trailer sitting beneath the handful of twisted shade trees that had now been stripped of their leafy foliage by the marching onslaught of seasonal change. Much of the other housing in the area looked like manufactured homes of the same gray coloring with graded dirt lawns and scattered Christmas decorations. The ground where Descheene had placed his foot as he got out was hard, and the light snow that had just begun fell silently against the warm windshield of his patrol unit and melted upon impact.

The small red sedan and beat-up pickup that sat quietly in the snowy night resembled the vehicles of everyone else who inhabited this community of less than two thousand. He closed the door of his patrol unit softly and walked carefully up to the trailer door. Old-fashioned large colored Christmas lights were laced around the edge of the roof, and there were lights on inside. Someone was up. He also anticipated they would be more than a little apprehensive; his experience told him that people always became nervous when the police arrived at their door asking questions late at night. He tapped his knuckles on the storm door and stood back. Around thirty seconds later, the inside door opened and revealed a large Latina woman wearing a loose-fitting white T-shirt and dark baggy sweatpants. Pink furry slippers covered her feet.

His belt radio squawked. Descheene absently reached around and turned down the volume. "Maria Sanchez?" he asked.

The woman nodded.

He introduced himself and told her why he was there. "May I come in?'

"Sure," the woman said apprehensively, stepping aside. "Would you like something to drink?"

Descheene opened the storm door and stepped in. "No, thank you," he said, then closed the entry door behind him just as the storm door clicked shut. "I'm here to ask you some questions about Angelina Martinez." He pulled his notepad and pen from his uniform pocket. "I understand she contacted you through social media about some baby clothes you had for sale."

The woman nodded. "Sure. I remember her. She was a nice girl."

"When was she here?"

Maria Sanchez waved him to a seat and wedged her large frame into a worn cloth recliner that rocked heavily with her weight. Her furry feet stopped the chair's rocking movement.

"She was here about five or six days ago," Sanchez explained. "Came by middle of the afternoon. After three, I think. I could tell by the size of her belly she was about to domino."

Descheene grinned and nodded, scribbled in his notebook. As he did, he noticed the recliner appeared to have been moved recently to its current location. The footprints of its rails had left deep impressions a few feet to its right in the dirty carpeting.

"Did she mention anything about the baby's father?"

Maria shook her head. "Not that I can think of."

Descheene said, "Did she buy any of the clothes she came to see?"

"Some. We had bought boys' and girls' clothes but were only selling the girls' clothes. She picked through them and took what she liked."

Maria Sanchez's breathing seemed strenuous, her size putting a strain on her respiratory system, and the way she had packed herself into the chair wasn't helping her situation. Dez could hear the quick, repetitive breathing circulating through her nostrils.

"My daughter lives with me," she continued. "She was going to have twins, but her daughter developed problems soon after birth and didn't survive. We decided we should sell the girls' clothes and at least get something for them since we weren't"—she paused to fight back understandable emotions—"going to need them."

"I'm so sorry," Descheene said. "How many outfits did she buy?"

The big woman thought briefly. "About six, I think. We had a few more, but she took the ones she liked."

"Is your daughter here?"

"She's asleep in the back bedroom with the baby. She had just put him down right before I got home."

"I see. How long have you been home?"

"'Bout an hour."

"Where were you?"

"I had some shopping to do and then picked up a couple of sandwiches from Blake's for us and brought them home."

"I thought you said she was asleep when you got home."

Sanchez shifted in her recliner. "I said she had put the baby down. She was still up, so we ate and she went to bed."

"I see. Did Angelina act upset while she was here, seem agitated in any way?"

Sanchez thought again, shook her head with enough emphasis to jostle her double chins. "No. She seemed fine. Just interested in the clothes. Like I said, she was a nice girl. Real cute, you know?" She looked at the Navajo Nation officer in front of her. "Did something happen to her?"

Descheene took a deep breath. The body armor under his uniform shirt often curtailed his breathing, but it was better than not breathing at all if that was the alternative. He said, "She was found murdered yesterday."

Maria Sanchez's shock was clear. "Oh my God!" she gasped. "Is the baby all right?"

"It's an active investigation," Descheene said. "I can't really comment further."

"That poor girl," Sanchez said. "What kind of animal would do that?"

"What's your daughter's name?"

"Monica. Monica Delgado."

Descheene scribbled again in his notebook. When he looked up, trying to formulate his next question, his eyes noticed something small catching the light against the base of a cabinet leading into the galley kitchen. He couldn't make out what it was, but he was working on how to figure it out when he said, "About what time did Angelina leave? It'll help us put together a timeline."

"Around three thirty, I'd say. She wasn't here long. Just long enough to go through the clothes."

"Did your daughter speak with her?"

"Of course," Sanchez said. "They talked about Monica's baby and about how much Angelina was looking forward to being a mother."

Descheene scribbled again. "It would be very helpful if I could speak with your daughter. She might remember something you don't."

"Like I said, she's resting with the baby." Maria Sanchez struggled in her chair, trying to gain a more comfortable position. "I was going to let her sleep until the baby woke up, which, if we're lucky, won't be for a couple of hours. He'll wake up hungry, so she'll need to feed him."

"How old is your daughter?"

"Twenty-two."

"Where's the father?"

"Who the hell cares. He's a useless asshole. She's better off without him."

Descheene's eyebrows rose, and he nodded briefly. "My sister told me the most beautiful thing in the world is the bonding of a mother and a child in the beginning." He grinned. "She said the emotions she felt while nursing her son were beyond words."

"My daughter can't do that," Sanchez offered. "She's not producing enough. It happens to some new mothers, so she's been bottle-feeding."

"Oh, I'm sorry. I didn't mean to—"

"That's all right." Maria Sanchez glanced at her watch. "Is that all you need for now, Officer?"

"Is that your daughter?" Descheene asked, noticing a photograph hanging askew on the wall behind Sanchez.

"Yes. That's her."

"Pretty girl," he said, studying the photograph of Maria Sanchez and her daughter next to a plant potted in Navajo-designed black-and-white ceramic. He glanced around the room quickly, making a mental note that the same plant now resided in a different pot on a side table. Descheene folded up his notebook and returned it to his pocket as he stood, then stepped toward the front door fumbling with his pen. "If anything comes to mind, please contact the station in Shiprock. And I might still need to come back to speak with your daughter at some point."

As Sanchez extricated herself from the rocking recliner with all the skill of a sumo wrestler riding a bicycle, Descheene absently dropped his pen by the cabinet base, then squatted down to pick it up. The act allowed his eyes to focus more closely on the item that had drawn his attention during his questioning of Maria Sanchez. The little snowman decorating the fingernail that rested awkwardly beneath the cabinet overhang against the kickplate told him all he needed to know. And Sanchez seemed big enough and looked strong enough to win a fight against a petite pregnant woman. He hadn't seen the daughter, but with her help, Sanchez could have easily overpowered Angelina enough to knock her out with the missing pot. That would have given them time to restrain her in some way, move her somewhere else in order to kill her, and remove the baby. His mind was reeling with plausible scenarios when he could feel the big woman's eyes on him. He stood up and thanked her again for her cooperation, and showed himself out.

Sitting inside his unit, he kept his eyes trained on her as she closed the front door. He hoped she hadn't been watching him too closely. Angelina hadn't been killed there, he formulated, because there would have been so much blood from removing the child. They had taken her someplace else for that. Descheene further hypothesized that the chair had been moved to cover any blood spilled from the initial blow from the now repotted plant. But there had been too much damage to her head to think that Angelina had been beaten to death in the living room. And given the kinds of wounds he had seen at the lake, she would have to have been moved while she was unconscious. Descheene had never seen the bathroom. For all he knew, she could have been killed in the tub and the baby could have been removed while her blood simply spiraled down the drain.

The more he thought, the more anger began to rage within him. He wanted to rush back in and arrest them both for the murder of Angelina Martinez and the kidnapping of her unborn child. But what if he was overthinking it? Making things fit his conjecture? He had seen nothing that led him to believe there had been a struggle. There could be any number of reasons for the plant to have been repotted. All the broken nail might prove was that Angelina had been there as Maria had already explained. But how could he even be sure the daughter was actually there? He hadn't spoken with her. And if they had killed Angelina, how could they have disposed of her body? He hadn't noticed any watercraft. Could they have put it in the Explorer and driven out to the lake before they burned it? Arson and forensics would hopefully have something in their report, but what DNA would be left to find? Hell, he thought, they could have done any number of things, but there were too many unanswered questions for him to be reckless at this point, and his probable-cause aspect was circumstantial at best.

Descheene stopped, took a deep breath, and exhaled slowly. He recognized that he needed to take a step back and calm down. He reached inside his shirt and pulled on the thin suede lanyard around his neck that brought with it his medicine pouch holding the bitter herb inside. He was protected. But when this was all over, he was going to have to reacquaint himself with the Blessing Way and Protection

Way ceremonies. He needed to find his way back to the natural order of life that the uniform often kept at a distance or, in some cases, even battled. He needed to remove everything that had begun to contaminate his life, such as fear, guilt, hate, envy, greed, jealousy and, like tonight, anger. He fisted his microphone and called dispatch for backup as he fired up his SUV. He drove back down the road and parked just past the far turn, waiting behind a stand of cottonwood trees in the dark.

Backup was ten minutes out.

CHAPTER NINETEEN

Lucy Nez whimpered as he ran his fingertips up the backs of her smooth, trembling legs, over the soft round curves of her buttocks, and then lightly up her arched back as she clung to the wall over the bench. The echoing rebuke from Nez jerked April Manygoats out of a fitful sleep.

"Leave her alone!" April yelled.

He slowly turned his head toward her, the crooked smile catching the glow of the single bulb as his gray eyes glimmered coldly.

"She's fifteen!" April pleaded. "She's in pain! She needs time to heal!"

"Pain is just another form of pleasure," he said. "If she's in pain, the more she'll scream; and the more she screams, the more I'll like it."

"If you want to abuse someone, why not me?" April offered. "I can take it. I might even like it."

He turned slowly again, then stood glaring back at her proposition. He studied her sitting there, chained and bruised and worn. "You don't know what I had planned for your friend tonight. How do you know you will like it?"

April tossed her hair out of her eyes defiantly. "Because I know what I like."

Lucy Nez continued to sob, strengthening April's resolve. He moved closer, squatting down in front of her, his eyes now glistening with anticipation.

"Oh, I'm sure you've never experienced what I can do," he said, the words seeming to slither out of his crooked mouth like the tongue of a poisonous snake. "And I don't want you to ever get used to it." His face moved to within a half inch of hers. April could smell the rankness of his foul breath. "I want you to scream and beg for me to stop because it hurts so badly you can't go on. And it will hurt." He put his big hands on his knees and pushed himself up. Smiling down, he added, "Because you intrigue me, I will spare your little friend tonight and let *you* experience the freedom of her pain."

April watched as he made his way over to a large ring hanging from the ceiling she had noticed earlier. Lucy Nez craned her neck to look back at her fellow captive, tears trailing down her young face, shaking almost imperceptibly and telegraphing the need not to set things in motion. But her plan had to work, April reassured herself. This could be their only chance. Her mind had already spun through every possible scenario she could think of—except the most disastrous. And that was the one she could never allow to play out.

When the large metal ring hit the wooden floor, the room shook and dust rose into the cold air. April's abdomen tightened as her heart suddenly beat faster at the aspect of the freedom through pain he was going to put her through. She hoped her child would survive whatever he had planned. She knew she could never tell Lucy she was pregnant. If she had, she'd never have agreed to play this game. And this was a game they had to win. It took all of her resolute strength to let Lucy see a face of determination and not one of fear. Even though she thought she had figured all the angles, April's mind was fighting back the frenzy of terror her nerves would not let go of.

"Tonight, we're going to play a little game I call Ring around the Rosie," he said, rolling the large hoop toward the area where April had been hogtied and hung in the air just days earlier. "Have you ever heard of sensation play? I have developed a rather unique variation of that."

April watched as he attached the steel cable from the winch to a welded ring on top of the hoop, then took the remote in hand. The electric motor whined against its weight until the hoop began to stand on its own, suspended in the air like something she had once seen in a Cirque du Soleil video on YouTube. April saw the shackles welded to the hoop and had a good idea of what was coming. She had done something similar to men who liked being dominated by a mistress. The ones who got off on subtle pain that led to intense pain that led to their kind of masochistic gratification. She swallowed hard and steeled herself against what she imagined was about to take place, knowing that a fifteen-year-old girl wouldn't have to endure it.

As the hoop dangled silently in the chilly air, he made his way over to April and released the padlocks that bound her wrists and let her shackles fall to the furry floor. As he unlocked her collar, her shivering seemed to intensify— whether from expected terror or simply the air that filled the room, he enjoyed the feeling of control it gave him. The quivering lips, the frightened eyes, the supple skin dotted with an array of goose bumps; the dirty, slightly matted hair, and the solidly erect nipples. And then there was that aroma—the fragrance that always enticed his senses—the scent of sex that saturated the air from every pore of her body and fed his undeniable thirst. He grabbed her arms and got her to her feet. April managed to stand on shaky legs while still succeeding in keeping her eyes from meeting his. He admired her teenage body, the same body he had abused for weeks, and marveled at its resilience. He had shared with her the cleansing freedom that came from the experience of pain and perhaps with it the release of pleasure that—to him—so often accompanied it. Possibly, he thought, he had underestimated this one.

He guided her to the hoop, her dirty feet moving sluggishly across the filthy floor. He had made sure he kept them fed, just like he had with all the others before, but only to the point where it sustained their existence. He had never given them enough nourishment to gain any type of strength that would enable them to fight back. He felt her body shivering, quaking in his rough hands, a happening that brought with it an escalation of his anticipation of what they were about to share.

April let him lift her right arm above her head and felt the leather shackle strapped around her wrist and buckled into place. She pretended to groggily watch as her left wrist was shackled in the same manor. Her eyes now focused as the Master squatted down and spread her legs. She watched as he pressed his face against her crotch and inhaled her scent, allowing his tongue to taste it with a savoring desire. When he exhaled, she could feel his hot breath moist against her skin and feel her body tense repulsively at the sensation. She watched as her right leg was shackled, then the left. She was splayed open now for his indulgence, but all that kept running through her exhausted mind was that she had to survive whatever was about to happen so their plan of escape could be set in motion.

He stood before her, noticing how her breasts rose and fell with every frightened breath; how her belly seemed to quiver against his invasive touch as he slid his fingers downward, crossing the invisible equatorial line most men knew existed to position them between her thighs. The moment his fingers slipped inside her she felt her legs try to pull away and her pelvic muscles tighten. April watched him lift his fingers to his mouth and close his lips around them. The slurping sound she heard made her cringe, but this was where she wanted him—focusing on her and not Lucy. When he pulled his wet fingers from his foul mouth, his tongue slid out in an effort to steal the last bit of her flavor from his lips. His eyes never left hers as he reached down and pulled a blindfold from his back pocket and displayed it.

"I'm sure you've seen one of these before," he said.

April nodded and recognized the corresponding flash in his eyes. As he moved the blindfold toward her, she began to shake her head erratically as if to make it seem as though she were fighting him. When it covered her eyes the world vanished, and she felt him secure it behind her head. With her sight now gone, her remaining senses became all she had. Her ears picked up every sound, her nostrils every disgusting odor, her fingers the cold metal of the hoop and her mouth the taste of her own blood as she imperceptibly bit into the side of her tongue.

She could smell his body now. She could smell the lagging scent of sweat and stale aftershave as it mingled with expensive cologne. She could hear Lucy Nez whimpering softly. She could hear his breathing more clearly and smelled the aroma of Mexican spices on his breath. Suddenly, she felt the tips of both his hands tracing the edges of her jawbone, down the length of her neck, over her shoulders and down the slopes of her breasts. His palms felt rough and warm, his fingers rougher as he cupped her breasts and softly squeezed them repeatedly. She jerked when his thumb and forefingers began rolling her nipples between them as if they were rolling tubes of modeling clay that would become his creation.

Lucy Nez watched as April took a deep, rattling breath. Lucy looked on as he reached into the front pocket of his pants and removed something she had never seen before. She watched as the tiny mechanisms of the black clamps opened and closed as he attached them to April's nipples. April moaned as their tiny mouths bit down on her erect flesh, knowing that her response would escalate his libido. Lucy continued to watch as he reached over and engaged the electric motor, lifting April and the large hoop further into the air. The hoop, now dangling freely from the cable, hovered no more than a few inches above the floor. Lucy Nez observed how his hand gently pushed the hoop so that it began a slow rotation.

"Now is when our fun begins," he hissed as he left her spinning slowly, walked over to his workbench, and returned with another toy. "They call this a tigress whip," he said. "It's made of leather with a nicely braided handle and four tails, or falls as they call them. At the end of each of those falls, past the four balls of bound leather, there are four more falls, giving the submissive the pleasure of sixteen tiny leather strips of gratification or sixteen miniature razors of pain, whichever I deem necessary."

Lucy heard his heavy footsteps move close to her. "Suppose I try this on you first? Give you a taste of what is to come?"

"NO!" April screamed.

Lucy Nez suddenly felt the drags of the whip caress her neck, carry themselves slowly downward, across the supple skin of her arched back, and fall lazily over her haunches. She waited for the inevitable smack of the whip against her skin, but nothing occurred. The anticipation that raced through her mind was more frightening than the reality of the falls of the whip smacking lightly against her ripe young backside. His laugh carried with it a humor of his own making. Thankfully, Lucy heard his footsteps move away from her as he returned his attention to April.

Lucy told herself to close her eyes as tight as she could; she didn't want to watch April suffer through the tortures he had knowingly planned for her. She hadn't even known this woman until the day they were thrown together, but she had chosen to take her place. Lucy's next regret was that she had no way of closing off her ears to all that would follow.

* * *

When his footsteps moved away, Lucy heard her friend's breath escape through shuddering gasps. Now that he had finished with her, April realized Lucy's sobbing had never stopped throughout her ordeal as he hammered the red welts into her skin and the resulting pain into her body. Her sobs and orchestrated moans had filled the small room throughout and echoed in her own ears. Behind the blindfold, she had simply closed her eyes and did what she had always done. She allowed herself to drift off to the island where the sun shone brightly and the sands were as white as refined sugar and the breeze that caressed her skin was cool and soft. Because that had been the plan. That had always been the plan. She had to put herself through this, she told herself, so that they both could live. And it had been up to her to try to create even the smallest chance of escape. If it worked, they would be free and could find food and clothes in the man's house and a car that would get them far away from here. And if it didn't, then Lucy would be left to survive alone. And April knew she wouldn't survive for long.

This was their chance, April believed, as he she heard him pull up his pants and buckle his belt. *This has to work.*

She *had* to be convincing. When he removed the blindfold, she let her eyes fold half-shut as her head seemed to sway uneasily on the axis of her neck. She let out one last breath before dropping her head forward. She then made no sound, showed no movement. *Be still*, her mind repeated. *Be still and control your breathing. You have to draw him closer. You have to make him release you.* She let her body go limp, buckling first at her knees, her tender wrists aching as they now carried the weight of all of her one hundred and fifty pounds as she hung lifeless in the hoop.

"You killed her!" Lucy cried out. "You killed her!"

He turned and moved quickly, running to lift April's weight, growling, "Not yet! Not yet! You can't die just yet. I need you to play with me while I teach the other how to play."

"You killed her!" Lucy cried again.

"Shut up!" he yelled. "Shut the fuck up!"

His hands moved quickly to release the buckles of the wrist cuffs. When her adolescent body fell limp over his shoulder, his hands went to work quickly releasing her feet from the leather cuffs that bound them in place. He turned, then fell to his knees and held her in his arms while his rough fingers grabbed her jaw and began shaking her head. Again, she let her actions breed the fear of unconsciousness in him as her head rocked from side to side and his anxiety increased tenfold.

"NO!" he commanded. "You will not rob me! You will not rob me!"

As he cradled her in his left arm, his right hand smacked her face in an effort to bring her back to the world he had created for his pleasure, but all that did was decorate her face red with the marks of his big hand. He placed her on the floor, then ran out the double doors, only to return quickly with a heavy five-gallon bucket of water. Standing over April, he dumped the bucket of icy sobriety over her motionless body. The flood of cold water washed away the blindfold and splashed over the floor around them, turning her body into a glistening, crimson-marked work of deviant art. Her body heaved and regurgitated the icy water that had clogged her throat. As she belched the clear liquid, her eyes startled open and she began gasping for each treasured breath she could fill her lungs with.

Lucy's cries now drilled into his brain like a thousand horns. "Shut the fuck up!" he yelled again, dropping the bucket and charging across the floor to his workbench. He ripped the machete from its wall peg and turned, breathing heavily from his weight, and moved toward her. "I said shut the fuck up or you're going to join your friend! I can always find another like you!"

Lucy watched his right arm lift the blade high with each heavy step he took. She turned her head away as his arm came down swiftly and planted the end of the blade into the bench that held up her body and cut into her narrow waist.

"Don't make me grow tired of you," he growled. "Or next time I'll bury it in your back and split you up the middle."

Suddenly, April came alive, forcing a powerful leg up with all the resolute strength she could gather, and drove a solid foot between his legs, sending him crumpling to the floor. The heavy bucket that had carried the water now danced across the wooden floor and clambered away from them. April quickly grabbed it as she got to her feet and brought it crashing down upon his head, laying him out prone on the floor with every fiber of hatred she had stored up inside her. Then, as she had done with the trucker, she drove a hammer-like fist solidly into his crotch, bringing him out of his semiconscious state and forcing him to focus on his testicular pain. April looked around frantically, noticed the machete sticking out of the wooden bench like the mighty Excalibur and scrambled to reach it.

Standing over him, she swung downward, relentless as she emptied all her unbridled anger and fear into the motion. He used his arms in a desperate effort to block each of her unyielding attempts to drive the cleaving blade into his body. Wrapping his large hands around her small wrists, he fought to keep himself alive. Jerking April off balance, he managed to roll over and bring her crashing to the wooden floor. When her head bounced off the wood with a thud, her efforts suddenly waned. With all the will he had remaining, he pulled the machete from her limp grip and sent a big hand crashing into her face. April's head jerked violently from the blow and her hair tousled then lay still. He was on his knees now, bleeding from the gash the bucket had left on his head, breathing heavily and holding the handle of the machete tight in his right hand as he drove his right fist into her belly.

April didn't move. Just lay there, limp and still and unconscious.

As he allowed his rage to temper, he got to his feet and stood over her body, his chest continuing to swell with every heavy, exasperated breath. Lucy's cries again filled the room with terror as she realized their plan had failed. Stumbling over to the workbench, groggy with the euphoria that came along with his unleashed anger and his throbbing groin, he buried the end of the machete in the bench where Lucy resided. Through her tears, she watched as he made his way to the workbench and removed a chain leash and a collar that resembled a bulldog's—spiked and studded—from a peg on the wall. Making his way back over to where April lay in silence, he placed the collar around her neck and locked it with a padlock, then attached the leash.

"Get up," he ordered angrily, kicking her with his right foot. "Get up!"

April remained still. Jerking the chain that pulled the collar, he watched as her consciousness slowly began to return.

"I said get up, bitch!" came a harder jerk of the leash, which lifted her from the floor into a sitting position. "C'mon, I said!" This time the jerk of the leash strained the muscles and vertebrae of her neck as it launched her to her feet in front of him. Through enraged breaths, he snarled, "You just earned yourself a night in the pit." He moved his face so close to hers, she could again smell his pungent breath. "And a permanent home among the rest of my playthings."

The fear of those words was noticeable in April's eyes. Her plan had failed, but at least Lucy had been spared the degradation … for this night. April heard the rattle of the chain as he stepped away from her. Against the screams of Lucy, he pulled her forward, pausing only briefly to pick up the tigress whip and bring it down hard across Lucy's concave back. Her screams quickly turned to cries as he repeatedly brought the whip down hard against her tender flesh in an unbridled frenzy.

"Stop it!" April yelled. "Stop it!"

He paused and turned. "You brought her punishment on yourself! If she is in pain, it is from *your* making!" Lucy screamed again as the tails of the whip continued to strike her young body, leaving scarlet welts until she finally succumbed to oblivion. April glared as Lucy's body lost all cognitive function and simply dangled in the air from the shackles and dropped unconsciously over the wooden bench, her young shoulders popping under the deadweight of her own torso.

Their captor stood there for a moment, admiring the girl's body as it hung suspended in the air by the chain running through the iron ring in the wall. The spreader bar between her ankles kept her legs wide while her feet twisted as her knees buckled. Her shoulders strained as she hung there with the full weight of her young body, her soft arms bound in a way that kept them together in what resembled a sort of backward prayer position.

This was *his* world ... *his* chamber of horrors. And they were merely his captive possessions. His lives to manipulate. Here, April conceded, he was God.

April's eyes filled with the tears of pain she had caused the young girl. Her eyes swelled, and her sobs made him turn toward her with ripe anticipation. He stepped over to the workbench, tossed the whip onto it, and grabbed two sets of leather cuffs from the wall of pegboard. When he turned, April saw the danger in his face. Her belly hurt and shook with her sobs as her hands covered her face. Hands he quickly removed and encased in one of the pairs of cuffs. They were fur-lined and soft against her wrists, but bound tightly nonetheless. He knelt down and strapped the other set—again fur-lined—to her ankles, placing her feet far enough apart that she could still walk as freely as the twenty-four-inch spreader bar would let her.

When he rose, he stared at her hard, with eyes still filled with pulsing rage. "Let's see if you can survive a night in the pit. Some can, some can't. Some just go mad. Still others beg me for mercy. And yet some just beg me to kill them when the dawn rises." He smirked, looked back at Lucy after he saw April's eyes dart toward her. "Don't you worry about her. You'll get to hear her screams as you sit in the muddy darkness of the pit and know there is nothing you can do to stop them from carrying on the wind."

April's body lurched forward as he picked up the jingling chain and led her to the doors. Once they were opened, she saw the twilight for the first time since it had been removed from her view weeks earlier. The dim night air chilled her skin as she was dragged out into it. Her body shivered quickly, goose bumps covering every inch of her naked flesh as she struggled against the stiffness of the spreader bar. Was it the twilight of morning or of the evening? She tried to clear her head to recognize the sun's position in the pastel sky, but after spending so many weeks held captive in what she now could see was some sort of large shipping container, she had lost her sense of direction and cognitive differentiation of night and day.

"C'mon!" he barked. "Keep moving!"

April focused on the low hills and higher mesas, but that was all the surrounding area she could pick out. There was a house off in the near distance, and some type of truck, and a tall windmill spinning freely in the breeze. Her heart sank when she realized he had been right—there was no way for anyone to hear their screams. He had made sure of that with the desolation of this place. Wherever she was, it was far enough from anyone who could possibly raise an alarm from something heard in the day or night.

April felt the dry earth beneath her shuffling feet, smelled the aroma of sage and other wild scents that were being carried on the desert air. She took a deep breath to absorb it, then stumbled and fell when he jerked the chain harder to keep her moving toward her fate. She felt her body tense in anticipation of crashing into the ground, knowing that the dirt would stick to her ravaged and bleeding body the moment she slammed into it.

Her body was rocked when her shoulder, followed by her head, struck the ground. She felt herself roll onto her back and lay still, her breasts pointing toward the now darkening sky. So, it was nighttime, she thought. As she gasped for each precious breath, the pain coursed through every fiber of her being. Still reeling from the fall, she felt her legs rise into the air, heard the jingling chain thud into the ground somewhere above her foggy head. Suddenly, she felt herself being dragged across the ground, the rough sand collecting between her spread legs, scratching unrelentingly under her buttocks, back and shoulders, and getting trapped in her oily nest of dirty hair.

"Stop!" she yelled. "Stop! Please! You can't do this!"

But he didn't stop. And he wasn't going to. Just as he hadn't stopped those many times before when the others had called upon him, desperately pleading for their lives.

What had felt like never-ending pain lasted for only a short minute, until April's legs simply fell to the ground. She had been left to deal with the pulsating pain that had scored her body like gritted sandpaper upon her skin. The pain that now electrically stung her shoulders, back and rump felt like a storm of hornets had landed and begun filling her with their poison. She wriggled against the agony, trying to get into a position where she could raise her head high enough to see what he was doing. But all she heard was the noise of something being dragged across the ground, then something being tossed onto whatever had been dragged. Her mind told her it could have been wood, but she wasn't sure. It wasn't metal because it hadn't made that kind of sound. No, she was sure it was wood.

Her eyes opened enough to see him standing above her, looking down at his naked prey, her blood and his own mixing together on her tortured, beaten body. April saw his big hands reach down and grab her cuffed wrists and lift her to her spread feet. She felt his thick fingers move over her face, get tangled in her hair and pull her head backward.

"You shouldn't have done that," he said. "Now it is only a matter of time, and that time is slowly coming to an end."

She fought him as hard as her remaining strength would allow. Had she felt herself running out of the last breath she would ever take on this earth where no one cared about her? As her fight began to diminish, he stared at her body one last time, glistening and heaving in the pale moonlight. The moon now colored her cinnamon skin, highlighting every inch of her frame. He marveled at its simplicity.

"The female form," he whispered, "is not only a gift from God, but the canvas he has given me to paint my most inner thoughts."

"Please," April begged weakly. "Just kill me. Get it over with. I can't take it anymore."

April's hair, dirty and matted against her head, was the only thing separating her scalp from his hand as it helped to keep her upright. Her eyelids began to droop as she struggled to remain conscious.

"Not yet!" he said, his voice an angered hush. "You have no idea what I'm going to put you through." He brushed away the few strands of hair that lay across her face. "After that, you will become part of my collection." He looked around at the vastness of his property. "They're all here, you know? All twenty-four of them. Each one in a specific area that reminds me of them. Sometimes I even go out and talk with them. And you know what? They are all very good listeners now. I never get interrupted." He stroked her cheek softly. "Don't worry, I'll visit you often, too. And you will be a good listener as well."

"How can your conscience not torment you?" April said. "Don't you see that what you're doing is wrong?"

The big man laughed uproariously as his right arm reached under her legs while his left supported her back as he lifted her into the air. "I don't have a conscience."

His biceps struggled and his back muscles strained as he lifted her into his arms, holding her as if he were getting ready to carry her over the threshold. Her head fell backward as he turned and began to walk. Dangling from her lack of strength, it swayed as he moved toward the dark hole in the earth he had uncovered. A large wooden door lay off to its right.

The pit.

She didn't know how, but she could smell the clean, fresh soil of the hole. He stood at the edge of the abyss now, holding her in his arms while the cry of a coyote and its mate echoed from somewhere off in the distance. Suddenly his arms gave way, and she felt herself drop into the darkness of the abyss. Before she could scream, she struck the bottom of the dank hole with a cushioned thud, the spreader bar twisting her legs awkwardly, the chains rattling loudly. Looking up, all she could see was his darkened shape staring back at her silhouetted against the stark contrast of a full moon.

At least she could see the stars, she reasoned. With cuffed wrists and the bar strapped between her ankles, she knew there was no way for her to climb out. But at least she could see the stars. Maybe her mother was looking up at those same stars and thinking of her. Maybe this would be their last chance to have a connection in this world. The cold air continued its creep through her skin and into her bones. She pulled her arms in close, covering herself as best she could, but her legs could not be tucked into a fetal position to gain the warmth she sought. She remained bare to the damp cold of the pit.

April looked around, unable to see much of anything in the moonlight. When she returned her gaze to the top of the open hole, he was gone, and a new sense of fright filled her weakening brain. Then she heard the same noise she had heard after he had dropped her legs to the ground. She focused on something thin spanning the opening of the hole, wavering as it hung in the air. A rope. It was a rope. The sound moved closer, becoming louder as it approached. Then a slowly moving darkness began to block out the moon and take away the glimmering stars. It was the large wooden door she had seen lying on the ground. He was pulling it over the hole, sealing her inside with nothing but the darkness to keep her company.

"No!" she cried out. "What are you doing? Stop! Please! Don't leave me here!"

He stopped briefly to reappear at the top of the pit, his dark silhouette now filling the area between the wooden lid and the remaining edge of her earthen tomb. "Tonight," he said, "will give you time to think about what it feels like."

"What it feels like?"

"To know that mine is the last face you're ever going to see."

CHAPTER TWENTY

Backup arrived in the form of officer Tamara Dan. She pulled her white crew-cab Dodge pickup beside Brandon Descheene's unit as the driver's window disappeared into her door. Descheene quickly noticed she had pulled her hair back into a ponytail, as she often did before beginning her shift. He also took note of how her face seemed to glow softly in the ambient lighting from the truck's dashboard instrumentation. He was still working on finding the nerve to ask her out, and that frustrated him. After all, this wasn't high school. He shouldn't be nervous. He was a grown man. And a cop. A person chosen to serve and protect.

"You're lucky I took the call, Dez," she said. "I was heading back to end my shift. What have you got?"

Descheene told her.

"You have a plan?"

"I'll take the front door; you take the back. I'm guessing there's an egress door out of the back bedroom. If the daughter's there with the baby, she'll probably wanna run, so we'll need to take that option away."

Tamara Dan said, "What made you suspicious?"

"You heard about the body out at Morgan Lake?"

Dan nodded. "Yeah."

"The body had a missing a fingernail. One of those stick-on jobs with a snowman design on it. I found a missing nail inside the trailer under a kitchen cabinet, by the kickplate."

Tamara Dan said, "Let's hope the mother didn't see you notice and get rid of it."

"Don't even say that," Dez said. "As far as I know, there are two women in the trailer—the mother and her daughter. The daughter supposedly has a child, which I'm betting is the dead woman's baby."

"Did you see them?"

Dez shook his head. "The mother said her daughter was sleeping in the back bedroom with the child. A boy, she said. From what the dead woman's boyfriend told me, they were expecting a girl."

"So, all you've got is a broken-off piece of fingernail?"

"That and the fact that it looks like they've moved some furniture around to cover up something, and a photo on the wall that seems odd."

"What kind of odd?" Tamara Dan said.

"It's just weird," Dez said, "but I have a really bad gut feeling to go with it."

Dan took a deep breath and exhaled, weighing the situation. "Let's go."

Brandon Descheene circled Dan's pickup and headed back to the trailer with her following close behind. When they pulled up, Tamara Dan drove around to the back side of the trailer, bouncing roughly off the graded road and over the uneven ground and small brush. By the time she exited her pickup, she had instinctively turned down the volume of the police radio on her hip and had her service-issued Glock 22 in her right hand. As she approached the trailer under the pale glow of a first-quarter half-moon—known as *ooljéé' nit'ą́ą́ nádaal* in her language—the moonlight was producing enough illumination for her to take surefooted steps. Listening carefully, she could hear Descheene knocking on the front door and announcing his return.

Tamara Dan placed her back quietly against the side of the single-wide, keeping her breathing relaxed and measured. She flexed her fingers around the grip of her pistol, now made more comfortable with its new backstrap, which contoured it well to the palm of her hand. There were no steps leading from the back door of the trailer, so Dan moved cautiously toward the back bedroom door as Brandon Descheene knocked again. She heard the front door open and Dez ask to enter. She had no way of knowing if his gun was drawn, but with the occupants being possible suspects in a brutal murder, it was an educated guess that he had it unsnapped with his hand on it, ready to exit its holster at a moment's notice.

Tamara Dan could hear movement in the back bedroom. It sounded like the frantic desperation of a person getting ready to bolt. Dan moved herself in front of the bedroom door and reached up for the doorknob. All she could barely see through the curtained windows were shadows of someone, possibly the daughter, moving around erratically, followed by the agitated cry of a baby that had just been woken from a sound sleep. Her right arm rose, the Glock 22 now pointed at the door, as the fingers of her left hand encircled the doorknob. Her heart was pounding, her nerves electric, her eyes focused.

Suddenly, the door flung open, knocking her backward to the point of stumbling and falling. A figure jumped from the trailer and quickly ran past her in a blur. Tamara Dan spit from her lips the grains of sand that had been kicked up when she fell, and got to her feet to give chase. Every sight and every sound now became focused on not causing harm to the child the woman was clutching in her arms. Dan could see the fluttering of long hair and a white blanket as the woman ran, darting through the scrawny trees behind the trailer, trying to be as evasive as possible.

"Stop!" Dan yelled, her breath remaining steady. "Navajo Police! I'm armed and will shoot!"

The woman disregarded the warning and continued to run, now striking out across a barren field that had already been tilled for winter. Officer Tamara Dan radioed she was 10-43—in pursuit—and took off running. The undulating earth made Dan's feet and ankles work harder than they would in a standard foot chase on solid ground, and she had been in many of those over her short time on the force. Whether it had been chasing after someone whose family had reported them belligerent with violent tendencies, or hurtling after a suspect who had fled from a reported meth lab, she had done it. But running through a field under a moon that was playing hide-and-seek with the clouds took extra effort and required more stamina as the chase continued. At least she wasn't the one carrying the weight of a crying baby.

"Stop!" she yelled again. "There is nowhere for you to run!"

The woman continued to disobey her orders, probably knowing full well she would not shoot because of the child, Dan reasoned. She thought of Descheene. She wondered how things were going on his end. Was the mother giving him any trouble? Probably, she figured. And to the point, was the piece of fingernail still where he had seen it?

The woman running with the baby was closer now. Tamara Dan had found another gear and had moved up behind her enough to where she could see the gray hoodie and matching sweatpants the suspect was wearing. Tamara Dan's breathing remained measured and controlled, her thighs feeling strong and powerful. Probably, she figured, from the hours spent on the thigh machine at Anytime Fitness in Farmington and jogging on the treadmill. The only drawback to that regimen was that the treadmills faced the parking lot. Nothing she liked better than working out in the glaring sunshine in skintight athletic wear while being gawked at by the occasional pedestrian male.

With the woman's arms filled with a bawling baby, Tamara Dan holstered her weapon and picked up her speed, using her arms to crank up her determination. The frantic woman began a sloppy zigzag pattern, stumbling and recovering, and occasionally looking back over her shoulder at the approaching officer, still managing to keep up her evading pace. The weight of Tamara Dan's bulletproof vest and gun belt, along with her nine-millimeter pistol, extra clips, radio, stun gun, handcuffs and other items necessary in the performance of her duties, seemed to hang like a belt of weights around a diver's waist.

Unexpectedly, the woman's legs buckled, and she dove to the ground with a resounding thud, being mindful enough to roll as she fell in order to land on her back and not the child. Officer Tamara Dan dug her heels into the tilled dirt of the field and pulled her pistol only as a method of persuasion.

"Put the child down!" she ordered.

The woman, out of breath and gasping for oxygen, did as she was instructed.

"Roll over!" Tamara Dan ordered. "Roll over, now!"

The child cried a frightened wail, nestled snugly in a now dirt-covered blanket.

The woman rolled over, face down in the dirt, and put her hands behind her back without Dan having to ask.

Tamara Dan quickly holstered her weapon and handcuffed the woman. Then she keyed her shoulder mic: "Ten-twenty-six, Dez. I've got the daughter, child is safe."

A split second after she released her thumb from the mic, Brandon Descheene responded. "Nice work. I've got the mother."

By the time Tamara Dan returned to the trailer with the woman in handcuffs and the baby now quiet in her arms,

Brandon Descheene had already put the mother in the back of Dan's crew-cab pickup.

Dan asked, "You find the nail?"

Descheene pulled small a Ziploc bag from his pants pocket.

Dan grinned. "You're lucky."

"You should have seen her face when I picked it up after I cuffed her." Dez opened the passenger-side rear door of Tamara Dan's pickup and held the baby while Dan got the daughter inside, then closed the door.

"She give you trouble?"

Descheene shook his head. "Nothing I couldn't handle. Took me a few to get her cuffed. I did a cursory search of the trailer and found traces of blood in the cracks of some of the tub grout and around the drain. Looks like that's where they took the baby. Guess they figured the blood would just wash down the drain if they just cleaned up the rest."

"You find anything they may have cleaned it up with?" Dan asked.

Dez shook his head. "My guess is it all burned up in the dead girl's SUV the county guys found earlier."

Tamara Dan nodded, then smiled thoughtfully. "You look good with a baby in your arms."

"You think?" he said. "Nah."

"So, I guess I'm taking these two in?"

Dez looked at her, gently bouncing the baby in the white blanket in his arms. "If you don't mind?"

Dan smiled. "Nope."

Dez said, "Did you check to see if the baby's a girl?"

Dan shook her head. "You can," she said, grinning.

"I'm not gonna do it," Dez said. "You're a woman. You do it."

Tamara laughed at his awkwardness, walked closer, unfolded the blanket, and checked under it. "It's a girl. Looks like you were right."

Dez smiled. "I'm gonna take her to NNMC and have her checked out. Then I'll call the father. I think he needs to know his daughter is alive and safe."

Tamara Dan gently rubbed Descheene's arm. The Northern Navajo Medical Center was close by, so there was no need for an ambulance. And the sight of him holding the baby showed he had a tender side she hadn't seen before.

"I'll get these two booked and get started on the paperwork," Dan said, "even though it's past my shift." She walked around to the driver's side of her truck. "When's your next time off?"

"I've got an early shift tomorrow," he responded, "so I'm clear tomorrow night."

"Same here," she said. "You wanna grab something to eat after work?"

The moderate smile on Descheene's face hid the excited thumping in his chest. "Sure," he said. "You into Mexican, barbecue, or steak?"

"Nah." She smiled. "I'm a cheap date, *shi bae*. I could go for a skillet breakfast at the Village Inn. Haven't have one of those in a while."

Brandon Descheene felt his heart dance a joyful beat. Out of the blue she had referred to him as one would a boyfriend. The baby girl made a contented sound, and Descheene looked down at her peacefully sleeping, then looked at Dan. "I'll wait for forensics to get out here before I head to the hospital. My guess is, they'll probably end up pulling the pipes under the tub." Dez looked down again at the child in his arms. "Poor kid," he said, "doesn't even know she hasn't got a mother."

CHAPTER TWENTY-ONE

When Arthur returned to the hotel, he took the big wolf dog out for a walk, which always seemed to be more of a tug-of-war because Ak'is didn't care for being leashed. Like Arthur, he liked his freedom. Arthur watched as Ak'is left several liquid calling cards, along with a healthy deposit that he bagged and threw out, then stopped at the hotel's snack alcove for some snacks on their way back to the room. Once there, he undressed down to the boxer briefs Sharon had bought him, grabbed his phone and began searching for truck stops in and around Albuquerque. Ak'is hopped easily onto the bed and stretched out at the foot, took a deep breath and exhaled. It seemed a full stomach and an empty bladder meant contentment.

Arthur's internet search revealed five truck stops around Albuquerque with two beyond the realm of probability on the outskirts. If those five turned up no leads, he would have to restructure his thinking or open his search up wider. As he had already learned, April had been going home, a trip that would seem arduous for a teenager with no money. And the chances of finding a driver heading in the direction of Sheep Springs was out of reach of even the longest odds in Las Vegas. But a pretty young girl hitchhiking on I-40 would have a good chance of being picked up by someone and driven somewhere. Even in today's climate of distrust, a desperate girl in a desperate situation would try anything that would get her back to her family.

Arthur woke up the next morning knowing the task at hand. He remembered the small map on his iPhone from the night before and visualized it. Roady's Truck Stop was too far south, and one of the two TAs was too far east. That left the TA just north of the I-25 and I-40 confluence, the Pilot, Flying J, Love's and the Route 66 Travel Center farther west on I-40. Arthur's gut was telling him to hit all of those since they would all be in her path, seeing how she would be heading west, and a girl looking to escape and make her way back to her true life would take the fastest way possible. His gut was also telling him that he was hungry.

After showering and dressing in a clean blue shirt and white tube socks, Arthur pulled on the same jeans he had worn for the last few days before tugging on his boots. He grabbed a hot coffee from the continental breakfast at the hotel, along with a doughnut. He tossed a few pieces of crispy bacon onto a plate he had taken from the polished stainless steel buffet warmer for Ak'is and headed back to his room. He grinned to himself as he remembered Sharon always urging him to substitute fruit instead of junk for the first meal of the day. Somehow, he just couldn't get the memory of the pineapple she made him try out of his mouth. As he navigated the carpeted hallway, he remembered her surprising him one morning with his travel mug full of creamed coffee and a small bowl of cantaloupe chunks dusted in a soft sprinkle of sugar. He remembered his face as he put a chunk in his mouth and chewed slowly. *The things you do for love.*

Ak'is stood at attention when he entered the room, ears perked and nose in the air, mesmerized by the overwhelming aroma of bacon. Arthur closed the door, walked over to the wolf dog and placed the plate on the floor in front of him. The dog licked his lips and devoured the bacon before Arthur could even fill his collapsible water bowl, let alone sit down to enjoy his own doughnut and coffee.

Arthur looked at his friend. "I guess we're going now."

Ak'is stared at Arthur with what he could only interpret as a smile. Arthur gobbled his doughnut while packing his duffel, left the card key on the dresser and tossed the disposable coffee cup into the trash. The then two climbed into his truck and headed out to the first truck stop with the photo that April's mother had given him that snowy morning in his kitchen tucked safely into his jacket pocket.

* * *

Arthur parked the Bronco in the lot marked for cars and RVs at the Travel Center of America truck stop off I-25, just north of its confluence with I-40. It was eight fifteen in the morning. The Bronco was still warm when he left Ak'is watching him walk away through the windshield. He headed across the large parking lot, past the Valero gas pumps stationed in front of the red, white and blue retail center for the normal four-wheelers, to where the big rigs were parked.

Arthur guessed there were at least sixty rigs parked in the lot on the north side of the truck stop. If he spent only three minutes questioning every driver, he calculated it would take him around three hours to work through them all and find out if anyone recognized April Manygoats. And with four more truck stops to check out, he figured, this would take him close to midnight if there were as many truckers in each lot. About now was when he wished he had two-legged help instead of four.

Arthur finished the TA around noon. He had shown the photograph of April to every trucker he could find in the lot and no one had recognized her. He explained to the restaurant manager at the Country Pride why he was there and that he wanted to be able to show any truckers who were having lunch the photo and ask them if they had seen her. The manager walked him around the restaurant as he did, but no one having their breakfast disturbed recognized her either. Arthur drew the line at asking anyone in the showers, so he grabbed some beef sticks and some sweet tea and headed back to the Bronco.

Ak'is seemed happy to see him—or at least the beef sticks. But the way he was dancing around in the passenger seat told Arthur that a bathroom break was needed. And badly. As soon as Arthur opened the passenger door, the wolf dog lunged past him. Arthur closed the door and walked with him across University Boulevard to the only strip of green grass available. It was a nicely manicured area, long and narrow, against a chain-link fence next to the Utility Trailer building and seemed to have been put there to decorate the entrance to the Super 8 motel. After Ak'is relieved himself, they wandered back to the Bronco, drove back to the interstate and continued west.

The Love's at Sixth Street and Frontage Road was smaller, and there weren't as many big rigs, so it didn't take him long to work his way through anyone who might have come across April. No one had. By the time he made it to the Flying J, it was quarter of two and the sun had arched its way westward across the sky, but the cold chill of the high thirties made Arthur keep the engine running and the heat pumping in the Bronco.

The Flying J sat on a large rectangle of asphalt on the western fringe of Duke City on Ninety-Eighth Street and housed the travel center for tourists and truckers alike, a nice-looking Denny's, and a Conoco gas station sheltered beneath a large T-shaped carport. It was located less than six miles south of Petroglyph National Monument with its seventeen miles of volcanic basalt ridge that separated the planned housing developments that had been built up to the east from the real west that still lurked beyond West Mesa. Arthur counted ninety-three rigs as he drove slowly through the parking lot. Trailers that had no tractor attached to them possibly meant they were being washed or getting repaired, so his list had just shrunk by sixteen. And that only left seventy-seven drivers to find and question.

Arthur parked the Bronco in front of the Denny's—facing Ninety-Eighth Street—and walked over to where the rigs were parked. Most were conventional long hoods, but a handful of cabovers stood out among the flock. Most of the diesel engines Arthur heard idling had drivers in the cabs working on their logbooks, and the rest chugged in place while their operators were in the center buying something or eating or getting some needed rest in their sleepers. He caught a break in that most of the drivers didn't mind being bothered when he handed them a business card and told them why he was wandering the parking lot with a young girl's photograph.

Arthur didn't wear a watch. In fact, the only time he had was during his years in the Marines. Outside of that, he'd always said he was on Human Time. He'd often heard growing up that the European confines of time seemed to get in the way of acting at the right place in time. Having a timepiece tell you when to do something simply supported the illusion of regimented action. The telling of time had been created by those who wished to control man, to regulate his minutes, hours, days, weeks and years through the fear of losing or wasting time. By the look of the sun's further advancement, Arthur could tell it was close to four o'clock in the afternoon. After wandering back to the Bronco to give

Ak'is another bathroom break, he was making his way back to finish the rest of the rigs when a cabover Kenworth hauling a covered wagon—as Billy called trucks with black tarps covering their trailers—pulled into an empty slot vacated by one of his earlier questionees.

As Arthur approached, the air brakes whooshed and the Cummins diesel turned silent. Arthur watched the driver's side door swing open and the driver begin to climb down. The man was dressed in a long-sleeved company shirt, jeans and cowboy boots with a chain drive wallet in his hip pocket and a Cardinals ball cap covering his head. He was aware of Arthur's presence, which seemed to slow his descent, and looked curiously at him as his feet reached the asphalt. "Can I help you with somethin'?"

Arthur handed him a business card thinking it was a good thing he had brought a box.

The driver closed the cab's door and locked it, then studied the card.

"I've been hired by the family to locate their missing daughter," Arthur explained. "I've been hitting all the truck stops in the area asking drivers if they've ever seen her."

Arthur held out the photograph of April.

The man's demeanor changed from cautious to nervous. "Naw, I haven't seen her."

Arthur's radar picked up on the edginess in his voice and the cursory glance he had given the photograph. "Why don't you give it a good look this time," Arthur suggested. "Maybe something will come to mind."

The man pulled a handkerchief from his other back pocket and wiped his sweating face. Seemed unique, Arthur thought, for a man to be sweating in such chilly weather, unless he was sick. Arthur said, "Are you all right? You look ill."

"I'm fine," the man snapped. "Let me see that picture again."

Arthur held it up.

"Yeah," he said. "I seen her. Gave her a ride some weeks back."

Arthur returned the photo to its safe place inside his jacket. "Exactly how many weeks?"

"'Bout three, I guess. Give or take."

"Where'd you pick her up?"

"TA off of 25." The man returned the handkerchief to his pocket. "She asked me where I was headed, and if I'd like some company." The man broke eye contact briefly, as if to look around the open lot in hopes of locating someone he could call in case he needed help. "I figured her for a lot lizard looking to make some money playing the skin flute, if you know what I mean? Figured that ride crap was just a way to get her twat in the cab."

Arthur understood. And it never surprised him how crude some men could be when it came to talking about women. "How did she look?"

"Like a girl ready to suck some dick for a ride. I've seen her kind all around truck stops and pickle parks for years. Once you know what to look for, you know what to expect."

"And what do you need to look for?"

"Some of the girls are clean and sober, but she looked haggard and strung out. Hell, it looked like she needed a fix of something."

Arthur noticed the gold band on the man's left hand. "So, you, being the standup husband you are, offered her a ride."

"Yeah, I gave her a ride. But look, I don't want no trouble. I gotta wife and a kid."

"Maybe you should think about that the next time you want some oral pleasure." Arthur took a step closer. "How far did you take her?"

"She jumped out when I got to the Love's in Milan. The little bitch made like she was gonna do it, then punched me in the balls."

Arthur grinned. "Smart girl. See where she went?"

"Like I said, she jumped out of the truck and took off running across the street to the Enchanted Mesa Travel Center. That's all I saw."

"Are you sure?"

"I was in pain, man," the trucker reiterated, grabbing his crotch. "She fisted my nuts good."

"Think," Arthur stressed. "Anyone else pick her up?"

He shook his head. "Not that I saw. Not saying somebody else couldn't have."

Arthur said, "Think hard."

"Hell, I don't know!"

"Think harder."

"Fuck, man, I'm tellin' you I fucking don't know. Why don't you go ask them? They're bound to have cameras around there. All I did was fill my tanks and move on."

Arthur turned and walked across the parking lot knowing the gut feeling that had urged him down this path was right. But he had no time to think about that. Now he had a definite direction and a location where someone had seen April last. If he was lucky, there would be video of her at the travel center. If not, then he was back to only knowing that was how far she had gotten in her quest to go home before someone else had picked her up. And maybe for the last time.

Milan was almost seventy-five miles and more than an hour's drive away, but it was still a straight shot on the interstate. The sun had set with all the pastel colors of twilight brushed across the evening sky by the Creator's hand, and it was a sight Arthur never grew tired of. Especially when he and Sharon would sit on the edge of the canyon on White

Mesa and watch the spectacle unfold. They would huddle close enough for him to smell her scent and feel the warmth of her body under their chief's blanket. Her aroma always filled him with a calmness, a feeling that with her was where he was meant to be. That no other place he could find would be as perfect.

Arthur's gut rumbled and reminded him that beef sticks weren't really considered a healthy diet, and he was sure Ak'is' gastrointestinal makeup was telling him the same thing. Before leaving, he grabbed some more snacks for the pair of them, then put the Flying J in his rearview mirror as he drove under the interstate deck and watched the speedometer climb its way up to seventy-five before merging onto the westbound lanes of I-40, praying there was video of April Manygoats that would bring him that much closer to finding her.

CHAPTER TWENTY-TWO

Arthur was rolling toward the Enchanted Mesa Travel Center on I-40 with his headlights now on since the twilight had flourished and ended with a glorious blaze, and a bright but smaller full moon had taken over. Ak'is stared at the white, blotchy orb through the windshield, this round micro moon calling to his inner wolf. The sky was a black expanse that sparkled with an array of scattered diamonds that seemed to harness the tiny moon's glow. Arthur had called his wife's cell because he knew she'd still be at the station.

"How did your session with Dr. Peterson go today?"

"It was fine, I guess," Sharon said. "She has a fish tank now. Says it's calming for her patients to watch the colorful fish. I'm not so sure." Sharon exhaled. "She keeps telling me we're making progress, but I don't know about that either. I guess I am. I mean, I guess we are. I just wish you were there."

"I know," Arthur said. "As soon as this is over. I'm tracking a really good lead right now, so things might break open."

"Dr. Peterson is asking me questions like she doesn't believe you're invested in dealing with our past." Sharon waited for a response.

Arthur moved the phone away from his ear, then put it back, "You know I am. I told you I'd be there with you, and I will be, but there's a nineteen-year-old girl somewhere out there that needs to be found. We don't need another red dress hanging in a tree."

"I understand all that," Sharon said. "And I know you care about what happens to us—"

"I'll be there as soon as I find her." Arthur changed direction quickly. "Is Billy at the house?"

"Yes. He's here. He's been falling asleep on the couch in the den when he's not binge-watching Netflix."

"Let him. He lives with his grandmother and his sister, and they don't have much. When I called him, he was delivering firewood to some of our elders."

"He's a good young man," Sharon said. "And honoring our elders is always a good thing. You said you had a lead? How promising?"

Arthur filled her in about his meeting with the trucker. "I'm heading to the travel center now. He said they have security cameras—maybe they caught something."

Ak'is turned, stepped on the center console and jumped into the back seat. He lay down, took a deep breath and exhaled.

Arthur said, "Did you do the four thirty and the five thirty broadcasts?"

"You know it. I'm anchoring the ten o'clock, too." Sharon huffed a short laugh. "I'm a busy girl."

"Wonder Woman, huh?"

"Damn right. Better watch out or I'll throw my Golden Lasso of Truth around you."

Arthur was perplexed. "You think I lie?"

"Don't all men?" Sharon said jokingly. "But you're better than most. Even though you snore."

Arthur smiled. "*Ayóó'áníínish'ní.*"

"I love you, too."

"Even my love handles?"

"Especially those," Sharon said. "They give me something to hold on to during our passionate throws of copulation."

"Well, that certainly makes it sound appealing," Arthur responded wryly.

"What do you think I am," she joked, "crude? I'm an educated woman."

* * *

Arthur took the exit to Horizon Boulevard in Milan and turned right. Left would have taken him to the Iron Skillet Restaurant and, beyond that, what used to be the Cibola County Correctional Center. Arthur remembered reading back in 2001, the year he had received his DD 214 from the Marines, that seven hundred prisoners had staged a nonviolent protest over prison conditions; that ended with them all being teargassed. Twelve years later, a smaller number had done the same thing resulting in a better conclusion. By the time Arthur had joined CBP, most of the prisoners held there were UDAs. When the whole facility was shut down and reopened in 2016 as an ICE detention center, Arthur had already left the Shadow Wolves for his so-called quiet life. He sighed at the loss of those days as he navigated the merging lane across from the Pinon Drive cul-de-sac, slid across the open lanes and swung the Bronco onto Willow Drive.

The Enchanted Mesa Travel Center was brightly lit. The carport over the gas pumps glowed like a supernova as he drove beneath it and parked the Bronco in a slot by the Kachina Café and got out. "No howling," Arthur said, pointing his finger at Ak'is. "You'll scare the tourists. Remember last time?"

Ak'is looked at him indignantly, adjusted his front paws on the passenger seat, and licked his lips.

As Arthur walked across the bricked entrance, which had been laid out in a pattern resembling a large Navajo rug, he took note of the security cameras stationed on a light post, covering all areas in four directions, so he knew there had to be footage—depending on how long that footage was kept. When he entered the travel center, he was greeted by a ceiling mural depicting fluffy white clouds set in a robin's-egg sky. Arthur studied briefly the large cloud containing horse images and the smaller cloud carrying a handprint in red with the fingers splayed.

Arthur noticed a young Native woman behind a jewelry counter filled with shining bracelets, necklaces, watchbands and rings displayed for tourist consumption. Her long brown hair tumbled softly over strong shoulders that were hidden beneath a crisp black blazer. The hair framed a face with deftly brushed-on eyebrows above a pair of rich almond-shaped eyes that looked as if they had been created in dark chocolate. Her eyes flanked an attractive nose that resided perfectly over full pink lips that she had delicately traced with some kind of lip liner. Beneath the blazer was a red blouse and, below that, matching black pants.

She looked him up and down as he approached. "Hi there," she said, eyes sparkling. "How can I help you?"

Arthur pulled a card from his pocket and gave it to her. "I'd like to speak with whoever operates your security system."

She studied the card, looked at him inquisitively. "You looking for someone, Mr. P.I.?"

Arthur grinned. "That would be a conversation I'd have with your security guy."

Her eyes suddenly lost their sparkle, and she pointed with her chin. "Door to the office is over there." She handed him back his card. "Swanny'll be glued to his monitors, like always, so just knock."

"Is it a secret knock?"

"What?"

Arthur smiled, said, "Thank you," and walked through the myriad of Native and non-Native souvenirs to the door marked OFFICE in white letters. Arthur knocked the rhythmic shave-and-a-haircut-two-bits knock and waited to see what happened. When the door opened, a redheaded kid with freckles, about twenty years his junior, stood in front of him eating a Twinkie and wearing a black T-shirt sporting the yellow Nirvana smile logo on it beneath a gray long-sleeved hoodie. His faded, pre-ripped blue jeans led down to a dirty pair of yellow-and-black Nikes. If nothing else, Arthur concluded, the kid was color coordinated.

"Can I help you?" he said while chewing.

Arthur handed him the card the girl had given back to him. "Are you Swanny?"

He took the card and looked at it. "Unfortunately," he said. "Got stuck with that in the Navy. Last name's Swanson, so I guess it kinda fit. You're a P.I.?"

"I'm looking for a missing girl that disappeared six months ago," Arthur stated, "and I'm hoping you can help me."

Swanny looked puzzled as he slipped Arthur's card into his pocket. "Six months ago?"

"Like I said, six months ago she disappeared; then she reappeared here when she was dropped off by a trucker three weeks ago. The trucker told me he saw her come into the center, so that means she may have been recorded by your cameras. I'm hoping you have footage that might show if she met anyone here and if she left with them."

"Okay, Magnum, you gotta warrant?"

"I'm not a cop," Arthur said. "Cops have warrants. I'm just the guy hired by the girl's parents to bring her home."

"So, no warrant," Swanny replied flatly, taking another bite of Twinkie.

Arthur ran his options through his mind quickly. "Look, kid, one of two things is going to happen here—I'm either gonna call two of my police friends who won't like being woken up at this hour and they are going to contact the local cops and have them come out here with your warrant, which'll waste even more precious time, or I can appeal to your strong sense of civic duty"—Arthur pulled out his wallet and held out a fifty—"right?"

Swanny stuffed the last of his Twinkie into his mouth, wiped his hand on his jeans and grabbed the fifty. "There's a lot to be said for civic duty," he mumbled.

Arthur grinned. "I thought so."

"Step inside my inner sanctum," Swanny said, waving a hand around the room. Arthur entered. The kid closed the door behind him as Arthur admired the array of twenty-two-inch flat panels stationed on the kid's wide, two-tiered desk to his right. Five screens sat on the top shelf, five on the bottom. Each had eight different squares showing different angles of the parking lot and gas pumps and various interior shots of the center. An ergonomic keyboard lay on the desktop in front of a contoured mesh rolling office chair with a Twinkie wrapper tossed aside and resting by a large drink from the Kachina Café.

Swanny dropped into the chair and spun toward the keyboard and began typing. "About three weeks ago, you said?"

"Yes," Arthur acknowledged, pulling a straight-backed chair from its spot against the wall, "so go back to a few days before, the last week of November."

"Gotcha." More typing. "All our recordings are kept on a digital five-hundred-gigabyte hard drive that can store more than six months of high-quality video, so if she was here, I'm sure we got her on camera."

"How many cameras do you have?"

More typing. "Around twenty. We've got the usual over the pumps, the registers, and the entrance, then there's the ones all over the parking lot, too."

Arthur said, "Even the café, right?"

Swanny's typing ended with a final hard tap of the enter key. "Yep."

"Can you pull up the cameras by the pumps and go through those first?"

"Sure," Swanny said. "Watch the middle monitor. I've started it from the Thursday before the last week of November."

Arthur pulled April's photograph from his pocket and kept it close. He watched as the travelers pulled in, filled their respective vehicles, paid at the pump and drove off. As the digital images raced across the screen, Arthur's eyes remained glued to the middle monitor as the days turned into nights and the nights back into days.

"I worked for this really cheap-assed place once that had me on a system that stored ninety days of video from thirty-two cameras recording at least five or six frames a second using both analog and megapixel, storing video on a ten-TB system—"

Arthur took a moment to stare at him. "I don't have any idea what the hell you're talking about."

Swanny pulled a drawer open, retrieved another pack of Twinkies, opened them and closed the drawer. "Okay, the system we use here is a five-hundred-gigabyte—which consists of five hundred and twelve thousand megabytes—and there's one thousand twenty-four megabytes to a gigabyte."

Arthur kept his eyes glued to the moving pictures on the center monitor during the unsolicited rambling computer lesson.

"The ten-TB, or terabyte," Swanny continued, "at the other place saved way more video but got to be too expensive because ten terabytes equals roughly ten thousand gigabytes—"

"Stop!" Arthur barked. "Reel it back!"

The kid stuffed the rest of the Twinkie into his mouth and let his sticky fingers work the keyboard.

"Go back about five minutes," Arthur instructed. The picture on the monitor moved everyone in reverse, then paused and ran forward. "There!" Arthur pointed to the girl in a Coca-Cola T-shirt, jeans and sneakers, carrying a backpack. "Can you get a facial on that girl?"

"I can try," Swanny mumbled. "Give me a minute." More typing slowed down the footage to the point where it could be stopped when the girl turned to look back, presumably, Arthur figured, to see if the trucker was following her. "Can you blow that up?"

"What is this man, an episode of *Law and Order*? If I do, it's gonna be grainy. Let's see if any of the other cameras got her." The kid's fingers danced on the keyboard, worked the mouse a little, and the view changed from the gas-pump portico to the cameras on the light pole he had passed on his way in. "There she is, but her back is to us. Damn!" His fingers clacked again; the screen changed to a view from inside the travel center facing the angled sliding entry doors. "I got her!"

Arthur looked closely at the girl as she entered. The kid paused the video, which showed a full-face view, and took a screen shot. Arthur held up the photo Melanie Manygoats had given him. The girl in the photo and the one frozen on the screen matched, and for the first time Arthur felt he was that much closer to bringing her home. Even though three weeks had already passed since the video was recorded. "Can you see where she goes? Can you follow her?"

Swanny worked hard to quickly swallow the remainder of his yellow cake and said lightheartedly, "Does a politician lie?"

Arthur watched the picture move again and they could see that she walked over to the café entrance and stopped. It seemed as though she was looking periodically at something, or someone, in the store area Arthur had walked through to get to the office. She stayed there for what looked like a little over two minutes, judging by the timer ticking away in the bottom right-hand corner of the screen. Arthur stood up when a man in a suit walked up to her and started talking to her. He noticed the man was careful to always keep the back of his head to the camera. He had probably done this before, Arthur figured, which meant he either had a wife or had taught himself to be extremely careful by noticing camera placements.

"Follow them," Arthur told the kid.

Swanny did as he was told. After a little conversation, the man led April into the café, still being mindful of camera placement. He was larger than April, with a bulbous head and stocky body, but that wasn't saying much—she was a nineteen-year-old teenager. He gave her some money, and she went to the counter to order while he wandered to a table and put his back to another camera. *This guy is good.* April got her food and brought it over to the table, where they talked while she ate. The man ate nothing. Then came the moment when April got up and disappeared for a few minutes.

Swanny looked at Arthur. "Bathroom?"

Arthur shrugged. "Maybe."

Arthur and Swanny watched as the man took something from inside his coat, removed the lid from April's drink, and tapped the contents into it. He had re-covered her drink before she returned, swirling the liquid to fully absorb whatever drug he had slipped into it. Swanny looked at Arthur with an expletive. April returned to the table and sucked down more of her drink, telling the man whatever she was telling him.

Suddenly, Arthur saw April's head drop and pop back up. After it happened again, the man got up and helped her from the table, grabbed her backpack and guided her out of the café and out another door. Swanny got his fingers working and pulled up footage from an outside parking lot camera facing the rear entrance. There was still no clear view of the man's face as he maneuvered her to a late-model Cadillac Escalade, opened the rear passenger door behind the driver's seat and poured her inside. Arthur watched him close the door, seat himself behind the wheel, back up and drive off.

Arthur barked, "Can you find which way he's heading?"

Swanny startled and jumped to it, finding another camera angle that caught them turning out of the lot and heading toward the interstate.

"Damn it!" Arthur said, slamming his fist on the table with the keyboard, making it and the kid's large drink hop briefly.

Swanny looked up. "Sorry, man. The dude never showed his face. How fucked-up is that?"

"That's because he knew where the cameras were. This guy's a pro."

"Wait a minute!" Swanny said with inspired glee. "Just because we don't have his face doesn't mean we have nothing."

Arthur watched the kid's fingers fly across the keyboard like Elton John's on a Steinway.

"Bingo!" Swanny said. "I got a partial plate because of that shadow. And see that depression in the right rear quarter panel? Somebody hit that dude's SUV. Maybe your cop friends can match the partial plate to an accident report?"

Arthur grabbed Swanny's right shoulder and shook him thankfully. He had been so preoccupied with the video he hadn't noticed the damage to the SUV. "That just bought you another fifty. Can you send a still of that and the girl to my phone?"

Swanny nodded. Arthur's phone vibrated a few seconds later.

"Thanks, kid." Arthur tossed another fifty on Swanny's keyboard. "You may have just saved that girl's life."

Swanny smiled broadly, scooped up the money.

Arthur's thumbs worked quickly on the keyboard of his phone as he sent a text containing the photos to Detective Lance Gilberto and Captain Jake Bilagody. With it, he added the words, "April's last contact."

On the way out of the store, Arthur felt as if some of the weight had been lifted from his heart as well as his shoulders. For the first time since he had started down this path, he had something to go on—an actual lead that could possibly break his way. The partial plate and description of the SUV would be fed into law enforcement computers and hopefully something would trigger a red flag. And there was no way in hell he was going to use April as bait going up against the Cuban if all this led to her being found. There had to be another way for that to play out. Since Garcia expected a call from Arthur once he had located his runaway property, coupled with the fact that he had paid him fifteen thousand dollars to ensure her return, he was hoping Gilberto's contact in the APD, Eduardo Espinosa, could locate an undercover cop they could pass off as April.

Ak'is was waiting patiently in the Bronco, and when Arthur opened the door, he dove out and ran to the side of the café, hiked his leg against the wall and began to turn the tan adobe into a dark patch of wet. Arthur looked around, awkwardly filled with embarrassment, making sure he held no eye contact with anyone who might be watching this event unfold. When Ak'is lowered his leg, he turned with a definite look of relief on his furry face. Arthur's phone suddenly vibrated in his jacket. He pulled it out and tapped the green accept button.

"Where'd you get this photo?" Jake Bilagody said sternly. Arthur wasn't used to that tone. He had heard him use it with others before, but never with him.

"From surveillance video taken three weeks ago at the Enchanted Mesa Travel Center in Milan," Arthur told him. "I just saw how everything unfolded with April Manygoats the last time anyone saw her. Some guy drugged her, put her in that SUV, and drove off with her."

"Are you sure?"

"Hell yes, I'm sure," Arthur insisted. "I just told you I watched it happen!"

Jake's disappointed breath blew into the phone.

Arthur said, "What's up? Did you get a match already?"

"I don't have to get a match," Jake said, the anger and disbelief that had edged his voice initially already deteriorating rapidly. "I think that SUV belongs to Gordon Lockerby."

"Who's that?" Arthur said.

"My realtor."

CHAPTER TWENTY-THREE

Arthur was dumbfounded. "How can you be sure?"

"Remember that day I told you he had some houses for me to look at?"

"Sure."

"I met him in Farmington and followed him around. His Escalade had a dent in the right rear quarter panel just like the one in your photo. He told me somebody hit it in a parking lot a couple of days earlier but he didn't know who since no one left a note. He said he was going to take it to Webb Cadillac over on Main Street to get it fixed, but he never could find the time because he was so busy. I ran the partial plate and vehicle description after I received your text. There are only a handful of dark-colored Escalades in our area, and his is one of them. The coincidence is too strong for me. My gut tells me it's him."

"He won't be at his office now," Arthur pointed out, climbing into the Bronco after Ak'is. "It's after nine o'clock."

Jake huffed. "That doesn't matter. He's a realtor. Realtors are always available. Besides, I've got his home address. I'm heading over there as soon as we hang up."

"I won't be there for about two and a half hours," Arthur warned. "Can't you send someone to his house? You can't arrest him on suspicion because he's out of your jurisdiction and he's non-Native."

"I've got thirty-six officers protecting a population of twenty thousand people in a district that covers three states,"

Jake said. "You tell me if I can spare anyone. Besides, I don't like being a desk jockey. Never have. I've been this way for over twenty-five years; I'm not gonna change now."

Ak'is pretended to listen to the one-sided conversation from his usual spot in the passenger seat—ears perked, tongue dangling, eyes staring intently. Arthur decided to push the point. "What if this guy is working with someone? Grabbing girls. What if he's trafficking them?"

"For all we know," Jake said, "he could be a serial rapist or one of those killers that hides in plain sight. Look, I've got too much on my plate right now to argue the point with you. Did I tell you that old Hector Tom fished a body out of Morgan Lake the other day? Delores Mendoza says the woman was pregnant and someone cut the baby out of her after they beat her to death."

"Damn," Arthur sadly.

"Tell me about it. Dez was following a lead on that. He was waiting on backup, last I heard. We're pretty spread out tonight. Look, I've gotta go."

Arthur said, "Copy that."

* * *

Jake Bilagody pulled his jacked-up Suburban into Gordon Lockerby's driveway at ten fifteen p.m. The streetlight that lit up Lockerby's small area of Farmington made visible the two-story home in a style that resembled pueblo design in tan stucco. The wide two-car garage sported a paneled brown door flanked by two coach lights, and the front door, which was hidden under a slightly arched portico, was lit by a coach light matching the ones decorating the garage. The yard was typical for the Southwest, if you could afford it: a sea of small stones anchored a few larger rocks, a short, tumbled-brick wall raised a plant bed sporting vegetation Jake didn't even recognize as indigenous, and there were a couple of bare trees thrown in for texture. About the only thing he recognized was the gas meter standing alone looking like some kind of *Star Wars* droid.

Taking a breath, he rang the bell, then pulled out his badge and stood there, resplendent in his crisp uniform and polished black leather. In the interim silence, he studied the decorative wood and cast-iron bench that sat to his left, followed the richness of the mahogany front door. High-dollar, for sure, he thought. *The things you can have when you have money.* Soon the tumblers of the locks began to sound and the door was opened by an elegant blond woman in her mid-fifties dressed in jeans, a cream-colored blouse, and bare feet with painted teal toenails that matched the tips of her long fingers. She reminded him of the Gena Rowlands of thirty years ago.

The stare he received never got old, and it never changed. Most people never had a police officer knocking on their door after ten o'clock at night.

"Can I help you?" the woman said.

Jake smiled politely. "Mrs. Lockerby?"

"Diane," she said.

"I'm looking for Mr. Lockerby. Is he home?"

The blue eyes stationed below the blond hair didn't seem puzzled by his question. "Might I ask why?"

"I just need to ask him some questions about a missing girl." He showed her his badge. It didn't seem to impress her.

"Not that bitch again?"

He folded it and put it away. "I'm not sure what you mean."

"The conniving little bitch he sent to real estate school. Anna something or other. Don't tell me they've finally found her?"

Jake shook his head. "I wouldn't know. I'm concerned with a young Navajo girl that's missing. We have video of someone looking like your husband picking her up at a travel center in Milan three weeks ago and driving off with her."

Suddenly, her blue eyes searched the street for the prying eyes of neighbors. "You'd better come in, Officer."

"Captain," Jake made a point of saying as he removed his hat and wiped his feet.

Diane closed the door and allowed him to follow her into the kitchen. It was all white, like the rest of the rooms in the house that he could see, but displayed pine cabinets and fancy lighting far above what Jake was looking to afford. But if he sold his house, used what he had saved, he would be able to afford something small and comfortable.

Jake watched her pour a glass of bourbon from a bottle of Jim Beam Single Barrel she already had sitting on the black stone island, mix it with splash of water from the faucet and swirl it around. She took a sip before saying, "My husband is always helping someone. I'm not surprised he gave some girl a lift."

Jake thought a moment. "If you'll forgive me for saying, it seemed to be more than a lift." He watched her sip her bourbon again. By his observation, she seemed to be a woman who kept in shape, obviously by exercising at some fitness center in town, or she had her own workout room somewhere in the house. She also looked like a woman who had been keeping up appearances and lying to herself about her husband's caring ways toward other women for a while. Whether she had become used to the lifestyle he afforded her, or she had felt trapped in a marriage with nowhere else to go, she had chosen to stay with him for one reason or another. It was hard to be out there on your own after what seemed like a lifetime of being married. Jake knew that firsthand.

"It looked like he may have drugged her before he put her in the car," Jake said. "I know that sounds rough to hear, but we really need to locate him."

Jake noticed how her body seemed to stiffen at the revelation. "I see," she said. "Would you like a drink, Captain?"

"No, thank you. You mentioned a girl before—Anna someone—tell me about her."

Her blue eyes seemed to be taking her back in time, opening up doors in her mind she had kept closed and unleashing fears she had kept hidden behind them. "She was an eighteen-year-old senior he met at a jobs fair the local high school put on five years ago before graduation. Claimed she'd watched all those house-selling shows on TV and thought it seemed like a good way to make big money." She took a long sip of her whiskey. "I guess no one ever told her Farmington wasn't Los Angeles. Anyway, my husband took an interest in her—but then again, he always took an interest in anyone younger than me. Especially after our only child died."

"I'm so sorry," Jake said.

"Thank you. After it happened, Gordon told me our son had died because of what I had done three years earlier."

"And what was that?" Jake asked, taking out a small notepad to begin writing.

Diane Lockerby took another sip. "Seems I committed the ultimate sin that ruins all marriages, even though he was why I committed it. I had an affair."

"I see. But you and your husband stayed together."

Diane huffed a laugh. "You're cute." She took another sip. "The story really begins, Captain, when my husband grew up as a juvenile delinquent. A product of a broken marriage when he was nine, he developed a rebellious side. What do they say? Life, for some, is nothing but a pathway of shattered dreams? That was my husband's childhood. But all that changed when his mother met his stepfather ten years later. From the way Gordon told it, he was a big man and wasn't the kind who spared the rod—or, in his case, the back of his hand." She took a breath. "Anyway, fast-forward to nineteen years ago. When he questioned me, I admitted that I was seeing someone and told him why. I guess he wanted to keep me, so he got down on his knees and went through the motions of begging and apologizing for doing whatever had driven me away. He knew I wanted a child, so he told me he wanted to give me one." She swirled the golden liquor in her glass. "Less than a year later our son was born. Two years after that, Gordon took him to the lake. He loved feeding the ducks and geese. Then I got the call."

Jake could see a dampness developing in her eyes.

"Seems Gordon had turned away just long enough for our son to wander off." She wiped her eyes, briefly self-conscious of this stranger in her house. "When they found him, he had drowned in the lake. Probably chasing geese, the police figured." Diane's gaze seemed lost in the past. "Our marriage died that day along with our son. And Gordon blamed me."

"Why?" Jake said.

"Punishment," Diane Lockerby told him. "Punishment for my having that affair. He even went as far as to tell me it should have been my lover's son that died and not his." She shook her head mournfully. "Today he just goes through the motions of being a married man. We are simply together, but alone." She toasted Jake with her half-empty glass. "Hell, we haven't had sex in fifteen years." She swallowed a mouthful Jim Beam. "I know he's been getting it from somewhere, but I gave up caring about it a long time ago. Gordon has certain … needs. Needs I can't—no, won't—fulfill."

Jake looked at her.

"My husband is a fantastic Realtor, Captain, and a good provider, but he has developed a dark side over the years since our son's death." She swirled her remaining liquid again. "I believe they call it BDSM."

Jake's eyebrows rose.

"He likes to tie women up and do things to them. Does that surprise you?" Diane waited. "I bet it does. Maybe he's punishing women who like it as a way of punishing me? Or maybe he's the one being punished. I don't know, and I don't really care."

Jake cleared his throat. "You were telling me about the girl."

Diane smiled. "TMI? Sorry. Sometimes my mind wanders. Gordon used to get calls at his office, and a few times here at home, from her friends and family because he had paid for her to go to realty school. He figured she had probably changed her mind, like teenagers do, when the real-world smacks them in the face, and she just bailed. He wrote it off as a loss and swore he would never do that again."

"Did he have any contact with her before she went missing?"

"I don't think so," Diane said. "I do know that when the girl's parents filed a missing persons report, the police questioned him about her. He denied having any knowledge of her whereabouts after sending her to Albuquerque." She poured herself another drink, this time with no water. "There was a curious thing, though—a few days after the police were here, the girl's family received a typewritten letter from her thanking my husband for taking a chance on her, but saying that she couldn't see herself selling houses. She said she had met someone and they had left Albuquerque looking for adventure. The letter told them that she was okay and for them not to worry. The police verified her signature." Diane took a sip of straight Jim Beam. "Because she was eighteen, and therefore considered an adult who had every right not to be contacted, the investigation came to an end."

"No one ever gave a thought to foul play?" Jake asked. "Checked out Albuquerque?"

Diane shrugged. "Guess not."

"Can you recall anyone else your husband ever helped?"

She rolled her eyes in thought. "There have been so many over the years. He always took an active part in helping youth and people less fortunate, I'll give him that."

"Anyone you can think of in the last year?"

"Are you sure you don't want a drink, Captain?

"Yes, ma'am."

"Ma'am?" Diane said. "You can call me Diane. Hell, we're about the same age, aren't we? Ma'am makes me feel like my mother."

Jake grinned politely, repeated his question using her name.

"Before the schoolgirl, Gordon had this vision of being a philanthropist wanting to help unwed mothers. Don't ask me where he got that idea. Guess he loved thinking of a building someday with his name on it. He decided he could help them by providing them funding for housing, on a small scale, as well as job counseling. The first girl he helped was a nineteen-year-old name Jessica Langdon who had just given birth to a baby girl. Gordon paid for her to stay in a hostel, bought her some professional clothes, and sent her to Denver for some kind of job preparation." This time she downed the remainder of her glass like a college kid on spring break. Jake could see she was beginning to put things together in her mind. "A few weeks later the police came to our door again. Seems the girl's relatives had received a letter from her saying she was all right and not to worry. Apparently, she ran off to Montana with some guy named Bill."

"Bill who?"

"I have no idea."

"What did your husband tell them?"

"He said he'd heard from her twice after she got to Denver." She paused, thinking. "The letter was typed, but signed by the girl, too. You know what seems strange, now that I think of it? My sister and her husband had been trying to adopt a baby for years but were pissed off over all the damn paperwork they had to fill out and the hoops they had to jump through to make it happen. It just seemed fortunate at the time, but now . . . a day or two after the girl's letter had said she had run off with the guy, Gordon offered to help them adopt a baby girl whose mother had committed suicide. Drug overdose, I think it was."

Jake, who had been scribbling in his notebook, stopped to look up. "How did he help them?"

She poured some more Jim Beam but this time added two ice cubes from the stainless fridge. At this rate, Jake figured, she'd be on to the next bottle before he left.

"They told me they gave Gordon five thousand dollars in order to make the paperwork go smoothly." She looked at Jake as he wrote. "Do you suppose somehow this was the baby of the girl who went to Denver?"

"I don't know. But I'll be sure to look into that." Jake stopped writing, put away his notebook. If Gordon Lockerby was into sadomasochistic sex, perhaps he was filling his need with kidnapped girls he figured no one would miss. And if he had gotten involved with that type of sex, something had to have been the catalyst. Maybe some dark secret he'd kept hidden, or maybe he stumbled across it online and got off on it. You could find anything on the web these days. What was once a promising new world of enlightenment had become a degenerate's evil playground. And maybe—somewhere over the years—just filling his sexual desire gave way to other, more hidden cravings.

Jake said, "Does your husband have an office here in the house?"

"Of course. He converted one of the upstairs bedrooms into an office." She swirled the bourbon in her glass. The ice clinked. "Would you like to see it?"

"I think I would."

"Don't you need a warrant or something?"

"I'm just outside my jurisdiction, so you're perfectly within your right to say no. But if you do, I'll just have to make a call. But that will cost the girl we're looking for more valuable time she may not have."

Her eyes sparkled as she sipped her drink, then smiled. "Right this way, Captain. No point in wasting time."

The office was at the top of the stairs and to Jake's left. It overlooked the flat roof of the arched portico over the front door. A smattering of stars shimmered in the cold, dark sky, with a twinkling satellite delivering cell phone service or cable TV while rotating along with the earth. A streetlight pouring its cone of light onto the street outside lost its control of the room when Jake hit the light switch. Diane continued to drink from her glass as she leaned against the doorjamb, legs crossed at the ankles. All she needed was a cigarette, Jake reflected, and she could be Mrs. Robinson.

The room looked like any other home office in any other home in any state across the country. There was a broad oak desk covered with paperwork, files and binders; a high-backed office chair sat empty in front of it and turned to one side. A computer with a tower took up space on its top, and a printer sat on top of a short oak file cabinet that matched the desk. Five or six cardboard file boxes with dates and years scribbled on them sat beneath the large map of New Mexico decorating the opposite wall from the desk. Jake walked over and studied the multicolored pushpins that decorated it.

"Gordon buys one of those maps every year," Diane explained. "He writes it off, too. Business expenses."

Jake said, "What do all these pins represent?"

"The red ones are properties currently in escrow, the blue ones are his properties still on the market, and the yellow ones are the retail properties he's handling."

"Once properties are closed, does he pull the pin?"

Diane sipped at her drink. "Yes. Then any paperwork he has goes in one of those boxes."

Jake grunted, his eyes roving over each of the pins and the numbers printed on the small tags they pierced. "What are these numbers?"

Diane walked over and stood next to the Navajo captain. He was a good-sized man, she thought. A little taller than she was and that's what she liked. She liked his face, too. It looked as strong as he appeared to be. And those hands of his ...

"Those are the MLS numbers," she said.

"What?"

Diane smiled. "Multiple listing service numbers. Every property on the market has one." Diane sipped her drink again and paused. "Huh?"

Jake looked at her. "What?"

"That pink pin up there," she said. "There's something odd about it. I'm not in here much, but I'm willing to bet that's not an MLS number pinned to it."

Jake said, "How can you be sure?"

Diane adjusted her eyes to investigate the tag beneath the pin. "Because there are too many numbers. The one with pink pin, north of La Plata, looks like a parcel number."

"What's the difference?" Jake said.

"MLS numbers," Diane explained, "have nine digits. The pink one there has eighteen. That, coupled with the fact that the La Plata one is out in the middle of nowhere, it has to be a land parcel." Diane wandered over to the desk, set her almost empty glass on one of the manila folders, and pulled open a file drawer. Jake walked over as her fingers crawled through the green hanging row of Pendaflex. "Gordon always has his files separated by region," she explained. "Then by MLS. Since there's no listing number, he might not have a file for it. At least not in here."

"Why would he have chosen a pink pin, do you think?"

"Honestly, I haven't a clue, Captain, but if it's pinned to that map, it means something."

When she reached the back of the file drawer, she pushed it shut and headed for the three-drawer cabinet holding up the printer. Jake watched her work her way through each of the file drawers and close them. Then she stood, hands on what seemed to Jake to be slim but firm hips, and looked around the room. The moment she sucked her bottom lip into her mouth and lightly bit it, Jake had to divert his eyes. Just looking at her, he contemplated, she was quite a woman. Too bad her husband was such an ass.

When she walked past him on the way to the double closet, Jake picked up on the faint scent of perfume. It wasn't like anything Nizhoni, his ex-wife, had ever worn. In fact, she hardly wore any perfume at all. But this ... this was a sweet aroma that had the desired effect on his male libido he was sure the bottle had promised. He pulled it deep into his lungs and savored it briefly, then let it out as he followed her to the closet, trying to keep his mind on the job at hand.

"What do you expect to find in there?" he said.

"Anything he'd probably want to keep from me, I'm sure he'd lock up in the safe."

Diane pulled open the double doors to reveal a closet full of boxes holding fresh reams of Boise printer paper stacked neatly along with more storage boxes of dated material and a Sentry floor safe. Diane squatted down and began spinning the combination dial.

Jake said, "You know the combination?"

"Nope. But I might be able to figure out what he would use for it, if we're lucky."

Jake watched quietly as she spun the dial to zero, then worked from there, right, left, and right again. She tried the black lever handle. It didn't budge.

"His birthday?" Jake said.

"Just tried that."

"How 'bout your anniversary?"

Diane snorted a laugh. "Do you remember yours?"

"March 2, 1996."

Diane turned, impressed. "Your wife must love you."

"Not anymore," Jake said. "We're divorced."

Her tone turned somber but hopeful instantly. "I'm sorry."

"Don't be. I've gotten over it. I know she has."

"Well, that's good to hear," Diane said, returning her attention to the safe. "He probably picked something stupid like men always do. No offense. He's a big Denver Broncos fan … when did they win the Super Bowl last?"

Jake thought. "Twenty sixteen, I think."

"Do you remember the score?"

Jake shook his head. "Are you kidding?"

"Look it up," Diane said.

Jake pulled his phone from his pocket and typed in the question. The phone kicked back an answer immediately. "Panthers ten, Broncos twenty-four."

Her slim fingers spun the dial and began at zero again. Jake looked on as she turned right to ten, left twice to twenty-four, then right again to sixteen. She looked up at him and grabbed the handle. When she turned her wrist, the handle cranked downward with a metallic clank. She turned her head and smiled, then pulled open the safe door. Jake moved closer as she removed a group of papers from the safe, stood and walked over to her husband's desk. She picked up her bourbon glass, knocked back the remaining liquid, and set it on top of the computer tower.

"Like I said, if he's keeping something from me, it'll be here."

Jake stood by, doing nothing he could call outstanding, and watched her rustle through the envelopes and papers until she came across an envelope with the words *The Parker Initiative* written on it. Removing the folded bundle of papers from the envelope, Diane read through them. "This is it," she said. "These are the closing documents for the sale of the land near La Plata."

Jake said, "May I see those?"

Diane handed them to him, and Jake flipped through them. "Is there any reason your husband would have purchased property without telling you?"

She shook her head and shrugged. "No idea."

"Has he ever mentioned this Parker Initiative?"

"No. But Parker is my maiden name."

Jake looked at her. "Can you make me a copy of this?"

"Sure." Diane walked over to the file cabinet, turned on the printer, and ran the documents through. When the copies were completed, she handed them to him. Jake thanked her. Diane returned the originals to the safe, along with the rest of the papers, closed the door and spun the dial. When she returned to the desk, she picked up her empty bourbon glass and held it in the palm of one hand with her other hand wrapped around it.

"You said you think he drugged that girl?"

"That's what it looked like," Jake said, folding the papers into thirds and stuffing them into one of his front pants pockets. "He had to help her into his SUV."

"How can you be so sure it was him?"

"The license number, and the dent in the right rear quarter panel."

"How do you know about the dent?"

Jake scratched his chin, weighed the possibilities of answering, then did. "Your husband is my realtor. He showed me some houses the other day, and I made a comment about the dent."

"Oh," she said, surprised. "I see." She led him back downstairs to the kitchen, where she poured herself another three fingers and dumped in two more cubes.

Jake said, "Where is your husband now?"

She took a long, slow sip of her golden liquid, then swallowed as if she felt the numbing burn descend her throat. "He said he had to go to Phoenix yesterday morning for business. He packed a small bag and chartered a plane from Four Corners Regional to Phoenix Mesa-Gateway Airport. He said he'd be back by Friday morning."

"Makes sense," Jake acknowledged. "It's about a seven-hour drive. Would you happen to know what charter company he used?"

"Mesa Aviation, I think."

Jake picked up his hat from the kitchen island and set it on his head, thanked her for her help, then showed himself to the door. Diane followed, drink in hand. Jake opened the door and stepped out under the cover of the arched portico. The night air had gotten colder. He shivered noticeably and handed her a business card. "You'll let me know if you hear from your husband."

She took it, studied it front and back. "No home number?"

"My direct line is on the front. It'll route to my cell if I'm not in the office." He tipped his hat. "You've been a great help, Mrs. Lockerby."

"Captain," she said, "if Gordon's been doing what you say he's been doing, he's been lying to me for years. And if you can prove it, it won't take me long to become the ex–Mrs. Lockerby."

Jake nodded but said nothing and walked back to his truck. After climbing in and closing the door, he turned the ignition and radioed in as he waited for the heat to build up enough to banish the cold air from the dash vents.

"Have someone pull all the missing persons reports for the last six months for females between fifteen and thirty. Also, have someone check out a company called the Parker Initiative."

"Ten-four, Captain," dispatch said.

"Tell them to dig deep. I want to know everything about the Parker Initiative. And get hold of Four Corners Regional and see if a Gordon Lockerby chartered a flight out of there to Phoenix yesterday."

"That all could take some time, sir."

"I want it by the time I get back," Jake replied, checking his dash clock. "Tell them they have thirty-five minutes."

CHAPTER TWENTY-FOUR

Arthur was an hour out of Shiprock, moving up Highway 491, when his phone buzzed in the center console of the Bronco. He didn't recognize the number, but the area code was Albuquerque, so he answered it and put it on speaker.

"Arthur Nakai, please."

"You got him."

"Mr. Nakai, this is Detective Eduardo Espinosa of APD. Detective Gilberto asked me to call you."

"I expected a call this morning," Arthur said.

"There's a lot going on here," Espinosa said.

"There's a lot going on here, too," Arthur said. "Gilberto tell you what's going on?"

"He filled me in. I don't mind saying you're taking a big risk with your life, and the girl's."

"I've discovered a lot more since I spoke with Gilberto," Arthur said, filling him in on what he needed to know. He kept the fact of April's kidnapper to himself; that had no bearing on what he was hoping to set in motion against Garcia. "Garcia is expecting me to bring him the girl. I have no intention of doing that. I was hoping we could work together on this."

"We might." Espinosa said it carefully.

"We'll need a policewoman about April's size and weight. Dark hair."

Espinosa was quiet, thinking. "I may have to pull someone off something else, but I'm sure I can set that up. What's your play?"

Arthur noted the stars in the sky and the moon hanging clear and bright. Whatever snow had managed to linger on the terrain was probably lying under the moonglow and reflecting its radiance. He saw the lights of a jet crossing the sky, then the silhouette of the plane against the large hanging moon.

"Garcia's expecting me to contact him," Arthur said. "When I do, I'll set up a meet to turn over the girl only to him. That's where you come in. Can you station your people around the drop-off point? When Garcia comes to collect his property, you can have him."

"What makes you think he'll show?"

"I'll tell him I'll only deal with him, and he needs to bring some cash for my trouble."

"You sound pretty sure of yourself," Garcia said.

"He wants the girl," Arthur explained. "He has no other choice but to deal with me. He wants to make an example of her to the other girls of what happens when you try to leave. When he's all yours, you have to make sure you locate the girl I spoke with—Nikki. I don't know what they did with her after we made our little deal, but I'm sure if she's not already dead, she's wishing she was."

Espinosa agreed. "I'll get things moving here. Let me know when you've contacted him." The cop paused, weighing the tactical operation in his mind. "Just so you know, I wouldn't even be doing any of this if it wasn't for Lance vouching for you. Plus, the fact I checked you out. You're not just some jagfuck sticking his nose up our ass. You're a brother. I was in Iraq in '04 as part of a convoy transport mission. We were on a road we'd traveled numerous times that normally had a shitload of people on it … but that day there wasn't a fucking soul out. You know what I mean? Quiet as hell."

Arthur said nothing. He knew exactly what he meant.

"I was in the third of five Hummers running point, when all of a sudden we took fire from insurgents."

"An ambush."

"Fuck yeah. We took fire from both sides. Not long after that, we were hit by an RPG." Espinosa paused. Arthur knew the detective was seeing it all again as he recited it. "The guy next to me lost both legs below the knee and one hand." Espinosa exhaled. "Not a fucking scratch on me. Can you believe that shit? It's not even funny how fucked-up that is. Anyway, by the time the Cobras arrived to give us air support, we'd been exchanging fire for about half an hour. I never thanked God so much for rockets and machine guns." Espinosa hesitated, the memory hitting home. "Five of us got Silver Stars. One got the Navy Cross. For valor in combat, they said. I say bullshit. You know what I mean? Medals are for fucking track stars."

"I know that when you're in that situation," Arthur said, "you do what you're trained to do—and not because you'll get a strip of ribbon with a chunk of metal attached to it. The mission becomes one simple fact—if it has a weapon, kill it."

Espinosa said, "Damn right. We'll be ready to move when you call."

"Copy that." Arthur hung up.

Arthur slowed the Bronco and took the left that led him across the southbound lanes of 491. He heard his big tires burp across the reflective white cattle guard and ended up stopping under the portico of the Little Water Express next to a gas pump. The 351 Windsor powerplant—the heartbeat of his new pet—drained the thirty-two-gallon tank every four hundred and eighty miles, but what did he expect? He could have found one that came with a straight six, but that had been out of the question since Arthur's love for power outweighed his sense of frugality. And having the Windsor with the four-wheel-drive gave him that power.

After filling the tank, he parked the truck in the dirt and let Ak'is out for his normal ritual of watering the earth. After loading him back in the truck, Arthur went inside and grabbed some more snacks from a display and a bottle of sweet tea from the eight-door cold section. The Navajo girl behind the red, white and blue counter loaded down with energy drinks, fidget spinners and Luv Pops smiled at him. Arthur glanced down at the wire racks full of the Navajo Times and Indian Country Today by his leg as his phone began to vibrate. Arthur answered while he fished out his wallet.

"Where are you?" Jake said.

"I'm in Little Water getting gas." Arthur paid for his snacks. "What did you find out?"

"The more I learn about this guy," Jake said, "the more my gut churns."

Arthur left the convenience store and headed for the Bronco, snacks and sweet tea in hand. "I'm listening,"

"According to his wife, Mr. Gordon Lockerby had a thing for helping young women."

"Wife?" Arthur said. "He wasn't home either?"

"Nope. She told me he was in Phoenix for business. Said he'd chartered a plane from Four Corners Regional, but that was bullshit. They had no record of any flight chartered by a Gordon Lockerby." Jake filled Arthur in on Lockerby's past, along with the adoption of the supposed child. "While we were searching his home office—"

"We," Arthur said. "How'd you manage that?"

"After his wife began to add things up, she became extremely helpful. Anyway, this guy had a map on the wall showing all of his current real estate dealings. When Diane spotted an unusual pin in it, that got her thinking he'd been hiding something from her."

Arthur climbed into the Bronco, put the phone on speaker, and began opening snacks. "Now it's Diane?"

"Stop."

"What? Is she pretty?"

"I said stop." Jake sighed. "This is where it gets interesting … One of the pins in the map turned out to represent a five-and-a-half-acre parcel out in the middle of nowhere northwest of La Plata purchased in 2014 by the Parker Initiative."

"Never heard of it," Arthur said before taking a sip of sweet tea and a bite of one of the snacks. Ak'is sat patiently, continuing his close watch on the unopened package of beef jerky.

"No one else had either," Jake replied. "So, one of our civilian employees—a real tech wizard—dug deeper into it. The Parker Initiative is owned by the Halfway Corp., which is owned by New Beginnings Incorporated, which, in turn, is owned by Tabula Rasa International."

"Tabula what?"

"Rasa," Jake reiterated. "Didn't you learn any Latin in the military?"

"Sorry, no," Arthur said, "I was too busy learning Dari and Mesopotamian Arabic so I could stay alive."

Jake grunted and went on. "Tabula Rasa, roughly translated, means 'clean slate.' You know, like a mind that has been wiped clean of its past in order to absorb new ideas." Bilagody paused, seeing if it would sink in. When

Arthur gave no response, he said, "Like a place for young girls and women to leave behind their past and discover a new path."

Suddenly, a light bulb didn't just come on in Arthur's mind; it exploded. "Holy crap!"

"Exactly," Jake said. "And guess who owns Tabula Rasa?"

Arthur swigged some sweet tea. "Gordon Lockerby."

"Bingo!"

"What did your guy do, search the dark web?"

"I don't care if he dug up Jack Webb, if it got me answers," Jake answered. "The only problem for me is that the parcel's off the rez. I'll have to call in the state or the county and maybe even your friend in the FBI himself, Frederick Thorne, to handle it."

"I was hoping he'd retired," Arthur grumbled.

"I think he's only fifty. You don't see me retiring, do you?"

"You're different. I like you."

Jake laughed. "I bet when Thorne was a teenager, he had one of those Toyota pickups with the EFI badge on the side of the cab. Only, in his case, it stood for Egotistical Fucking Idiot."

Arthur's laugh made him choke on a crumb of corn snack. Ak'is perked his ears and stared intently as his friend swigged some more tea and swallowed. Arthur tore open the jerky package and gave his furry friend its contents.

"If that's where Lockerby has April, having a swarm of cops and Feds showing up will only put her in more danger."

Jake said, "That's if he hasn't gotten tired of her in the last three weeks."

"April's mother told me she knew her daughter was alive because she hadn't come to her in a dream," Arthur said. "I was always taught that our visions were to be respected and believed. When Sharon was missing, I never saw her come to me like she had walked on. It's what gave me hope."

"I'll get hold of the operations captain for San Juan County," Jake replied. "We picked up a carjacker that got loose from them a month or so ago. Arrested him on the rez. By law we can't arrest non-Natives so we had to take them to the closest jurisdiction off the rez, so we dropped him at Kirtland. I'll have him send a deputy to meet you in La Plata."

"No offense, but I need someone I can trust," Arthur countered. "And I already called them."

"Who?"

"Better you don't know."

"Kid, you're always putting me in a bind," Jake argued.

"I'll make a deal with you," Arthur said. "If he's not alone, I'll call you. If he is, I go in."

Jake remained silent, then: "You think he's alone?"

"Most sociopaths," Arthur said, "rarely have a partner. And if he's been working at a job all this time, that's what keeps him focused during his cooling-down period between the kidnappings and possibly murders."

"Murders?"

"Nobody's turned up saying he took them, have they?"

Jake pondered the inevitable. "None that I know of. Maybe instead of killing them, he traffics them. Or worse— his wife told me he likes BDSM. Maybe he tortures them before he kills them."

Arthur's heart sank.

Jake continued, "That same civilian employee pulled me a list of all females between the ages of fifteen and thirty that have gone missing in the past year. It was staggering. There were eighty-six in the Nation—fifty-five of them were found alive, nineteen were found dead, and twelve are still missing. April and Lucy Nez are among the ones still missing. I've cross-checked those disappearances to places where Lockerby has homes for sale and nothing matches. I even tried to hedge my bets and got a warrant to have OnStar track his Escalade, but there was no signal to be found."

"How could that be?" Arthur said. "Even if you don't pay for the service, they can still track you."

"Their best guess is, he found the box and pulled the wires. Tells you how to do that on the internet."

Arthur shook his head. Ak'is finished the jerky. "I know what I saw on that footage. I don't think he's trafficking her. I think he's just a freak. And freaks hide in plain sight. They could be your neighbor, your postman or the person who bags your groceries."

"But he's got a wife," Jake said. "It was hard for me to keep little things from Nizhoni, so shouldn't she have been able to pick up on something as big as a double life?"

"These freaks are often married with kids and even go to church. You may be a great cop, Jake, but you're terrible at hiding things."

"Like what?"

"Remember when you were dieting last time? You kept telling me the whole thing was a sham."

"It was."

"Bullshit. I bet you were grabbing lunch every day at the Sonic by the Navajo Shopping Center."

Silence. Then: "I love their SuperSonic Bacon Cheeseburgers."

Arthur simply grinned. "Where's the parcel located?"

Jake told him. "You'll have to swing off 170 after you pass under that haul road the coal company built that led from the pit mine to the generating station."

Arthur said, "Copy that."

"Get off at the first left and follow it around the farmland that's there, then keep going into where the terrain gets hilly. It's pretty far back off the road. Google Earth shows there's some kind of old ranch house with some outbuildings that were part of a large stable that closed down years ago."

Arthur chugged down the rest of his sweet tea. "Depending how this goes, I'll call you. If we find April, I'll make sure she gets to San Juan Regional Hospital. Then I'm heading back down to Albuquerque."

Jake said, "*You'll* take her to the hospital?"

"The less you know, my friend."

"I hate it when you stonewall. What the hell are you going to Duke City for?"

"I promised I'd meet with a guy named Chino Ignacio Garcia."

"Who's that?"

"A guy who's about as likable as a piece of crap stuck to my toilet bowl."

"What the hell are you planning?"

"Something that will put an end to him." Arthur took note of Jake's apprehensiveness. "Don't worry. I'm working with a detective from APD's Juvenile Crime Section."

"Mmm," Jake grunted. "And this Garcia has no idea what's coming?"

"None at all." Arthur smiled. "But, hey, while I got you—you think you could swing by my house and hang out for a bit? Billy's there now with Sharon."

"You expecting something?"

"Maybe."

"Consider it done," Jake said.

Arthur added, "She gave him a gun."

Jake sighed. "Oh, great."

"Sharon has my SIG."

"Her I trust."

Arthur watched an old Jeep Gladiator pickup pull in under the portico. It looked like a mid-sixties model. The silver paint had hardened to a dull gray and the hood was an orange blotch of rust that matched the river of rust running from the driver's side mirror to the chrome door handle. "Garcia threatened her life and my business. If this thing turns to shit ..."

"I understand. I've got a few things to clear up here, then I'll head over."

"Thanks."

"Just let them know I'm coming," Jake remarked. "I don't wanna get shot."

As soon as Arthur hung up, he dialed John Sykes. "You RTD?"

Sykes replied, "Ready to deploy, LT. I'm with my dad at Bridges in Farmington. Just tell me where to meet you."

Arthur rattled off the location. "See you in a couple."

"Ooh-rah." John Sykes said.

CHAPTER TWENTY-FIVE

Arthur and Ak'is watched as the lonely nocturnal winds blew over the high desert landscape and rocked the loosely hung Christmas lights on the only house across Highway 170. The gentle winds periodically gusted enough to churn up a puff of dust from the topsoil of the graded road where the Bronco sat. The pair watched the dust swirl in the beams of the Bronco's headlights as John Sykes' big yellow Dodge Power Wagon emerged from under the coal company bridge. The headlights of both trucks crossed paths as the Dodge rolled off the blacktop and pulled up beside the Bronco.

Arthur turned down the country music flowing from KTRA and rolled down his window as Sykes did the same. Sykes blew smoke from his cigarette out the open window and let it dissipate into the night sky.

"That is one big fuckin' dog, LT."

"He's what you get when you mix a Siberian Husky with a timber wolf." Arthur scratched the dog's large head, his fingers almost disappearing in the animal's thick fur. "His name's Ak'is."

"Friend, huh?" Sykes nodded. "It fits."

Arthur asked, "How's your dad?"

"Doing okay." Sykes shrugged. "He hates the food, he hates the staff and the fact that he can't remember much anymore. It sucks to get old."

"We're all heading in that direction," Arthur said.

"It still sucks," Sykes remarked. "I guess I'm lucky he still knows who I am." He took a drag off his cigarette. "Life's a bitch, right? You're born crapping in your diapers and you end up back where you started." Sykes blew smoke out his nostrils. "You expecting trouble from this jamoke tonight or did you just want some company?"

"I don't know what to expect," Arthur replied, "but I like the odds to always be on my side."

Sykes smiled, his brown-haired, blocky head looking eager to get moving. "You know me, sir. Always up for a fight."

Arthur said, "How's the shoulder?"

Sykes worked the rotator cuff of the shoulder that had taken the bullet that night in the canyon from James Basher. "It's fine. A little stiff in this cold weather, but it's just another scar my girlfriend thinks is sexy."

Arthur watched an old blue sedan heading south disappear under the bridge, then joked, "I'm still surprised Rosheen puts up with you."

"I let her into my soul, brother," Sykes said, "and she healed it."

Arthur smiled. "That's what happens when you find a good woman."

Sykes grinned, took another drag off his cigarette.

Arthur said, "Bring any friends along? I've got my nineteen-year-old and three clips of hollow points."

Sykes nodded, "Nineteen-year-old plus ten with three clips wearing full metal jackets." Sykes exhaled the smoke and tossed the cigarette out his window onto the ground. "Who is this jag?"

"Name's Gordon Lockerby," Arthur said. "He kidnapped a teenage girl in Milan three weeks ago that's been missing for the past six months. Her mother hired me to find her. You remember Jake Bilagody?"

"Sure."

"Jake says this guy's heavily into BDSM, according to the guy's wife, so we can only guess the kind of hell he's been putting her through."

Sykes huffed. "How close are we?"

"About sixteen klicks. He's got some old horse ranch back in the country. If we catch him with the girl," Arthur warned, "don't take a shot unless you have a clear line of fire."

"Copy that."

Arthur turned the volume back up on the radio, shifted the Ford into gear and circled Sykes' Dodge, then headed down the graded road with the Power Wagon trailing close behind. Someone had requested a song online about guy whose girlfriend left him and had taken his truck and how much he was missing the truck. Michael J. was making sure it got air time.

As the Bronco moved through the night, Arthur noticed the suspension of this new truck didn't creak and groan as it bounced around like it was a Jesse Jones trophy truck in the Baja 1000. This one seemed to ride the flow of surface undulations like a luxury car. Maybe, he thought, when this was over, he would drop it off at Hosteen's 4X4 and have him jack it up and add some bigger off-road tires to get the transformation started. Yeah, he agreed with himself, that sounded like a plan. The only drawback was that he'd have to be seen in the pregnant banana on wheels—Sharon's yellow Toyota FJ—while the work was getting done.

Jake had said satellite imagery had shown a large house with some outbuildings a little over ten miles off Highway 170. If they could get close enough, John could recon the house while Arthur scoped out the remaining buildings. One of the questions that kept running through Arthur's head was,

Would Lockerby even have the girl here at all? It had been three weeks since she had been drugged and driven away from the travel center. Now it was two weeks till Christmas. Could he have already taken her somewhere else? Or had he already grown tired of her and done whatever he did with girls he grew tired of? Arthur wondered how much of the girl would now be left to take home.

The time on the dash clock meant that Jake would already be at his house on White Mesa with Sharon and Billy, and that thought made Arthur breathe easier, knowing he would be there if Garcia picked up on the double cross. And as long as Detective Espinosa was there to pull his weight, Chino Ignacio Garcia was going down for what he had done not only to April Manygoats, but to every other girl and woman he had used, abused, degraded and then discarded.

The farther both trucks drove through the night, the more Arthur could see why the horse stables built out in the middle of nowhere hadn't made it. You have to have a lot of space and comfortable stables for horses for it to be successful, but most were built closer to a town. Granted La Plata wasn't a metropolis, but at least you'd build close to something with a post office. This place was about twenty-eight miles from Farmington. To Arthur, or anyone with a brain, it seemed like folly at the start to even suggest building something that expensive in this desolate location. Not to mention the propane-charged generators it would take to keep it warm in winter and cool in summer and make sure the lights were on. And drilling for a well would have been expensive. All Arthur Nakai knew was that he would never have done it. The financial risk was way too high.

As the Bronco topped a hill, Arthur saw the large house squatting under the moon. He slowed, and John Sykes did the same. Both trucks stopped and went dark, engines off.

Arthur judged they were about two hundred yards from the house and about a hundred yards from the gated entrance, which was flanked by two brick pillars topped with copper spires. Both men climbed out of their trucks, followed by Ak'is, and jogged to the gate and flattened their backs against one of the pillars. Ak'is loped up and stood at Arthur's feet, tongue out and panting, waiting for orders.

"On five we go over the fence," Arthur instructed. "You make your way to the house. Check it out thoroughly, then head over to the large barn. I'll check out the smaller buildings and meet you there."

Sykes looked down at the golden eyes of the wolf dog, said, "Roger that," and took a deep breath, then let it out as if he were slowly lowering a three-hundred-pound barbell to his chest. "What I wouldn't give for a PTT about now and some night vision."

Arthur remembered Abraham Fasthorse's arsenal of equipment, which had enabled them to get Sharon back, and smiled. "No push-to-talks, buddy. Hand signals only. And we have moonlight. You still good?"

"Still good."

Arthur counted down to zero, and the two men climbed over the white tube fencing and trotted toward their objectives in a semi-crouch. Ak'is jumped through the bars and followed Arthur silently, his large paws swooshing as they hit the sand of the area and tossed it behind him. The air was crisp and clean, and the smell of sage that hung on it seemed as though it had been sent as a blessing by the Creator as they darted across the open area. Soon they hopped another white tube fence and darted past the salt brush, using the shelter of a few junipers that had been left to flourish on the main property.

Arthur held his fist in the air, and both men and Ak'is stopped. He pointed two fingers at Sykes and then toward the two-story house. Light escaped from the downstairs windows while the upstairs remained dark. The soft drone of a jet passed overhead, but Arthur didn't look up. Sykes nodded silently and took off toward the house, weapon drawn. Arthur let his eyes pick through the night and focus on the first of the three small outbuildings. In an instant, his boots dug into the sand, and he was off, covering the open ground quickly with his furry companion. When he laid his back against the cold cinder block of the first building, Arthur filled his lungs with chilled air and looked down. Ak'is was moving his head as if he were scanning the night for enemy combatants. Arthur's heart began to race, and he could feel his adrenaline pumping like it had during those predawn raids on Taliban positions in Afghanistan. His every sense now seemed heightened—his hearing was more acute; his sight was crystal clear; his sense of smell picked up every aroma and his whole body seemed charged with the electricity of battle.

Arthur moved slowly to the corner of the building and quickly peeked around it. Nothing. He then moved quietly toward the wooden doors and slowly removed the heavy iron bar that locked the two sections of sliding door together. John was probably at the house by now, he thought. He wasn't hearing any shooting, so that was a plus. Knowing him, he was looking for a way in—moving precisely and silently as he had in the Wolf Pack. Arthur lowered the iron bar gently until it hung from the left door, then, taking carefully placed steps, quietly slid the other door open. His fingers flexed around the grip of his Glock instinctively, relieving the vise that was his hand and replacing it with a more relaxed grip. Steadily, he peered around the open door and into the darkened interior of the building.

He could smell nothing but concrete and a mustiness that almost made him sneeze. Beyond the moonglow that shafted through the open door, he saw nothing and heard nothing. He entered for a closer look and allowed his eyes to focus. The building was empty except for a group of blue plastic barrels—the kind you could store rainwater in. He couldn't fault Lockerby for that. It was good planning. Still, there was no April and no Lockerby.

Back outside, he made his way to the next stand-alone building. Entering it in the same manner as he had the first, he came back outside with the same result. Empty. He looked toward the big house for any sign of John Sykes but saw none. He took a deep breath and headed for the third small building. Somewhere off in the blackened distance, Arthur heard the cry of a coyote. Contrary to popular belief, they do not actually howl at the moon; they howl as a way of marking territories or communicating a kill and calling the pack to join in the feast. Almost instantly, a responding cry sounded. Arthur smiled. He had always loved that sound because it spoke to his soul. It made him close his eyes and absorb their song into his being. As he walked, he studied the ground. It had been a long time since horses had left prints here, but a short time since coyote paws had crossed the land looking for pocket mice or any other type of rodent they might find to snack on. By the time Arthur Nakai finished checking the third outbuilding, John Sykes had made his way from the veranda of the big house, darted across the open ground, and met Arthur at the corner of the large main barn.

"No one in the house, sir," Sykes reported, keeping his voice barely above a whisper. "I searched all the bedrooms. Master bedroom was clean, except for a girl's necklace on the dresser and a bunch of girls' clothes hanging in the closet. In fact, every bedroom closet was filled with girls' and women's clothes. You don't think this asshole is into that type of shit, do you? Dressing up like a broad?"

Arthur shook his head briefly. "Trophies."

"Fuck that," Sykes replied. "The only hygiene products I saw in the master bath were for a man, and there were some dirty dishes left in the kitchen sink. Looks like he fed someone recently." John Sykes studied the large barn. "Damn, this thing is huge."

"I know. It's a freaking dream barn." Suddenly, Arthur's eyes widened. "Was that necklace silver and of a little Indian girl?"

Sykes thought briefly. "Yes, sir."

Arthur told him of the one Melanie Manygoats had described to him in his kitchen; the one her husband had made and daughter had been wearing.

"That's it exactly."

"Then the girl I'm looking for either is here or was here."

Sykes nodded.

"We'll breach the barn from both ends of the building. Take him by surprise. I'll come in from this end, you take the other. Better go around back. Those doors in front are most likely where the office is. If he's near them, he might see you passing by."

Suddenly, a terrifying scream split the chill night. It was sharper than the coyote's howl and telegraphed instantly the distinct measure of agony that had been used to create it.

"That didn't come from inside the barn, sir," Sykes said.

"It came from around back," Arthur agreed.

Both men scurried around the left side of the barn, Arthur in the lead. They sprinted alongside the sixty-foot end of the big barn and peered around the corner. The moonlight bathed a large beige shipping container—the kind of hooch they used to live in during what little downtime they had in the FOB. The girl's scream echoed again, and Arthur Nakai and John Sykes rushed across the open ground between the barn and the shipping container. Given the size of the container, the men knew it to be a what they called a high-cube—roughly forty feet long, eight feet wide and almost ten feet high and fit for carrying everything from overseas. Judging by its condition, it appeared to be on the newer side, so Arthur figured it was a one-tripper from China. A fact that could be easily corroborated by the police.

Both men flanked the double steel doors. Arthur held an index finger to his lips, readjusted his grip on his Glock again and reached for one of the handles dangling from the long locking bars. Sykes raised his weapon with a two-handed grip and gave a nod as the screams suddenly transformed to tortured cries and guttural grunts that now came in deliberate and measured intervals. Each man took a deep breath before Arthur jerked open the door. It slammed hard and loud into the side of the shipping container.

Sykes entered first, remembering the steps and motions that had become second nature during breeches in the hot zone all those years ago. Steps and actions that had been embedded into his memory like all the other survival training that had been hammered into him every day without rest. Arthur followed. Sykes went high, Arthur went low. Gordon Lockerby stood before them in nothing but a black T-shirt. He turned, his eyes wide and filled with astonished anger, his big hands continuing to latch onto the young girl's tiny waist as he made his final, powerful thrust. The girl's body glistened with sweat and was bent over, strapped and handcuffed to something that resembled a torture device.

"Back away from the girl, asshole!" Arthur yelled.

"Do it now!" Sykes demanded.

Gordon Lockerby's anger transformed his face into a grotesque red pumpkin above his slightly obese and naked bottom half, his body glaring a yellowish pasty white under the bare bulb. The girl gasped, cried and whimpered as she helplessly slumped in place.

"NO!" Lockerby shouted. "You're not supposed to be here!"

Arthur Nakai and John Sykes froze for a moment as Gordon Lockerby grabbed the handle of a machete and jerked it from the side of the wooden bench. Raising it high, he charged the two men, his still erect member and scrotum swinging from side to side as he crossed the fifteen feet between them at a quick pace. Arthur heard Sykes' weapon report a split second before his in the confined space. His ears rang with the high-pitched, deafening tone he had become accustomed to as he watched Gordon Lockerby crumple and plow into the floor in front of them facedown, the machete dropping from his hand and clattering away from him.

Sykes looked at Arthur. Arthur looked at Sykes. Both men breathed rapidly.

"Get the girl!" Arthur ordered.

Sykes holstered his weapon and complied without hesitation.

Arthur knelt down beside Lockerby and tossed the machete clear with the muzzle of his Glock. Using his upper-body strength, he rolled Gordon Lockerby onto his back. He was still breathing, even though there were four bullet holes in his chest oozing blood and soaking the black T-shirt.

"Where's April?" Arthur demanded.

Sykes ran to the girl and released her from her shackles, lifted her weakened body into his muscular arms and carried her out of the container. Ak'is followed.

Lockerby belched a spattering of blood from his twisted mouth. "You'll never find her." Arthur watched the red liquid of life spill from Lockerby's mouth like a pumping lava flow. "You'll never find any of them."

Arthur pressed his Glock hard under Lockerby's double chin. "Tell me where she is!"

Lockerby's face grimaced. His eyes squeezed shut and his hands tried to grab Arthur's wrist to pull it away, but his strength had waned to the point of uselessness. Arthur now felt the warm, sticky wetness of Lockerby's blood on his wrist. He pressed the gun barrel harder under the big man's jaw, the angry wolf raging within him, urging him to pull the trigger, all while the good wolf battled equally hard to keep his finger from pulling the trigger, waiting for the information that would free the young girl he had been tasked to save.

"The darkness is coming for you, asshole. And it can have you. Now, where's April?"

Lockerby fought to smile with all the defiance he could pull together. "You know what I loved about cutting all their throats? Hearing that same delicious sound they all made after the blade laid them open." Lockerby struggled to breathe, then gurgled, "You're never going to find her."

When Lockerby's eyes went dead, his hands fell away from Arthur's wrist.

"Where is she?" Arthur began to yell, pounding his fist into the dead man's chest with every repeat of the question. "Where is she! Where is she! Where is she!"

When no response came, Arthur stood, defeated, and walked out of the container into the cold night. His aching lungs filled with life as he grappled with the loss of April, the one girl he had been appointed to find. How was he going to look her mother in the eyes and tell her he had failed? How was he going to apologize to her father and her brother? How was he going to be able to look at himself in the mirror? He pinched the bridge of this nose with his thumb and forefinger, snapped his eyes shut tightly. He didn't even think about Chino Ignacio Garcia. Who gave a damn about him at this point? Let Detective Espinosa and the Albuquerque Police Department figure that one out without him. Arthur was done. He was done figuring; he was done playing the fucked-up odds that had led to this and he was done thinking he could make a difference. He inhaled again deeply and let it out in disgusted rush. Who the hell was he kidding? He couldn't even save a stolen sister. He was useless.

"Lieutenant!" John Sykes yelled from somewhere in the darkness. "Hustle up!"

Arthur sprinted away from the container in time to barely see John Sykes running after something in the night. Arthur's legs powered up as he ran to follow whomever or whatever Sykes was chasing. The muscles of his thighs and calves pumped as the adrenaline coursed through his body, giving him new life. His breathing remained steady as he moved quickly. Suddenly, he came to a stop close to Sykes. He was standing watching Ak'is claw at the ground around twenty yards from what looked to be an adobe-style watering trough. Arthur had seen them before, but these days they were usually built around a galvanized stock tank. Arthur jogged over to Ak'is, who paid no mind to him, consumed in his digging.

John Sykes said, "He's got hold of something!"

"Help me!" Arthur encouraged Sykes as he fell to his knees. "There's something's under here!"

Sykes dropped and began clawing at the sand. The moonlight gave them ample illumination for their endeavor, led by the big wolf dog. Arthur could hear Ak'is' rapid breathing in those brief spurts of air that meant there was a purpose to his actions. Ak'is' claws quickly hit something hard at the same time Arthur's fingers hit something that felt like wood. Arthur began to use his forearms to push sand out of the way. Sykes did the same.

"I found a rope!" Arthur yelled, springing to his feet. Ak'is backed away.

Using the strength of his upper body, he pulled the heavy wood laden with high-desert soil on top of it. Sykes grabbed hold of the rope as well and with the combined power of their legs they towed the heavy wooden door from over the darkened pit it revealed. Tossing the rope aside, the two men ran to the edge of the hole and gazed into it. The bright moonlight bathed a still body below.

Arthur jumped down the six feet and squatted down beside the girl. "April?" he said, brushing away the matted hair from her face and carefully lifting her into his arms. He felt her neck for a pulse. She had a weak one, and that made his heart beat stronger.

"John," he yelled, "find something to cover her with. Quick! We have to get her body temperature up!"

Sykes disappeared from view.

Arthur held April close, using the warmth from his own body to try to somehow kick-start hers. Her skin felt cold to the touch, and her breathing was faint, but she was alive. Gordon Lockerby had lied before he left this world, and knowing that was an incredible joy. As he held April close, he knew Lockerby's *chindi*—according to his traditional beliefs—were vacating his body and taking with them his lifetime of evil. They could have them, he thought, and were welcome to them. And the fact that Lockerby had passed inside a building meant that the *chindi* now resided in that building until it was either destroyed or abandoned or cleansed by ritual.

Sykes soon returned with a large blanket and tossed it down to Arthur, who quickly wrapped April in it. "I'll hand her up to you," Arthur said as he stood. April's eyes opened briefly and met his. "I've got you," Arthur reassured her. "You're safe now."

April said nothing. Just closed her eyes and returned to her unconscious world.

Arthur was used to carrying deadweight. He had done it several times during his tours and around the Arizona border. It always amazed him how much heavier the human body turned out to be once it became inanimate.

"Careful, John," Arthur warned as he lifted her up to meet Sykes' outstretched arms. "She regained consciousness briefly but then passed out again."

"She's probably in shock," Sykes said. He curved his arms underneath her blanketed body and lifted her up, then struggled to stand and moved away from the edge of the hole. When he reappeared, he got to his knees and offered a hand to Arthur, who grabbed it and used his feet against the dirt wall as leverage while his muscles, and those of John Sykes' arms and legs, pulled him back up to solid ground.

Arthur looked around, saw April lying a short distance away. "She's got a pulse, but she's cold as ice," he said. "We don't know how long she's been down there. Pick her up, and we'll take her to the house."

Sykes did as he was told, then said, "Lockerby dead?"

"Yeah."

Sykes redistributed April's weight for the trek to the house. "Can't say I'm sorry."

Arthur trotted beside him, past the open container door. "He mentioned there were more. I wonder how many."

"If he's been doing this for a while, who's to say."

Arthur pulled his phone from his pocket, tapped the screen and autodialed. It took a few seconds for Jake to answer.

"We found April."

"Alive?"

"Yeah, but weak and in shock," Arthur reported. "There was another girl here, too."

John Sykes let the strength of his powerful legs move him across the uneven sandy terrain while his arms kept April cradled against his thick chest.

Jake said, "You get her name?"

"No name yet."

"She told me her name was Lucy Nez," Sykes interrupted.

"John says she's your missing girl."

"Lucy Nez?" Arthur could hear Jake's relief. "So, you took Sykes with you?"

"When you need a job done, ask a Marine."

"Is Lucy all right?"

"She'll need a lot of help to work through what happened to her," Arthur said somberly, his breathing steady while he moved quickly. "April will, too. They both appear to have been abused sexually. Your guy's wife doesn't know the half of it."

"My God," Jake said.

"I think you should call your friend at county and have them get their asses out here—and tell them to bring along someone who knows how to work a GPR."

"Ground-penetrating radar?" Jake sounded confused. "Why?"

"Before Lockerby died, he told me there were others." Arthur paused. "He told me he liked the sound they made after he cut their throats. I found some plastic fifty-five-gallon drums in the barn. I bet he buried them out here somewhere."

"Sonofabitch. I can't believe his wife never picked up on this shit."

"He was good at keeping that side of him hidden," Arthur said. "Sociopaths usually are."

"That's over five acres of area," Jake said. "A walk-behind unit would take forever, and no one has the manpower for that."

"Ever heard of the CART system?" Arthur said.

"Nope."

"MIT did something about ten years ago along with some research institute for ConEd in New York. They made a radar system that can image something buried up to ten feet down."

"How in the hell do you know this stuff?"

"I read," Arthur quipped. "The thing has seventeen shielded antennas—nine transmitters and eight receivers. Using GPS, it can create a map showing all the underground anomalies. In this case, where the barrels are buried."

"I'll tell the operations captain to make some calls and locate one. What're you going to do now?"

"John and I are taking April to the house on the property so she and Lucy will be together and can get warm. We'll wait with them until county shows up, fill them in and give our statements. Then I've got to head back to Albuquerque."

Jake exhaled. "Garcia? What are you going to do without the girl?"

"I've been working on a plan with Eduardo Espinosa of the Albuquerque Police Department. I'll be their bait to take him down."

"I don't have to tell you how dangerous that sounds," Jake warned him.

"No," Arthur said, "you don't." Then: "Let me talk to Sharon."

There were the usual sounds of someone handing the phone over before Sharon's voice poured into his heart. "Tell me you're all right."

"I'm all right."

"Don't be flippant."

"I didn't think I was."

"Did you find April?"

Arthur filled her in.

"Thank the Creator. Is she okay?'

"That depends on your definition of okay. She's alive."

Arthur could hear his wife's distressed breathing over the phone. He could tell she was worried.

"When are you coming home?" she said. "It's almost midnight."

"Soon."

Sharon huffed. "Like I believe that. What was Jake calling dangerous?"

"Nothing. I've got to go back down to Duke City and set things up with a guy in their Child Exploitation Detail. They'll take it from there."

"Like I said, men always lie to their wives."

Arthur pursed his lips. "I'll see you in the morning."

There was a pause. Then a breath. And then a soft, "Be careful."

"Always," he said.

Sharon said, "Now I know you're lying."

CHAPTER TWENTY-SIX

"I've got the girl," Arthur said as he pulled up to the stoplight where La Plata Highway met Highway 64, the major bloodline between Chama, New Mexico, and Teec Nos Pos, Arizona. "I had to kill someone to get her, so that took extra time and effort on my part, and that'll cost you an extra five grand."

"As long as my property is returned to me intact, you will get your money," Garcia said.

"Don't you want to know if she's all right?"

Garcia laughed. "It doesn't really matter what shape she is in, as long as she can be made an example of. You see, Mr. Nakai, long ago I learned a merciless punishment is the best deterrent to further disobedience."

Arthur's emotions churned in his gut like a stormy sea while his hand tightened around the steering wheel. "I should be in Albuquerque around three a.m. Where do you want to meet?"

"Why not come here?" Garcia proposed. "That way I can give you the extra funds, and we can part as friends."

"We'll never be friends," Arthur replied. "And based on our last meeting, I don't like the odds. Home turf tends to put them in your favor. I was thinking of someplace a little more neutral."

"I have an industrial property on Woodward Road, by the railroad tracks. Just east of the Rio Grande. Do you know that area?"

"I can find it. Text me the address."

"I hope you have my ... property with you," Garcia said.

"Tucked away in the back of my truck. I had to give her something to knock her out, make her less combative."

"Some of my people can learn a lot from you, Mr. Nakai. I'll see you in three hours. And remember—nothing important to you is safe until I have what is mine."

Arthur ended the call, dropped the phone into one of the cup holders in the Bronco's center console. When the text carrying the address came through, his phone vibrated. Arthur picked it up and read it, then called Detective Espinosa.

"Everything's set," Espinosa reported. "I had to do a lot of heavy lifting to push it up the ladder, but I got you in. I'm looking at a city map right now. You have a location for the meet?"

Arthur dictated the address.

Espinosa said, "Thank God you didn't say his club— that would have put the whole operation in the Northwest Area Command." There was a thinker's pause, quiet enough for Arthur to hear the cop's steady breathing. "This way it'll belong to Valley Area Command, so nothing changes for us. I'll get with Northwest and have them move on the club at the same time we're taking Garcia down." Another pause. "Looks like we can only make entry from two points at that location, but there's a good chance they'll have those manned. We'll use two teams—one will stage by the BNSF rail yard on Hill Street, off Woodward; the other can stage at an empty lot over on Broadway. That way we'll be off radar until the last minute."

"The only reason I'm coming back down there is because of April," Arthur said. "And I'm going in alone."

"This isn't up for debate," Espinosa argued. "You're gonna do what I tell you or you don't go in at all."

"That's bullshit," Arthur argued. "Garcia's expecting me to deliver the girl, and if I don't show up with her this whole thing goes to hell." Arthur could feel Espinosa's frustration growing on the other end of the line. "He's expecting me," he continued. "If you go flooding in there with a shitload of cops before I can get him out in the open, he'll bolt. Or worse."

"Fuck me!" Espinosa grumbled. "Then you're wearing a wire."

"No way!"

"You're wearing, or you're out of it. Period. I've already put up with you as much as I'm going to."

Espinosa was right, Arthur grudgingly agreed. There was too much riding on this to be benched on the sidelines in the last minutes of the game. The only way to have a chance at bringing down Chino Ignacio Garcia and recovering all the girls whose lives he was destroying was to bridle his emotions and work with Espinosa.

"It'll be small enough they won't find it," Espinosa assured him. "We'll use a button mic or something. And I already have a female officer the right size and build of your Manygoats girl, so if you can keep her in the shadows, we might pull this off."

"Does she know what's at stake?"

"She's worked undercover for five years. She knows. She'll also be your backup until we roll in."

Arthur said, "Where do you want me to meet up with you?"

"I'll be with the team by the rail yard in the mobile substation. I'll text the address to you. When you get here, I'll introduce you to your new April."

"Sounds like a plan," Arthur said. "Oh, and, Detective?"

"Yeah?"

"You really need to calm down."

"Fuck off."

CHAPTER TWENTY-SEVEN

The motor-home-sized mobile community substation with the words *ALBUQUERQUE POLICE DEPARTMENT* emblazoned on it squatted beneath two tall, thick-trunked shade trees that stood beside a tanned wall that blocked out the unsightly view of the even larger unsightly mounds of dirt and busted slabs of concrete that hid behind it. Looking at its red, white, and blue coloring, Arthur was thankful this whole operation was taking place in the dark of night. Arthur shoehorned his Bronco into a spot left open between two marked squads by A & A Auto Parts and got out. Ak'is watched alertly from the driver's side window as Arthur walked up to a young cop smoking a cigarette and asked him to point out Detective Eduardo Espinosa. It only took a few seconds for the young cop to do so, and Arthur made his way toward him through the milling throng of officers waiting patiently to take down the prostitution king.

After the perfunctory greetings, Espinosa led Arthur into the rolling substation. It was filled with all the equipment you would think it would carry, along with some that came as a surprise. A young man stood and placed two small devices into his palm. Espinosa said, "We have a wireless receiver/transmitter that fits in your ear, or we can stick a button mic somewhere." Espinosa displayed both in the palms of his hands. "Either way, we'll pick up everything that's said. Your choice."

Seeing Espinosa for the first time, Arthur figured him to be in his mid-fifties. His mustache and goatee were a frosty gray while his eyebrows and hair remained a dense black. His slightly plump head sat atop an almost pear-shaped body, which gave the impression he wasn't missing many meals. Arthur eyed the choices Espinosa show him. The ear mic was smaller than an earplug and had a tiny antenna sticking out of it. The button mic was black and the size of a nickel and had a coin battery tucked into the back of it.

"Give me the ear mic," Arthur said. "At least my hair can cover it."

Espinosa handed the button mic back to the technician in the substation and placed the ear piece in Arthur's palm. "Stick it in. We'll try it out."

Arthur did just that. Then pulled his long black hair forward so that it spilled over his broad shoulders and covered his ears. "How do I look?"

"Like a stubborn Indio," Espinosa said.

Arthur grinned. "You should see my other impressions."

Espinosa checked his watch. "Try it out."

Arthur counted from one to five, then back to one. The tech gave a thumbs-up.

"Listen now to what I tell you," Espinosa stressed. "Don't pull any shit. You drive in, you meet with Garcia, you get the money and give us the word letting us know the transaction's been made and you've got the dough in hand. We'll take it from there."

"What's my safe word?" Arthur joked.

Espinosa didn't laugh. "Make something up."

Arthur gave it brief thought. "Tacos," he said.

"Tacos? Fucking tacos?"

"I like tacos. You ever had a Navajo taco made with fry bread?"

Espinosa shook his head. "*Madre de Dios.* Okay. You say 'tacos,' and we'll move in." Then he added, bringing up a thick finger and sticking it in Arthur's face, "You listen to me and listen carefully—you put my officer in any unneeded jeopardy, I'll have that new license of yours revoked and you prosecuted for endangering the life of an officer in the performance of her duties. That should get you ten to twenty easy. So don't fuck around."

"Copy that," Arthur said. "Where is she?"

Espinosa waved a hand, and the woman chosen to play April Manygoats in this nighttime charade stepped up. She gave a quick nod of acknowledgment to Arthur before focusing on Espinosa. She was dressed in a Coca-Cola T-shirt, jeans and sneakers similar to what Arthur had seen April wearing in the video from the travel center. Espinosa must have scrambled to get them, Arthur imagined, in order to have the best shot at pulling this off.

"In the shadows, she could pass for her," Arthur said. "Let's hope Garcia doesn't want a closer inspection."

Espinosa introduced them. "Detective James has spent the last five years doing undercover, so she knows what's at stake and how to handle it."

Arthur shook her hand. "Navajo?'

"From Crownpoint," Glenda James said.

As the two exchanged clan affiliations, Espinosa glanced at his watch again. "You'd better get moving," he said. "Don't want to keep that asshole waiting."

"You'd better lie down in the cargo area in the back," Arthur told James. "There's a blanket back there you can cover yourself with."

She nodded.

Once she was inside Arthur's Bronco, Ak'is looked on from the back seat, sizing up this new human's intrusion and cataloging her scent into an olfactory file. She didn't smell like Sharon, but rather of sweat and soiled clothes. The wolf dog's nose twitched and sniffed until he was satisfied before he lay down on the back seat.

"I haven't seen a dog that size in a while," James remarked. "Will he bite?"

Arthur said, "Only when I tell him to."

Glenda James smiled, got into the fetal position, pulled the machine-made Mexican blanket over her and got as comfortable as she could for the short ride to come.

"You'd better make sure your hair covers your face when you get out," Arthur instructed, "and remember to act docile and drugged up. We need Garcia to believe you're not a threat."

"Not a problem," James said.

"What kind of handgun are you carrying?"

"S and W nine-mil," James responded.

"Where?" Arthur asked.

"Small of my back, under my shirt," she advised. "I figured since my hands are going to look like they're tied behind me, that's where it would do the best."

Arthur nodded. "Is the S and W your personal weapon?"

Glenda James fingered her dark hair out of her face as Arthur fired up the Bronco and backed up. "We used to be allowed to carry our own up until a DOJ report came out after the new chief took over. Plus, there were some officer-involved shootings where some handguns and a suppressor used by one of the officers implicated wasn't range-qualified for use in the field. About seven years ago, I'm told, it was decreed that we were to use only what we were issued by the department."

Arthur shifted into drive and felt the rear tires dig into the rough dirt. The Bronco bounced along the unpaved surface of Hill Street until the tires hit the asphalt of Woodward Road.

"Sorry about the ride," Arthur remarked.

"No biggie," James said. "Beats sleeping in a dumpster for a week."

Arthur laughed as the Bronco thumped across three sets of railroad tracks and headed for the meeting with Chino Ignacio Garcia.

Glenda James said, "Espinosa says you really got a jones for this guy."

Arthur gave her the elevator pitch as they drove past the empty BNSF parking lot on their right and a couple of old mobile homes to their left. The tall shade trees that lined this part of the street seemed to be filtering some of the moon's light with their swaying leaves as they drove past skeleton-crewed manufacturing facilities, their parking lots dappled with a wide range of vehicles from their overnight employees. If it were daylight, Arthur reminded himself, he would be able to see the Sandia Mountains.

"You ever been to Sandia Crest?" he asked Glenda James.

"No. The outdoors isn't really my thing."

"My wife and I drove down last June and hiked the trail. She wanted to see the wildflowers. Get some pictures. Some kind of alumroot that's supposed to be only found there and one other place."

"Sounds interesting," James said in a disinterested way.

"Delightful story, Nakai," Espinosa said in his ear. "Any sign of Garcia?"

"Not yet. Lot's empty, but the gate's open."

"Remember, we're only seconds away. You say 'tacos,' and we'll swarm like flies on a fresh pile."

Arthur felt his adrenaline begin to flash as they approached Garcia's warehouse complex. Moonlight bathed the vast, empty parking lot behind the tall chain-link fence. Against the building, above entry doors that seemed to be staged at odd intervals, small lights gleamed brightly. Lights inside gave shape to the few windows that decorated this side of the long building. Arthur noticed a gigantic garage door that he could have driven a quarry dump truck through next to one of the smaller doors. Garcia and whoever he had brought with him must be already inside, Arthur reasoned.

"Be ready," Arthur said. "Cover your face with your hair and act like you're passed out."

Glenda James did just that, remained still.

Arthur slowed the Bronco as he moved through the open gate. If anyone was on the roof scoping them out, they'd see what Espinosa and Arthur wanted them to see—him and a dog, with Garcia's property stashed out of sight somewhere in the back.

A door opened to the right of the large metal door. Arthur tapped the gas and the truck surged forward. One of the men from Garcia's office stood holding the door open with a foot, making sure the assault rifle in his hands never deviated from its telegraphed intention. Being careful not to make any erroneous moves, Arthur pulled the Bronco up and rolled down the window.

"Where's the girl?" Assault Rifle said.

"In the back," Arthur responded. "And she's in no shape to walk. Open the big door, and I'll drive in."

Assault Rifle turned and looked into the building, relayed the request. Arthur told Ak'is to jump in the back. The big dog hopped over the seat and lay down behind Glenda James' legs. The large door of the facility suddenly jolted and made a groaning sound as it began to slowly rise. Assault Rifle returned his focus to the Bronco and made sure the barrel of his rifle followed the truck as it moved through the large open door. As soon as Arthur had cleared the door, it groaned again and closed with a steel slam that reverberated loudly in his ears and the entire vacant industrial facility.

Sitting in the middle of the long building, angled with their front ends facing each other, were a black Mercedes sedan and a white Range Rover. Arthur continued moving forward until he angled the Bronco to the right and turned off the engine an adequate distance away.

"Is he here?" Glenda James said. "Can you see anyone?"

"No one but the guy with the assault rifle behind us," Arthur said quietly. "They're probably in the two cars I'm looking at waiting for me to get out."

Arthur observed the length of the building and how it had seemed smaller from the outside. The Bronco's dash clock read three thirteen in the morning. The empty interior of the facility was painted a muted tan, and there were several entry doors painted the same, with EXIT signs above them between elongated rows of multipaned windows, the kind that would tilt outward to cross-ventilate the building during manufacturing. From his parked position, he could see three smaller garage doors on each side of the open interior and skylights that ran the length of the downwardly pitched roof above two bulky, yellow overhead cranes that spread their arms across the expanse and rested on beams supported by more vertical beams that gave the whole thing the look of elevated train tracks.

Arthur eyed the rearview mirror. "Assault Rifle's hanging back by the door we drove through," he told Glenda James and those listening in his ear. "If he opens the back, let Ak'is handle him."

"No problem there," she said, pulling her Smith and Wesson and keeping it tucked under the blanket.

"Espinosa?" Arthur said, "If this goes to hell, have your people breach the two large garage doors at each end of the building. I'm sure Garcia will be hightailing it out the back if shooting starts. I've got my truck blocking the front exit."

"Copy," Espinosa said. "Just make sure you get that front door up for us. We'll handle the back."

Arthur felt his Glock resting snugly under his arm in the shoulder holster, while the other one gave him even more confidence on his hip. He got out. The place smelled largely reminiscent of oil and grease and industrial disinfectant. The arc lights running the length of the center roofline were bright enough that they left no darkened niche for even a mouse to hide in. Leaving the driver's door open, Arthur moved around to the front of his truck, hands in the air and open.

A few more moments were allowed to click off before the doors of the Mercedes opened, followed by the doors of the Range Rover. Two large bodyguards emerged from the black E-Class. They, like Arthur, moved around to the front of the vehicle, their semiautomatic weapons seeming to be living extensions of both their hands. The wore expensive custom gray and blue suits, respectively, and took up positions of impressive intimidation. When the doors of the Range Rover opened, Chino Ignacio Garcia stepped out of the rear door facing him in all his ivory-suited splendor. Jonzell Washington quickly rose from the other side of the roofline, his face dark and focused. Arthur couldn't see his mode of dress, but he knew it had "low-life player" written all over it.

"I see you were able to find the place," Garcia said, his voice echoing throughout the vacant facility.

"Google Maps," Arthur said.

The Cuban smiled broadly. "You have my property?"

"You have my money?"

Garcia nodded.

"Then I have your property."

"Bring her to me."

Arthur lowered his hands slowly; the two suits from the Mercedes thumbed back their pistols.

Arthur said, "Let me see the cash."

Garcia snapped his fingers, and Jonzell Washington moved from around the Range Rover and began walking toward him. Carefully. Garcia pulled a pack of cigarettes from one of his suit pockets along with a gold lighter, based on the flash Arthur had seen in the arc lighting. As Jonzell moved closer—his right hand filled with five packs of banded bills—Garcia thumbed the lighter. The flame danced in front of the cigarette briefly, then vanished with an echoing click.

Garcia inhaled, let the smoke out leisurely. "Tell me, Mr. Nakai … did you ever think your life could change at any moment? You could have a heart attack; you could succumb to an unexpected illness or you could be killed before you leave here tonight."

"I try not to think negatively," Arthur said. "I leave that to the politicians."

Garcia choked back a laugh, took another drag from his cigarette. "I know you're armed. I'd like to see it on the floor before Mr. Washington gets over to you."

Arthur pulled the pistol from his hip and laid it down at his feet.

Garcia nodded. "Now kick it away from you."

Arthur did as he was told, consoled by the weight of the remaining pistol under his left arm. Arthur held up a hand. "That's far enough," he said.

Jonzell Washington stopped. "I swear I'm gonna kill you, motherfucker."

"You still selling that pipe dream?" Arthur said. "Toss me over the cash and let the adults do some business."

"Jus' keep talkin', motherfucker. I mean it. Jus' keep talkin'."

"The cash," Arthur insisted flatly.

Jonzell tossed it over.

"Good dog," Arthur said. "Now go back to your owner."

Jonzell's face strained with all the pent-up anger he was managing to keep in check only because of the company he was with. Arthur saw Washington's hands clinch into tight fists, the kind where you'd hear knuckles popping if this were a martial arts film showdown. Jonzell's arms began to shake from the fury coursing through his veins.

"This ain't over, fucker. This ain't over."

"Yeah, yeah."

"Mr. Washington?" Garcia beckoned. "Please step back over here and give our friend some room."

"Just wait," Jonzell reiterated. "You just fuckin' wait."

Arthur feigned dread. "Ooh, the anticipation."

Jonzell pursed his lips, turned on his heel and made his jaunty way back over to Chino Ignacio Garcia. The two looked like Al Pacino from *Scarface* met Wesley Snipes from *Demolition Man*.

"And now," Garcia said apathetically, "hand over my property."

"You know what I'm gonna do with this money?" Arthur said, holding up the packs of bills. "I'm gonna take some of it and get me some out-of-this-world Navajo tacos."

"We're rolling," Espinosa's voice said in his ear.

"You know the kind?" Arthur went on. "The ones made with homemade fry bread, diced green chilis, piled up with seasoned chili beans, diced tomatoes, shredded cheese, lettuce, onions, but no black olives. I hate black olives."

"As much as I applaud your obvious dietary fervor," Garcia said, "I must ask you to bring me what is mine. Now."

"Almost there!" Espinosa reassured him through the earpiece.

Arthur held up his hands in a hold-on gesture. "As I said, I had to drug her. She gave me a hell of a fight when she heard where I was taking her." Arthur walked around to the passenger side of the Bronco. "I don't think she likes you very much."

Garcia said something in Cuban Spanish, and the two bodyguards by the Mercedes raised their guns in Arthur's direction.

"If you have to shoot him," Jonzell said loud enough for Arthur to hear, "save enough of his ass for me."

Arthur waved a finger. "Be careful what you wish for." Then he tossed the money onto the Bronco's passenger seat. Once behind the truck, Arthur released the latch that opened the upper glass. "Stay," he whispered.

Ak'is didn't move.

Arthur tugged the latch of the tailgate, jerked it open and held it. He turned to the well-dressed flunky with the assault rifle. "You wanna give me a hand?" he said. "This girl's some heavy deadweight."

Arthur saw him glance at Garcia, then shoulder his rifle and step forward. In his ear, he heard, "We're through the gate! Silent running."

Suddenly, Arthur dropped the tailgate. When it slammed down with an echoing thud from the free fall, it gave him the hesitation he needed to see from Assault Rifle.

Arthur gave the Navajo command for attack.

When the wolf dog stood in the shadow of the cargo area of the truck, his deep growl rumbling like a looming thunderstorm, Arthur watched the eyes of Assault Rifle widen. As he struggled to retrieve his rifle, the animal bounded over the scrunched-up body of Glenda James and leapt from the truck, digging his bared claws into the man's shoulders, simultaneously tilting his head instinctively to allow his opened jaws to lock around his victim's open throat.

Glenda James tossed back the blanket and reached out for Arthur's hand. He grabbed it and pulled her out as guns fired and bullets ripped into the metal walls behind them. The Bronco's windshield spiderwebbed immediately in three places.

"Not again!" Arthur yelled. "I just got this truck!"

Glenda James returned fire. Peering quickly around the truck's right taillight, she squeezed off three explosive rounds in consecutive bursts.

Arthur looked back at Assault Rifle lying on the concrete floor, still and quiet. His throat was a mess of pumping blood and torn flesh, with Ak'is standing tall on his motionless chest. The dog's lungs filled and exhaled rapidly enough that Arthur swore his rib cage was having trouble containing them. Arthur heard something in his ear and darted toward the side door and jabbed a fist into the red button that ignited the motor that opened the large heavy door.

Quickly diving back behind the rear of the Bronco, he returned fire in the direction of the Mercedes from the left side of the Bronco. The Mercedes made a good backdrop for target practice as Arthur's breathing and resolve remained steady. His finger tugged at the Glock's trigger, sending off three bursts of two. The bodyguard on the left took four hits in the chest, reflexively discharging his pistol into the concrete. The slugs ricocheted off the hard concrete surface and sang away somewhere. Arthur couldn't tell where his last two shots had landed, so he continued firing at the other bodyguard as the first one fell in a landslide off the Mercedes' hood and spilled over the front of it.

The building's rear doors began to open, and the Range Rover spun to the right, tires screaming, and headed for it.

Glenda James and Arthur continued to fire, Arthur focusing on turning the shirt of the remaining bodyguard red, and James blowing out the back window and the right taillight of the fleeing Range Rover. As the large garage door lurched higher, the remaining bodyguard crumpled to the concrete. The opening door Garcia's Range Rover was heading for revealed a solid bank of black Chargers with flashing light bars like a theatrical curtain revealing an operatic stage production. Arthur turned briefly to see the same lineup behind him.

Streaming lines of blue uniforms suddenly flooded in through the large door and past the Bronco into the vacant building, their polished shoes clacking across the concrete in a tempo creating its own tune of justice. Arthur Nakai and Glenda James looked at each other, their chests swelling with each agitated breath.

"You all right?" Arthur said.

James nodded. "You?"

"Fared better than my truck." They both stood, looked at the damaged windshield through the open rear of the Bronco. Ak'is walked over and rubbed against Arthur's legs.

Glenda James squatted down and lost her fingers in the dog's thick fur, disregarding the blood around its jaws. "Maybe the city will pay for it?" she said.

Arthur holstered his pistol under his arm. "I'll send them a bill, but I'm not holding my breath."

James laughed politely.

"You two all right?" Detective Espinosa said, walking up to them.

They both nodded affirmatively.

"What the hell happened here?" Espinosa was pointing to the dead man with the torn throat.

"It's always good to have a furry friend," Arthur remarked as he walked around to the passenger side of his truck, reached in and pulled out the five thousand dollars Washington had given him.

"Here's the cash for the girl," Arthur told the cop. "I should keep part of it to replace my windshield."

Espinosa took it from him. "I'll have someone mark and bag it." He looked at the truck's windshield. "We have everything recorded, and I don't feel like impounding your vehicle right now. We know how it got damaged. Go back to your wife. But be ready to give us a full statement in the next couple of days."

"Thanks," Arthur said. He walked over to where he had kicked his other Glock and picked it up, shoved it onto his hip. "My backup," he said to Espinosa. "Oh, by the way, tell Garcia and Jonzell I'll be looking forward to attending their going-away party in court."

"Just so you know," Espinosa said, "the Northwest team raided the club while we were moving on Garcia."

"Did they find Nikki?"

Espinosa looked at the floor briefly. "I'm sorry, brother. They found what was left of her in a room in the basement."

Arthur's eyes squeezed shut. He swallowed hard, said nothing more and climbed into his truck.

Espinosa waved his hands in a wide gesture to open a path in the squads like Moses parting the Red Sea. When the Bronco's engine roared to life, Arthur backed out with a new purpose. He needed to find a place open at almost four in the morning that sold manila envelopes, because he had decided to make a stop on his way home. He was going to slip a few of those envelopes through the slot of Shirley Becenti's front door. Behind the glass where he could be sure they would be safe until found later that morning by the blonde in the boots. And he already knew what each envelope would have written on it: *From Nikki.*

CHAPTER TWENTY-EIGHT

Somewhere along the drive northwest to Bloomfield, the winter solstice had managed to slip quietly by. That meant the day was going to be around five hours shorter than the summer solstice, and Arthur was glad. He was tired. No, he was exhausted. And he was devastated by the recurring thought of little Nikki—a tragic little girl running from an even more tragic circumstance that turned into an even more horrifying end. At last, he believed, she was at peace in the hands of the Creator.

He didn't need to glance at his phone to know he was almost home. The morning sun broke over Angel Peak as Arthur's thoughts of Margaret Tabaaha swirled in his tired mind like those floating ghosts in old cartoons. He wasn't sure if it was the squinting glare of the rising golden orb or the memory of her dying in his arms, coupled with his thoughts of little Nikki, that brought the tears to his eyes. It was all still so fresh. He wiped the dampness from his cheeks as he ran the idea through his head about bringing it up with Sharon's shrink—Dr. Janet Peterson. Like the death of his father years earlier, Margaret's passing had left an undeniable hole in his heart and more than a heavy amount of guilt weighing on his soul. If he had arrived at her house even that much sooner would he have been able to stop her from swallowing the cluster of pills and drowning them in a bottle of whiskey? Or was that part of his past just another thing being kept alive in the compartmentalized rooms of his mind, where every box had been dated and labeled with the coinciding moments and events of his life? Perhaps, he thought, he should bring up the death of his father in-session? Get that out into the open so he could finally put it to rest.

Arthur slowed the Bronco and turned into the entrance of White Mesa Outfitters. Billy Yazzie's brown Galaxie 500 was nowhere in sight. It was a fair guess that he had been told to leave once Jake Bilagody had arrived. Arthur parked next to the Navajo captain's jacked-up Suburban and went inside after Ak'is hopped from the passenger seat, bounded from the driver's seat and hit the ground running, heading off into the morning searching for his own peace of mind.

Arthur's nostrils were soon greeted by the aroma of cooked pork, which still managed to hang in the kitchen from Sharon's cooking sometime during the night. He stepped cautiously around the table and chairs, being careful not to make any noise that would silence the snoring coming from the living room.

Jake's large frame was lying on their couch, putting its handcrafted quality to the test. Arthur picked up the remote and clicked off the flat panel that hung on the river-rock wall above the burl-mantled fireplace.

The sudden quiet woke Jake. "You just get in?" he said groggily.

"Yeah," Arthur said. "Nice to see you're awake and on the job."

Jake sat up, rubbed his eyes, yawned. "I asked my office manager to keep me informed of your escapade in Duke City. She kept in contact with her counterpart. When she reported everything went as planned, I decided I could afford to get a little shut-eye." He looked up at Arthur. "You look no worse for wear."

Arthur said, "I'm fine. I'm gonna have to get a new windshield, though."

"Don't let your wife see that. She's already nervous about you shamusing around anyway."

"What time did Billy leave?"

"A little after I arrived. I didn't really need him. Not with your pistol-packin' mama upstairs."

Arthur grinned. "She okay?"

Jake nodded. "Sleeping—"

"Not anymore," Sharon said, descending the stairs in her white tank top and shimmering ice-blue pajama bottoms and bare feet. "Don't let me see what?"

"Nothing," Arthur said, the smile on his face telegraphing that he was glad to be home.

"I think I'll go," Jake said, standing up. "Since I have to find a new Realtor tomorrow, or is that today? Besides, my bed is calling."

Arthur asked, "How's April doing?"

"Best as can be expected, considering the fact that she was pregnant."

Sharon was shocked by the revelation. "What?"

"I won't go into all the details," Jake said, "but she lost the child as a result of abdominal trauma. Let's just say Gordon Lockerby did a number on her and the other girl, Lucy Nez. The Nez girl kept repeating how April had saved her life." Jake looked at Sharon. "April's a strong-willed young woman, but Lockerby had her for three weeks prior to kidnapping Nez, so there's no telling how long it will take her to heal physically as well as mentally from the loss of the child and the abuse she took from this whole situation. My guess is years."

Arthur softly clasped Sharon's hand as she wiped away a traveling tear with the other. "Has anyone contacted her parents?"

"We did. I'm sure they've been at the hospital all night along with the Nez family. I've posted a couple officers there to keep any press from bothering them." Jake picked his hat up off the epoxied redwood-slab coffee table and placed it on his head. "I'll keep you updated."

"I'd appreciate that," Arthur said. "What about Lockerby's place?"

"April mentioned 'the others' being somewhere on the property like you did, so we did what you recommended and had a guy haul a ground-penetrating radar out there and start doing a grid search. So far we've dug up about ten of those blue plastic barrels."

"My God," Sharon gasped.

Arthur said, "I saw some of those in one of the outbuildings I checked out."

"It appears after Lockerby got tired of them, he killed them and buried them. Most were badly decomposed; the few that were still recognizable had been tortured as well." Jake exhaled. "This guy was one sick bastard." He looked at Arthur. "You were right. They hide in plain sight, don't they?"

"You think there's more?" Arthur said.

"I'd bet on it. Lockerby's wife said there were girls her husband tried to 'help' that were never seen again. I'm sure they're on the property somewhere. It's going to take some time to locate them." Jake nodded goodbye. "I'll show myself out."

Sharon wrapped her arms around the big Navajo captain and squeezed him tight. Jake looked at Arthur as Sharon kissed his cheek.

"Thanks for keeping me company," she said, "while this one was off playing Sam Spade."

Jake touched his cheek. He was going to hit the office before heading home, discuss some ongoing investigations with his lieutenant, and would be back at work later in the afternoon. "Anytime. Just don't make it a habit."

Arthur nodded. "I can't promise."

Jake said, "Walk me out?"

Arthur nodded and escorted his old friend through the kitchen and out the door. Once outside, standing by his jacked-up Suburban, Jake said, "Garcia says he gave you twenty grand. Espinosa wants to know where the rest of the money is."

Arthur smirked. "I gave him what he gave me back at the warehouse. That's all I got."

"Espinosa says Garcia is pretty emphatical. Says there's a corroborating witness, too."

"Jonzell Washington?" Arthur chuckled. "He's one to trust."

Jake said, "I vouched for you. You haven't got me sticking my neck out, have you?"

Arthur crossed his arms. "There is no other money. You can check my truck, my house and my only bank account. I gave it all to the detective."

Jake studied his friend closely, then let it drop before climbing into his truck. "That's what I told him."

Arthur smiled and waved, walked back into the house as Jake drove away. Returning to the living room, he found his wife where he had left her.

Sharon said, "I love hugging him. It's like hugging one of those big, furry stuffed animals."

Arthur folded her into his arms and held her against him. He could feel her body's anticipation moving beneath the thin veil of tank top and shimmering pj's. And he could feel the adrenaline pulsating through him like a returning king from a decisive battle.

"What do you say we put the clock away for tonight?" Arthur said.

Sharon's eyes sparkled, and her lips formed a smile he hadn't truly seen since they began their regimented attack on insemination. "What do you have in mind, old man?"

"Old man?" He pulled her closer. Close enough to feel her heart pounding through the tank top, which accentuated the fullness of her body; close enough to feel the hardness of her nipples pressing into his chest and her pelvis working slowly against his growing tumescence. "You're only five years younger than I am."

Sharon smiled impishly. "That's still younger."

Arthur grinned. "I see how you are. Just for that, maybe I won't give you the present."

Sharon's eyes sparkled with all the anticipation of a child at Christmas. "What present?"

"The one I got you in Santa Fe."

"Oooooh." She smiled. "Do tell."

Arthur reached inside his jacket, pulled out an elongated white box, and handed it to her.

Sharon promptly opened it and fingered back the protective cotton, revealing a beautiful six-string necklace of red coral beads.

"They're beautiful," she said, looking up at him. "I love them!"

Arthur smiled tenderly, then watched as she set the gift on the coffee table. "Don't you want to put them on?"

Sharon slipped her arms around him again. "Not just yet. You didn't have to get me anything, you know? Just coming home safe was gift enough."

Arthur took a few unspoken moments to stare at his wife.

Sharon said, "What are you thinking?"

"I'm remembering the very first moment I saw you."

"Why?"

"Because that was the day everything that made up my world stopped and became only you."

"Mmmm." Sharon smiled. "I knew I fell in love with you for a reason." Standing on her toes, she reached up and kissed his mouth—softly at first, then more passionately, until they were mingling their tongues together like thirsty adolescents. When they separated, she whispered into his ear, "Turn off the lights. Suddenly our bedroom seems too far away."

Made in the USA
Monee, IL
10 September 2021